Ashes
of the
Living

A Novel

To Surjit,

a great literary
colleague and an
even better
person!
Cheers!

John C

J O H N   C O X

Book Cover Design by Flor Figueroa | Designer at COLONFILM
Published by Dark Enigma Press LLC

Dark Enigma Press llc

Edited by Jenny Slade
Print ISBN: 978-1-7352775-1-6
EBook ISBN: 978-1-7352775-0-9

This book is dedicated to my sons John and Matthew, my brother Jeff, and my mother Marcia. Most of all, to my amazing wife Emma - even in the darkest places of fiction, your love and laughter are my guiding light.

Prologue

CARL WARREN OPENED his eyes to a wave of pain. The constant and invasive light blinded him, and his eyelids stapled themselves together. He recalled stories his mother used to tell him about how angels were real, and they glowed with a kind of holiness that made it hard for man's flawed vision to look upon. She hadn't been much in the caretaking department, but she was a fanatical believer in both angels and angel dust. The light was like that. Something so bright it was painful for his eyes to focus on.

Gradually he allowed tiny pinpricks of light in as his vision adjusted to the flood of illumination around him. Where was he? What had happened? His surroundings began to swim into focus as he squinted into the pain. He tried moving, but discovered he couldn't get up. He was lying on his back in a room he had never seen before. The whole ceiling consisted of nothing but long fluorescent bulbs and a chessboard pattern of plastic and tiling. The walls were the color of bleached bone and offered no advice as to where he was.

Carl turned his head and tried to get a more complete view of his environment. He saw to his right a Formica tabletop with a steel sink and detached cart. Other shapes lay on top of the table, but at this distance there was no hope of discerning what they were. Was he in surgery? It certainly looked like a sterile enough place to be inside a hospital. The air reeked of ammonium chloride and bleach, but underneath was a faint whiff of old blood. The kind of rusty spoiled odor that never truly dissipates. Hospitals were all like that. They smelled of death and cleanliness.

The room began to grow into sharper focus, and Carl guessed that he was in a room that was 20 by 16 feet in dimension. He tried moving his arms but found them restrained. His palms felt the cold surface of a steel table. His torso and legs were held by rubber restraints with gelatinous pads. His wrists, and presumably ankles, were bound with thick leather straps which seemed to offer no freedom of movement. He couldn't feel a knob or release lever for any immediate hope of escape. Why was he bound like this?

He forced himself to take deep, even breaths. This was not the time to panic. This was the time to think. There were no clocks to offer any source of structure to the passing of time. Had he been here for minutes or hours? Maybe days? Carl wasn't sure. He tried to think about what his last memory was and all he could recall was crashing into bed after a night of vodka and cheap draft.

A door on the left edge of Carl's peripheral vision swung open without a sound. He hadn't even a chance to notice it, and his heart betrayed him as it started to race. The earlier attempt at control was dead. The sound of footsteps brought into the room two men, but Carl recognized only one of them. He knew he was not in the hospital. He wished he were.

"Baxter, listen I...."

Robert Baxter held up his hand and Carl noticed, even in this situation, how the simple gesture demanded obedience. Protests dead on chapped lips. His captor walked over to the table smiling with an even set of white razors. Baxter was a tall man but lying on the table made him appear to be looking down from the peak of Saint Elias. His blue eyes were lit with a type of intelligence that made Carl look away. He preferred to look at the other man who still had not said a word.

"Will, I'd like you to meet Carl Warren." Baxter said, "You could shake hands, but well, Carl seems to have gotten himself into a conundrum of sorts." Baxter winked at Carl as if they shared some common joke. "Carl, this is William Thompson. He is sort of a 'jack of all trades, master of none' kind of guy." Will turned and walked over to the sink without saying a word. Carl could hear the sound of metal being picked up and then put down. The noise was a lot louder than it should have been. He tried to turn and see what was happening but the restraints were stronger than his body.

Baxter said, "Now that the introductions are out of the way, let me get right to the point. You are going to die, Carl. Most people prefer to die in their beds at home. A calm, dignified journey that would end by slipping into a tranquil dream. A one way trip to some sort of heaven after a fulfilling life. Unfortunately, none of that is going to happen to you. You are going to die on this slab in this room with me looking down on you." Baxter's smile widened. "You are going to scream until you feel blood crying from your eyes. The only questions are how long is it going to take and how painful is it going to be? Hmmm?"

Will wheeled the cart over until it fell out of his line of sight. He still couldn't see what had made the noises. Carl felt sweat sizzling on his forehead and his temples throbbed. There might still be a way out of this. He had to remain calm. Who knew what this was about? Maybe Baxter didn't know the whole deal. As long as he kept the reporter out of it, he might be able to come out of this alive. He had talked his way out of all kinds of shit before.

"Baxter, listen, I don't know what is going on but..."

Baxter interrupted "Let me tell you a story, Carl. A long time ago, the Greeks believed in a man named Tantalus who wanted to fuck with his gods. He killed his own son, boiled the flesh, and served the choice meats to them. He did this as a test to see if they would know the difference from their normal feasts. Of course the gods in their divine knowledge and wisdom did know and killed him instantly for his arrogance. But that isn't the interesting part of the story."

Carl could feel his voice raise an octave as he replied. "I have always done what you asked and you know that. Listen, I haven't fucked up once. Not one fucking time! You have gotten a lot of money working with me. I'm not sure......"

Baxter's stare dried up all of Carl's thoughts. The moment of odd quiet was enough to make anyone sweat. Then in the same dead voice he replied, "Carl, if you interrupt me one more time, I am going to rip off your ear with my teeth." The room shrank as he clicked his teeth together to keep from moaning.

Baxter smiled and continued, "Thank you. The ancient Greeks were fond of all kinds of irony. In the afterlife, Tantalus was placed in the middle of a cool, clear lake with a large fruit tree overhead. But when he stooped down to drink the water it receded away from his cupped hands and when he reached for the fruit above him the branches strained to stay just out of reach. So hunger and thirst gnawed at him with every second worse than the last. Eventually I like to think his body started eating itself. It was eternal damnation with no end, and each moment brought a new layer of pain and suffering. Since Tantalus offered a false feast to the gods, he could never have anything real for himself. It's a simple story but kind of funny, huh? Do you understand what I am saying?"

There had to be a way out of this if he could buy enough time. He had a chance if he played along. Just play along and everything would be fine. Carl wet his lips and said, "The punishment was right for the crime? That's it, right?"

"Exactly. You got it in one. Which brings us to your current state and why I am telling you this. You see Carl; you are one of the blunt tools. You aren't too bright, but at least you have enough stuffing in that head to know how to stay alive. In the past you were useful, but more importantly you knew when to shut up. Until recently anyway." Baxter smiled. He is enjoying this, Carl's mind screamed at him. Baxter said, "If you are going to rat me out, don't brag about it. Just do it. I keep my eyes on everything and everyone. Most people aren't good Samaritans, Carl."

"That was all talk! I wouldn't sell out! I swear it!" Carl's voice broke and his eyes burned as the sweat crawled into his sockets. Things were not going well. Will walked over to the other side of the table holding out to Baxter some sort of device and then a gun. Baxter held up the weapon for Carl to see more clearly. He said, "This is your personal angel of mercy, Carl. It is a Glock 30 with one .45 ACP round loaded in the chamber. A beautiful piece of art that even the Renaissance couldn't have envisioned. It is your ticket out of this place, friend. But that doesn't come until later." Baxter put the gun down on the table. Carl's spine could feel the barrel clang through the drenched clothes that clung to his skin.

Baxter held up two instruments that looked like miniature accordions. "These are a variation of the mouth props dentists use. They keep jaws open even when they are supposed to be shut. Typically they are made of silicone but, as you can see, mine are metal. The steel makes it easier since they lock into place. Now open wide."

Carl clamped his mouth shut. He had to get out of here! He twisted and strained. Nothing would give. The shakes started in his arms and worked their way to his skull, then down to his toes. He thought of a song he used to sing as a kid. Head, shoulders, knees, and toes....knees and toes.

Baxter's eyes grew dark. He said, "You want to listen to me on this. Don't make it harder than it already is. You definitely don't want to fuck with me. Open up now or it will get really messy for you."

Carl said, "Please don't......I will tell you anything you want to know!" Baxter reached down with a clenched fist towards his mouth. Carl thrashed his head trying to turn it from side to side.

"Hold him, Will." Two hands grabbed the side of his head. Strong hands. Carl tried twisting and clamping his jaws shut. His mouth cracked with a wave of pain. Had Will punched him? He reeled his head and tried to concentrate. The side of his face was on fire. Then he felt metal in his mouth as his jaw creaked like a rusty door blown open by a hurricane wind. He heard a faint click, and then Baxter's face spun into focus. He was smiling again which scared Carl more than being strapped to the table.

"This is what happens when you can't keep your mouth shut." Will handed Baxter a pair of pliers. Carl felt the hands on the sides of his head again. They were cold and callused. Baxter pushed down Carl's lip and grasped a front tooth with the pliers. He yanked back, and Carl screamed as he watched an arc of blood fly from his mouth. The pain exploded into a rack of agony. He wanted to cover his face, make the pain stop. His body screamed, but he couldn't move. Helplessness drowned his mind in a current of red.

Baxter said, "Turn his head, Will, and let him spit some of the blood out. Don't want him drowning on us just yet." Carl was abruptly turned and he gagged as his stomach muscles punched into his ribcage. He choked and gasped, trying to say something. Anything to make this stop.

Carl tried to focus once his head was moved back, but then he felt the pliers on another tooth just before his gums burst into fire again. Bile had begun to fill his throat and he tried to spit it all out. His head was turned again and he vomited from the pain.

His limbs strained against the bonds. He wished he could blackout but the nightmare wouldn't die. Baxter held the two teeth in the palm of his hand like they were sunflower seeds. He said, "I would take out more. Actually I would cut out that wagging tongue too, but I need some answers first. Speak to me, Carl. Tell me what I want to know. Who did you talk to?"

Carl tried to speak but couldn't stop coughing. He would give all the money he owned just to wipe his lips. He gasped while Baxter waited patiently. Will Thompson spoke for the first time. "Baxter, maybe we should just…" Baxter glanced at him and shook his head once. Will didn't speak again.

Baxter said in an almost gentle voice, "Come on, Carl. Next we move on to the heavier work. Don't make it be that way."

Carl nodded and croaked, "Ok…….please just….I didn't talk to the police or anything."

Baxter nodded "Of course not, because then you would have been arrested. Got to look out for yourself, you know. Stay a free man. Keep going."

"I found...a reporter. I called her last night. I thought with her connections she could pass...."

"Give me a goddamn name, Carl."

"Emily Morgan. I.....I....I don't think she even believed me. She asked to speak in person and needed 'proof of legitimacy' or something."

"Where?"

"I am supposed to meet her tomorrow night. Nine o clock at this bar. I gave her directions and..."

His next words faltered to a halt as Robert Baxter's face darkened. His eyes became an ice storm contained in the sockets by sheer hate. He grabbed another tool that Will had laid on the cart and held it up. It was a long ice pick and Carl began to howl in panic. He tried to thrash his body on the table, but couldn't move at all. His head was grabbed by the vice hands that had held him before. Baxter said in a voice edged with nails, "I can abide liars and thieves. I can abide people who kill their own mothers for an ounce of coke. I can abide the best and the worst in this world but I simply cannot abide stupidity!" The ice pick descended and pierced Carl's left eyelid with an audible pop. The thick, mucous-like fluid of his eyesight streamed down his face, and he could not stop screaming.

An hour later, Baxter and Will walked out of the door and into the empty warehouse they had chosen to use over the last few months. The room they had just left was the only area that had been cleaned. Baxter had no use for the rest of the building. It was probably the last time they would be coming here. Baxter talked as they moved through the open space. His stride was graceful and light for such a tall man.

"Have someone take care of that worm. I think we have everything we need." Robert Baxter liked respect even when he was in a good mood, let alone right now, so Will rarely looked into his boss's eyes. He nodded and focused on the overhead rafters where it looked like rust had been the choice color rather than an affliction. Will didn't talk a lot, which was probably one of the reasons he was still working for Robert Baxter. The warehouse was silent, and the sound of their footsteps sounded magnified in the open space. The crunch of old tile sounded like gunfire.

"We are going to have to move very quickly on this one, Will." Baxter said, "I doubt this Emily Morgan has anything of value if I am being honest. It sounds like all she had was a potential lead on a potential story. But potential has brought down kingdoms; let alone what it could do to our little operation. We can't hesitate. You need to find out exactly who she is and more importantly where she lives. You need to do it now. I want you, and anyone else you need, over at her house in less than twenty-four hours. At her door, Will. At. Her. Door."

"How do you want it handled?"

"Have you ever seen a leech? Usually people don't even know when a leech is hooked into their skin. That's because the leech is small and releases an anesthetic so the host doesn't know it's there. Make no mistake though, the leech steals from you. It will eat your blood until it is full. Now if you have a leech on you, the best route is to pry it off, or you could wait until it is done eating. But I always thought the right way was to teach the leech a lesson. It is draining part of your life away, and it doesn't give anything back. I prefer the old ways we had of dealing with leeches. Sometimes those old ways end up being the lessons that hit the hardest."

None of it made any sense to Will, but he waited, knowing he would hear the answer. They had reached the outside of the warehouse. Robert Baxter turned toward Will and said, "Burn her, Will. You burn her and everything that is important to her. Make sure there is nothing left. Don't make me repeat myself."

CHAPTER 1
A New Kind of Dead

THE DILAPIDATED BUILDING stood outside of his front windshield like the bones of a primordial beast. Inside the old Mustang's steel frame, Detective Tyler Morgan put the car into park and stared at the crude surroundings while letting the air conditioning wash over him. He closed his eyes and breathed in deeply a blast of the cool, controlled air. Tyler wished he had his arm around Emily or could hear Grace's sweet laughter. It was late afternoon on a muggy July day and Chicago's summers were notorious for being almost as cruel as its winters. This month had reached record temperatures, and traffic had raised tempers with each degree. The Chicago police department had seen a rise in crime recently, especially in some of the more crowded districts. Mostly domestic disputes or an occasional cocaine bust, but every once in a while someone decided the best place to leave a bullet was in an arm or a skull. Summer time could be relaxing, but it could also incite violence.

He had received the call thirty minutes ago, but his car's flashing light had not completely cleared the way through the busy downtown area. He had gotten stuck in traffic as people crawled through the streets trying to cut through and begin the day. He had used all the tricks of a seasoned local driver, but so had half the city. The other drivers gave way only grudgingly. The buildings passed by with a sluggish speed he didn't like. Too damn slow. He had pulled up less than a minute ago, but it felt like being a day behind.

Fortunately, he saw Chris Wessler's car and noticed with wry amusement that he had followed standard protocol to the letter (for a change). There was already a perimeter set up around the building. Yellow tape canvassed a good portion of the area like morbid gift wrap. He had done well with the prep work, and Tyler was sure Chris was waiting for him inside. They had been partners for two years now, so Tyler was familiar with how Chris would be putting together the scene and waiting to hear his partner's thoughts and analysis. Familiarity and experience made them an effective team.

Tyler opened the door and stepped out of the car to a wave of humidity. The sun beat down on his back as he walked toward the apartment building. He could feel beads of sweat begin to rise under his shirt. Usually a small crowd of people would gather around crime scenes like this. The police lights and the possibility of seeing dead bodies attracted all kinds. What was that saying about being horrified by a train wreck but not being able to look away? Today though, only a few of the diehard watchers had shown up since the crime took place inside an apartment. More importantly, it was just too damn hot. Tyler waded through the thin line of people as they parted around him. Being six foot three and built like a linebacker wasn't always a good thing, but sometimes it could be a definite advantage.

He stepped over several bricks from the framework lying on the ground. The sidewalk was interspersed with milk thistle and oxalis. He walked up the front steps and into the entranceway hall. The floor paneling was some sort of cheap wood, and the nails holding them down rose and fell like waves as Tyler stepped down the hall, listening to every groan. He climbed the stairs to the second floor, thinking of the first apartment he and Emily had rented years ago off of East 63rd. That was long before they had moved to Wicker Park. It hadn't been much, but it had been home. He wondered if the people who lived here would still feel the same way about this place after today.

Chris Wessler was waiting at the top of stairs, talking to another officer. Chris or Tyler would always try to interview the first officer on the scene before entering the location of the crime. Chris was wearing one of his loud silk shirts that he was notorious for. This one had a beige and teal floral pattern that hurt Tyler's eyes. He and his partner were opposites in every way except their heights, as Chris was six foot four, making the two of them the tallest in their division. Chris was loud, brash, and, most importantly, a good friend. A lot could be said for having a partner you could work with.

Chris nodded and turned to the patrol officer, giving his thanks. The officer passed Tyler, presumably to ensure the security of the perimeter. Chris pointed down the hall, asking him to walk towards the apartment door. Already Tyler could hear the staccato machinegun beat of cameras documenting the dead. He hated that sound more than any other. It got louder as they walked down the hall.

Chris said, "Well, it's about time you got here. Goddamn traffic, right? I got my head chopped off trying to get OCD to let us work with Vice on this one." He tilted his head in a hangman's pose.

"Is it the same as the others?"

"Different part of town, but yeah, almost exact same pattern, so I assume so. I just got here a few minutes ago though, and wanted to wait for the grim prodigy to arrive."

"User or dealer?"

"Looks like user. Christ, it could be both. Half of the users are the sellers anymore, especially in the case of Abyss. Seems to be the next big thing. Like we needed another next big thing."

Abyss, also called White Abyss or A.B., was an opioid drug synthesized from morphine. It was a derivative of the opium poppy that made heroin a high demand drug. A key difference was that the level of dependence seemed to be even worse with Abyss. It had strong hallucinogenic properties, especially if it was used intravenously, which made it incredibly dangerous. No one was sure what caused this effect. The user experienced a feeling of euphoria that lasted for hours, putting them in an almost catatonic state. This is where the name came from. More often than not the user also experienced an extreme sense of paranoia and loss of reality that led to violent, erratic behavior. Tyler's wife, Emily, had done a story on it a couple weeks ago. The Chicago Narcotics division was working on trying to figure out how it was synthesized and where it was coming from. Abyss was a rising star in the illegal drug industry, destined to darken Chicago's skies for some time.

Tyler stepped out of the hallway and into Hell. The apartment reeked of urine and stale Doritos. He could almost hear the cockroaches burrowing through the cheap pseudo wood tiling that was a popular pick for the walls of the building. He moved into the living room where a man's corpse was curled into a defensive fetal position. A wife beater t-shirt was stained almost completely red and the cheap carpet underneath the body had become a maroon lake.

Chris said, "As far as we can tell this man's name is Chad Gosman. Unemployed for at least a year. Used to be some sort of factory worker when there were still jobs available. No con status or record but we have just started looking. He was shot at least four times in the chest."

Chris leaned down to point at the side of the head while being careful not to touch the body. "Looks like he almost got a headshot based on the bullet lodged in their TV. That was probably the best piece of furniture in this place."

They walked into the kitchen passing a glass animal menagerie and an image of a sunflower in a cracked frame. Tyler wondered if it was the default picture now being used for art. The kitchen was carpeted in two different colored rugs. One was tan with several dark stains and the other was an orange and dark green blend, which hadn't been in style since the 1980s. Both had been stapled to the floor. The faucet in the sink dripped every thirty seconds onto a Taurus .38 Special Snub nose. Drip. Drip. Drip. The gun looked almost brand new and shined under the constant hydration.

Tyler already knew the ballistics would match between the gun and the bullets in the very dead Mr. Gosman. One chair leaned against the sink where a young woman sat hunched over as if in prayer. On the floor lay a large butcher's knife. It was the kind that comes with any generic cutlery set with a pseudo-woodblock and dull sharpening stick. The woman had long strawberry blonde hair tied back in a ponytail and wore what looked like a white tank top, though it was hard to tell with all the blood. It could almost be pink.

Tyler put on a pair of latex gloves and kneeled down to look into her face. Chris stood inside the doorframe giving him a moment before saying, "Her name is Kate Land. At first I thought the landlord was saying Katelyn. We don't know much about her yet, though she seems to have stayed out of trouble and had some sort of legit job. We are pretty sure she was on Abyss when this happened. There is an empty syringe on the table. Toxicology reports from the ME should be able to provide us more detail."

Tyler reached his hand under Kate's chin (no longer a nameless corpse). He looked at Chris with arched eyebrows. Chris said, "All placement pics have been documented." He lifted her chin, being careful to only touch the jaw. Rigor mortis hadn't quite set in, which was unusual since it had probably been at least three hours, but every person was different. It looked like the small muscles of the face were still pliable, meaning they still retained some level of adenosine triphosphate. Below her chin lay the cause of death. A giant, maroon cut started at the outer left side of her throat going towards the right like the half smile of a second mouth. The mouth grinned at Tyler in a wet smirk.

"Has Special Unit looked at this?"

"Yeah, they said she sat down in the chair and used the knife to cut her own throat. Looks like she did it in the most painful way possible. Crazy, crazy."

"They're right. Look at the angle of the cut. It's all wrong from an attacker perspective but for self-imposed it would work with a backhand grip on the blade. Did you see this second cut?"

"What?! Where?"

"Right below the first. It is easy to miss because of the mesh effect between the two. See?" Tyler lifted her chin a little higher. The second angry cut mark looked a little clearer, but Chris shook his head. Tyler pointed to the wound. "This means she cut her own throat and stopped. My guess is she lost her grip on the sticky knife and tried to cut again. By that point, she was probably too weak and barely conscious from the loss of blood. She would have been dead in less than a few minutes after that."

"That is fucked up. Really fucked up."

"Do you know what type of will it takes to do this?" Tyler asked, "This isn't some half-baked death wish wannabe, Chris. This is someone who has either completely given into despair or has no idea what is real anymore. Dreams are reality and reality is a nightmare. This is a new kind of dead. The worst kind because it is going to hurt a lot more than just the individual. We need to talk to Narcotics and find out how rampant this type of stuff is. From the looks of it, Ms. Land wasn't rich, so how is she buying this so-called super drug? If the manufacturers have found a way to synthesize this stuff cheaply, then we are going to be seeing a lot more of these."

"No shit? I will talk to Ramirez and King about it." Chris said, his brow furrowed in thought. "This situation looks pretty self-contained, but I will confirm with SU about the potential for any other intruders. No sign of break-in, but never hurts. What about semen or vaginal fluids?"

"If so, it was probably consensual and not relevant. This doesn't feel like sexual assault, but it doesn't hurt to check for that as well. We can't rule out anything yet. She isn't going anywhere unfortunately so let's be thorough."

Tyler stood up and stared down at the top of the woman's head. Her hair was parted perfectly down the middle. What had she seen in the final moments of her life? Demons? Angels? Was she even really Kate Land anymore? The story was nothing but a gaping hole ready to pull Tyler in. Sometimes it was better to not think about the dead, but Tyler couldn't help it. Most of the time they spoke more loudly than the living ever could. He walked out of the kitchen away from the half smile in the throat of a corpse.

LATER THAT NIGHT, Tyler finally got home. They had gone through the process of interviewing the neighbors for witness statements, but no one had heard anything outside of the gunshots which was eerie in and of itself. One woman had confirmed the landlord's statement that Kate and Chad had been around each other for at least six months and had seemed very intimate. "Not sweet at all, but I know they were together." These were the words coming from a young woman who breastfed her fourth child while talking to Tyler and Chris.

Tyler could only shake his head. Everything had to be cataloged and filed with the promise of future interviews. Every piece of evidence had to be bagged and tagged on even the slightest chance it would need to be reviewed. Even open and shut cases called for a lot of paperwork. By the time Tyler left his desk, it was already past ten.

For Tyler, the sun rose and set during these few moments at his apartment in Roscoe Village. He opened the door without a sound and put down his keys in the bowl next to the kitchen sink. Tyler's feet followed their usual pattern and walked down the hall to see Grace. His eight year old daughter's room was bright saffron with splashes of color on her walls from her many paintings which Tyler had "helped" put up.

A mobile made of dowel rods and hanging wire was suspended above her bed with all of the origami animals Tyler had made for her. Tyler's usual scowl softened into a smile in the bright environment. Emily said that he looked like he was ready to kill someone after work until he walked into Grace's room. Tyler doubted some people at work would recognize the way he looked right now.

His daughter lay asleep curled up into a ball, cushioned by an igloo of blankets. Grace slept like this year round regardless of the temperature. There was a strand of her long hair peeking out from the pillows. It seemed to move in time with the steady breaths of deep slumber. Tyler pressed his fingers to his lips in a kiss and then to the foot of the bed, not wanting to wake her. Grace tried to stay awake under her covers waiting for him to come home every night. She rarely made it, but Tyler had promised long ago he would check in on her and keep her safe. It was a promise he always kept.

The wooden floorboards creaked as Tyler walked down the hall, reminding him of the dead he had seen today. He brushed the thought aside as best he could. Many detectives took solace in a wide variety of activities to overcome a lot of the horror and violence they witnessed in their profession. For some, it was television, sports, or music, while for others it was food or alcohol. Tyler found comfort in his family. They kept a part of him separate from his job. A gentler part that could laugh once in a while. Tyler never smiled more than when he was here, safe with his family.

He opened his bedroom door to find Emily smiling at him from bed with a soft lamp glow illuminating her eyes and long hair. She pulled back the blanket, and Tyler was surprised to find her naked. "Come here, detective," she whispered and patted the bed with her hand. Tyler smiled and shut the door behind him. Life was sometimes hard, but it could also be pretty damn amazing. He lowered himself onto the bed where Emily's arms waited for him.

CHAPTER 2
The Dream Life

TYLER COULD FEEL rays of sunlight touching his face before he opened his eyes. He had always been a heavy sleeper and struggled to recall his dreams. He stretched and started to rise when he heard the familiar thump of eight year old feet on the wooden floor. It sounded like a herd of buffalo rather than a little girl. He lay back down and began to snore.

"Daddy?"

"Daaaad?"

The footsteps retreated backwards a few steps and stopped. Tyler waited with a smile on his face. The footsteps started again and became thunderous as they raced toward the bed. Tyler lunged out of the sheets and caught Grace in the air just as she pounced. "Yaaaah!" he yelled and they collapsed in a pile of blankets and wrestling moves. Grace Morgan's laugh sounded like her mother's. It was soft and genuine. She snuggled in next to him and wrapped the blanket around both of them. Tyler again doubted his fellow officers and detectives would recognize him right now.

"How do you always know, Daddy?"

"What, besides the fact that I am a world famous detective? Simple, Angel Eyes, because you always try to pounce on me like a little tiger!" This prompted Grace to giggle, and Tyler felt the day was off to a good start. Almost on cue, Emily's call for breakfast sounded and they raced down the hall. Grace skated ahead in her socks across the floor. Tyler picked her up and carried her the rest of the way.

Emily smiled at the sight and put hands on her hips in mock frustration. She said, "Where are you taking my child, caveman?" Tyler plopped Grace down in a chair next to his and sat down, rubbing his hands over the aroma of hot pancakes and spicy sausage. Tyler poured orange juice as Emily brought over Columbian roast coffee. Tyler and Emily never started a day without coffee. They had met several times for dates at a coffee shop off North Broadway when they had begun to see each other. Nothing brought people together like a fresh roast. She said, "Where do you get that appetite from, Mr. Morgan?" as Tyler piled his plate with the warm breakfast.

Grace walked over to get silverware while Tyler whispered, "I don't know, I am really hungry this morning so I must have gotten a lot of exercise last night." Emily smacked his arm as they started to eat. It was the one time each day the entire family was together, and he savored it more than the tasty food. The kitchen echoed with conversation in the confined space. Tyler didn't mind one bit. He let the good part of the morning wash over him in a cocoon of warmth.

They enjoyed the breakfast and each other's company, but all too soon it was time to get going. He got up, taking their plates along with a kiss from Grace. Emily said, "Tyler, don't forget to be home by 8:00 tonight. I have to leave here by 8:30 at the latest."

"I still don't get why I can't come with you." Tyler said, "Almost seems like a rape situation to me, meeting some crazy guy at a bar because he has some sort of vague lead for you."

"We talked about this, Tyler. I can't have my own personal squad of CPD protecting me every time I am checking information or meeting someone for an interview. You would only intimidate him, trust me, and not just because you are a detective. You know how you get around people you don't like, thank God I have never been one of them. I won't leave until he is long gone, plus I can always call you if there are any problems."

"A phone call doesn't help if you are in a life or death situation, Em."

"True, but that is why I am meeting him at Eddie Velvets. That place is always crowded, especially after work. I think it is because of the cheese steak. They will keep going until last call, and you know it. Plus it's my job." Emily mocked a pout as she put silverware into the dishwasher. "If I can't meet a potential witness and get some serious evidence, my career in journalism is over before it ever took off."

"If he really does have anything dangerous or illegal, you have to tell me about it, ok?"

"Yes, Mr. Serious Detective." Emily held up her fingers in a scout oath and a smile. Grace also held up her fingers with a giggle from the sink. Tyler couldn't help but laugh. Emily had that effect on everyone, especially himself. She was tall and slender at five foot ten with long brown hair and deep almond eyes. A beautiful woman with an even more beautiful personality. Tyler couldn't remember a day without hearing her laugh or seeing her smile. He wouldn't have wanted to anyway. Even their fights most of the time turned into a joke.

Emily was a reporter for The Chicago View, a relatively new newspaper and website trying to compete with the Times and Tribune, as well as all the other smaller circulation newspapers, not to mention blogs and forums online. Being on a newspaper still trying to find its feet in a digital age and working full-time in Homicide took a toll on their time together, but somehow Tyler, Emily and Grace managed to find enough to enjoy each other's company.

Tyler helped clean up and then went to get his jacket out of the bedroom. He unlocked the cabinet where his gun lay in a Kydex holster. He owned two 40 caliber Glock Model 22's with fourteen bullets loaded in the magazine and one additional bullet in the chamber. Normally, police detectives would carry one specific handgun and have some sort of secondary weapon as a backup, but Tyler loved the model so much he had gotten two. He kept the spare at home unless needed. The cabinet was locked again and the key went back into the pocket of his pants.

Tyler put the gun in the holster and hooked it to his belt inside a dark blue jacket. A cobalt and royal blue tie had been a present from Emily and went on with years of practiced ease. The mirror showed him as an imposing man with no signs of gray hair yet. Emily kept saying she wanted him to have some at the temples, so he had joked about buying some dye. Tyler straightened the mirror due to his height and left the bedroom.

He went into Grace's room and thumbed through a stack of vibrant origami paper lying on her small desk. He selected several light green pages and placed the rest back. A year ago, Tyler had made Grace a paper crane when she told him how much she loved birds. She had laughed with delight and every month since they would make an origami animal. Each time, they would practice making the animal together until Grace could do it herself. Tyler had made scores of frogs, horses, and giraffes but this time he was going to make one guaranteed to be a favorite. Grace had never gotten a hummingbird so he would work on it today during lunch. It had become a hobby for them both.

Tyler gave a kiss on the top of Grace's head as he made his way toward the door. Her eyes smiled at the paper in his hand, but she knew better than trying to guess. He smiled back at her, knowing she wouldn't ask. It would give something for both of them to look forward to today. Emily handed him a fresh cup of coffee with a kiss as he walked out the door. A little slice of paradise before a typical day of hell.

Tyler said he loved them as he carried the steaming cup of coffee and origami paper out of the apartment. He turned to shut the door and saw his wife and daughter waving with smiles on their faces. It was a perfect moment and would be the last time he would see his family alive.

CHAPTER 3
Aces Over Kings

"You're dead, Morgan!"

Tyler Morgan looked around the room and it seemed everyone's eyes were on him. His opponent smiled as he said the words that would either save him or damn him to a horrible fate.

"Hit me."

Chris Wessler turned over the card and laid it in front of Tyler. It was an ace of hearts which meant Tyler had twenty-one. He had won.

"You son of a bitch! That has got to be the goddamn luckiest hand I have ever seen. I guess being a cop genius isn't enough huh? You have to be a top gun gambler too. What are the odds? Seriously what are the goddamn odds? I should punch you."

"Bring it on, tough guy." Tyler held up his fists in front of his face as Chris took a mock jab at him. People around them shook their heads, used to the display but watching on nonetheless. Tyler had come up with playing blackjack about a year ago to settle tasks that neither detective wanted to do. They called the game Aces over Kings and it was their way of avoiding problems. The cards helped to relieve stress and saved a running tally of who did what. Unless Chris lost several times in a row, then came the accusations of cheating, Tyler thought with a smirk.

"Ok, you can review the logbook and fill out the evidence file report. Thanks Chris." They had spent the morning working on documenting evidence, pictures, and placement. Forensics had wasted no time searching for fingerprints, fibers, hairs, or anything else the naked eye might have missed. They also had notated their interviews with neighbors along with contacting family. The ME hadn't given the final analysis yet, but Tyler guessed outside of some sort of great toxicity revelation, it would show a high level of Abyss.

"You know we should play for money again. Haven't done that in at least a month. What do you say?"

"I love getting extra cash, Chris. The only difficulty I have is explaining how badly I beat you to Emily. Before I retire to an island, we should probably talk to Penton and Lyle. See if they have heard anything further about this new heroin variant before the case is closed."

"Ok smart ass, let's go."

Chris stood up and they began their walk over to Narcotics, grabbing a cup of coffee on the way. It wasn't a far trek, but it was good to talk to the different departments in person if at all possible. A lot of times you could pick up information through facial expression that a phone call or email just couldn't convey. It reminded Tyler of the COVID-19 policies that had caused some people cabin fever and how much he had missed working with others directly during that time.

Charles Penton and Casey Lyle had been working Narcotics for about three years. Homicide had worked with them collaboratively multiple times. More than 70% of all murders in Chicago were drug related which meant a lot of interdepartmental communication. Some police departments liked to encourage rivalry, but it was frowned upon by the CPD. More harm than good usually came from being overly competitive with co-workers on your own team. Tyler liked working with the Narcotics team and always enjoyed hearing Charles bellow at them about how messed up the world was or amusing them with a somewhat exaggerated story of his bravado.

When they reached Narcotics, however, only Casey Lyle was sitting at his desk. Chris pointed to the empty desk as a question. Casey leaned back in his chair and said, "Out for a late breakfast or early pre-lunch, who knows?" A running joke had given the duo the nickname of Straw and Bale, as Charles Penton was known for his enormous appetite and compact frame going to fat, while Casey was the thinnest police officer in the precinct. He looked like a palm tree with a crazy hairstyle and muted, khaki colored clothing. Unlikely as the partnership seemed, Tyler had never heard anything but good things about the pair.

"How's it going, Homicide?"

"Before we close the Land case, just wanted to get a little more background on the latest round of Abyss sightings." Tyler replied, "This has been what, your third one this week?"

Casey nodded and stretched out his arms to encompass several stacks of files that had been placed on both desks. There were more folders stacked on top of a four foot filing cabinet. The amount of documentation was impressive and depressing. "Third or fourth, I am beginning to lose count with all the other fucked up stuff going on. The case rate is taking off, which is definitely not a good thing for the division. I have never seen or read anything like this. The hallucino-genic properties alone prove it is some sort of synth custom, but we have no idea where the drug is coming from. It is a web in a web in a fucking web. We cut down a few strands by taking out the dealers as we find them, but they always got the drug from someone who got it from someone else. Abyss is becoming the drug of choice and we have no real connections to tell us how to stop it."

Chris said, "I thought it was expensive. How can it be so popular? That doesn't make any sense. The economy hasn't improved enough for people to just start buying all kinds of designer drug shit. "

"Well, it was expensive at first, but we think that was because of trial and error production." Casey said, "Now the creators must have a steady supply of whatever chemicals they are using to create the stuff. They use some sort of logistic system to import and synthesize in a safe location. My guess is right inside the city, since we haven't heard much from our counterparts in New York or Detroit. Most of them have had 5 grams or less which is pure base level 12 stuff. No real suppliers."

Tyler nodded. It seemed to point to an origin here in Chicago. Casey leaned back in his chair and rubbed the top of his head in frustration. He said, "We could be facing a lot more cases than we even know. Most of the time, the toxicologist is going to find morphine, or at least monoacetylmorphine. Since it is a variant of heroin which breaks down immediately in the body, it is hard to really understand the trend. By next summer, we could be facing an epidemic of massive proportions due to the extremely distorted perception these users have. I would venture to guess that long-term exposure to this drug would result in insanity, but a lot of them end up killing themselves anyway. The high has to be amazing to warrant taking such a risk."

Tyler shook his head. What they had was a drug that wasn't traceable to the source, had a side-effect of potential insanity, and was growing right here in their city. It was a modern day Bubonic plague. The Black Death would stalk the streets once again. He had hoped Charles or Casey would have some sort of specialist knowledge to point to the people responsible, but that wasn't the case. No special hanging file or software database to answer all his questions. Unfortunately, it seemed like the murder of Chad Gosman and Kate Land's suicide would be only the beginning. Tyler had a headache.

"We need to stay on top of this." Tyler said. "We'll keep you in the loop for any contacts, names, or relevant information we see in Homicide's cases. Can you let us know if you find any links that tie any of our cases together? If we keep communication open, we might be able to solve both of our problems before this gets out of control."

Casey nodded his head, already turning back to the mountain of files in front of him, his massive hair bobbing from the jilted movement. He pushed a stack away from his keyboard with a sigh and began typing. Tyler and Chris left Casey to his work. Chris muttered to himself until Tyler nudged him. Chris said, "It is good to loop everyone together. Will make it easier to see a pattern but this Abyss shit has already gotten really fucking depressing. How much worse could it really get?" Tyler shook his head. Rhetorical questions were almost never worth answering.

CHAPTER 4
Will

WILL THOMPSON SAT in the back of a brown Dodge Ram van with an H&K USP semi-automatic pistol in his lap. He tried to keep the gun pointed towards the side of the seat, which was hard with the constant jarring of the no-shocks piece of shit vehicle. He thought the van would be up for antique status pretty soon. It had come with two men in the front seat who talked constantly back forth like a pair of chained parrots. When he worked with any outside help, Will always preferred to have them in front of him, if at all possible. It didn't matter whether it was in a bar like where they had met, in a vehicle, or even when you were killing someone. It is far easier to shoot someone in the back than turn around, pull out your gun, and try to double-cross your teammate.

He had recruited some local help for this task mainly because most of the last crew was dead. That was a shame since Will had enjoyed their company far more than these idiots. They hadn't bothered him with a lot of questions, and they didn't talk this much. Still, what was that saying about trusting a junkie as long as you had the supply?

The long pause up front meant he had been asked another

question, and Will had to recall what they had said. Something about what exactly had to be done? He replied, "We need to kill the woman. Anyone else is collateral." The one in the front passenger seat named Leal turned around and repeated the word. "Collateral?" His face was a blank slate, and the question was more about the word itself, than any hidden implication. "Yes, collateral which means you kill or burn anything else in the way. Baxter doesn't care as long as the woman is dead. Then you get paid. Easy enough now shut the fuck up." Payment was fifty grand and, more importantly, a hefty bag of Abyss. The drug was fast becoming granular bits of red gold.

Will had made the arrangements using Baxter's name as he often did. He was the right hand, the physical presence of their business, but Robert Baxter was the bogeyman. The man behind the curtain was always the more ominous threat. People always feared what they didn't know or understand. In this particular case, he didn't blame them. Even Will tried to stay disconnected by working through his contacts, but sometimes you had to get your hands dirty. At least if you wanted to ensure it was done right. Sometimes you had to be there with your hands around someone's neck to keep their hands off yours.

Finding Emily Morgan had been easy since people were ultimately loyal to themselves. A little money went a long way in the age of social media. Her history, career, and family information were easily attainable, but it didn't matter. All that mattered was that she was gone and no questions. At least no questions that had real answers. Everything else was a detail that could be looked at later, or most likely ignored. It would keep Baxter happy, which in turn made life easier for Will. It was the best for everyone really.

They arrived at a small apartment building as the sun began to set. The driver, whose name was Harris, put the van into park and turned the keys to off but left them in the ignition. Both of the front seat occupants turned to look at Will, who turned around to look at the small steel drum in the back of the van. Inside the metal container was a highly volatile accelerant mix of gasoline, kerosene, paint thinner, and God knows what else. It would help the fire get hot enough to destroy their passing like brushing footprints in the desert. Hopefully it wouldn't burn the entire building down. Of course that was also collateral too, so no great loss.

"Not enough time or resources," Will muttered as he unzipped the black bag they had brought to carry the drum. He fed the drum into the mouth of the bag, covering up the metallic sheen. He didn't want their visit to be memorable to anyone who might see them.

Will turned around to face his one-time only co-workers. He said, "Ok, short and simple. She dies, and the place burns. That's it. No multi-tiered objective here but if we fuck this up we might as well pour the accelerant on ourselves. Ok, any questions? No, well…"

The one named Leal raised his hand like they were in school, though assuredly neither had made it as far as Lincoln Park or Phillips Academy. He looked at Harris, and they both nodded before he licked his lips, his voice coming out in a whispered caw. "What about the woman?"

"What about the woman?"

"Well, we are going after a woman and she is dead. Guaranteed dead. So it isn't like she is going to say anything, and you know…….." The implication was obvious as the words 'you know'. Will considered shooting both of them in the face, but this idea of theirs, no matter how repulsive could only make it look more random as a homicide. Besides, he still needed human shields. "Fine, bring the rope. I don't care, but let's make this quick." The doors creaked open as the men got out of the van. No one would notice their entry into the apartment complex or their departure amidst the confusion of the fire.

CHAPTER 5
End of the Day

Tyler stretched as he walked out of the door of CPD towards his car. The humidity grabbed him and clung to his clothes even at this time of night. He and Chris had finished most of their paperwork. It amounted to either citing the case as dead, in the water, or closed. The ME's report had not come back yet, but he had already gotten a call with a summary that tied to their initial theory. The ebb and flow of the case was logical for such illogical behavior, and all the loose ends tied up. No hidden gunman or secret conspiracy, but the cause was still disturbing. It gnawed at him like a type of cancer and the effect was bestial.

He sat down inside the Mustang as the springs in his seat groaned like an old man. "What are you bitching about?" Tyler muttered to his car, as he turned on the Bluetooth settings, looking through his preset stations before settling on INXS's "Never Tear Us Apart" which was a favorite of his. Hell, the whole Kick album was a masterpiece. The saxophone solo echoed ethereally through his car as he felt tension leave his body inch by inch. Things were already a little better, knowing he was going home after a long day, but his shoulders still ached. Maybe he would get them rubbed tonight, Tyler thought with a smile as he put the car into reverse.

Tyler had met Emily almost nine years ago to the month. It had an almost surreal and mythic feel to him now. He had been a rookie patrol officer on his lunch break, hoping to find an Elmore Leonard novel and pick up an issue of Men's Health in a dying bookstore. He had walked by the Classical Literature section and had seen a stunning, brown-haired woman holding a paperback. He had stopped so abruptly that he almost tripped. The book she held was one of his favorites, Swift's *Gulliver's Travels*. Tyler had walked up to her without even being aware that he had done so.

Within an hour, they had discussed one of the novel's themes concerning whether mankind was inherently corrupt or could be corrupted (Tyler had thought inherently corrupt even though that was boring), and within two hours they had moved on to politics. They had been kicked out of the section during the restock by a clerk with arched eyebrows. Tyler's lunch break was far over, and he left with the promise of a deeper discussion over dinner. He had taken her a Gerber daisy on their first date, which she still had. The flower was pressed in a photo album in their bedroom.

Tyler had never truly been in love before, but it had come naturally with Emily. Within a year, they were married, to the surprise of everyone. Even then, Tyler knew he had his perfect counterpart. Emily was his exact opposite in so many ways, which is why they meshed so well. She was subtle to his brashness and soft to his dour nature. Nothing in life was ever perfect; certainly not their relationship, but he wouldn't change a minute of it. Not even a damn second.

Tyler's view on the world changed once again when Grace was born.

His daughter was a ray of light that made each day a little better. She used to laugh out loud from her crib for no reason, which would make Emily and Tyler laugh with her. Tyler still called Grace his Sunshine or Angel Eyes. Even today, the baby nicknames were hard to let go.

Before ten months had gone by, Grace was crawling and reaching for crayons and pencils. Her interest in art was a gift that neither of her parents possessed. Tyler was hard-pressed to deny that she was already more talented artistically at eight years old than he ever would be.

Grace's artwork brought a hush of amazement from her teachers, but her personality shone through her laughter more than any visual depiction. Tyler glanced down on the passenger seat where the neatly folded origami hummingbird sat waiting to hover about Grace's room. He couldn't wait to see the look on her face tonight.

The Chicago traffic crawled through downtown with its usual end of day sluggishness like a lumbering, dying beast. It seemed that he would get every green light going to work and every red light going home. "I'm probably not the only person who feels that way," Tyler said to himself. The sky had taken on a reddish hue, though a mass of dark nimbostratus clouds gathered, intent on drowning the city one raindrop at a time. He should be able to make it home just before the storm hit. The only guaranteed precinct topics were what was going on with the Bears and what the weather was going to be like. Tyler didn't have any comments on either subject.

Tyler put on his signal as he turned into Roscoe Village. If there had been a passenger in the car with Tyler, they might have noticed he looked more at ease as he drove towards the complex. The lines on his face would smooth and then disappear. His grip on the steering wheel loosened, and he would lean farther back in the seat. Tyler was never aware of this process, but he would catch himself exhaling a long held breath. It felt like he was coming up for air after being at the bottom of the ocean. He was ready to spend time with his family. This was the best kind of reward for his work today. It was all he ever needed. All he ever wanted. Tyler continued his relaxed drive until he reached home. Where he would see the flames.......

CHAPTER 6
Six Months Later,
Blessed are the Dead

Tyler awoke with a start. He felt the stiff cushions of the couch beneath his legs. Sweat trickled down both temples and settled along his jaw. He had been dreaming about his family again. He sat up to a roaring headache as he kicked over several bottles of God knows what onto the floor. The fabric of an under shirt clung to his back even though it was going to be a cold January day outside. Snowfall so far had been light, though meteorologists predicted with fifty percent accuracy that a large blizzard would hit Chicago any day now. How long had it been? Six months and two days since that night where his home had burned down. Six months and two days since his family had died. Sounded like the end to a terrible joke.

Tyler stood up, trying to shake the thoughts out of his head as he battled the headache to the bathroom. The new apartment was almost halfway through the first year's lease, but it still felt strange and alien to him. The walls weren't the color of his "real" apartment and the layout was cramped and unwelcoming to him. It had been the first place he had found on the market. He had signed the lease without even thinking. The landlord had smiled when showing him the place, but it was more for the deposit than anything else. It was just walls to shield Tyler from the weather, nothing more. There was no such thing as a home anymore.

He barely had time to flick the bathroom light on as he stumbled to the toilet and urinated what was left of the liquids inside him. He waited to see if his body would need to lean over and vomit as well, and for a moment he thought he might, but the feeling passed. Maybe later if he could find the time. He passed by the sink and glanced at the reflection in the mirror. A foolish mistake that grounded him to a complete halt.

Tyler barely recognized himself anymore. His eyes had a bloodshot quality that made mockery of the dark circles underneath. They looked more red than white like he was wearing fake Halloween contacts. The patchy beard had begun to appear on his face again. Tyler had stopped shaving for a while, but whenever he had to go out, people stared at him like he was an Abyss junkie. Shaving hadn't helped with that very much, but he still turned on the razor whenever he had to leave. When was the last time he had gone outside? That hadn't been for at least a few weeks. Right? He had lost track of time.

The flicker of a memory crossed his mind. Shaving with Grace standing by his side smiling. Oh, she had laughed when he chased her around the house with a can of Harry's shaving cream. "Noooo, Daddy! I don't want to be messy like you!" Always a giggle that would start his own laughter and then.....

Tyler held up an arm to ward off the thoughts. His muscular frame was still there, but it had begun to take on an unhealthy sheen. Tyler still worked out, more as a way to try to block the memories rather than actually caring about his health anymore. No amount of pushups could take his memories away. One day, he had collapsed on the treadmill and blacked out. Later, he awoke to find himself face down on the floor. Only alcohol helped with any of it, and sometimes his choice of cure could be worse than the poison. He was drinking far too much at this point, but he was past caring about such things. Here he was, a stranger in his own mirror. A stranger in the only body he had ever known. What a fucked up notion.

Tyler had been granted a leave of absence for a few months after the deaths of his family. He had buried himself in looking for any information concerning the murders. He had pushed hard on anyone associated with Emily personally or professionally. He hated the looks on his former neighbors and coworkers' faces. He could almost hear the sound of relationships snapping like cheap matchsticks. All of his Criminal Informants and then other officers' CIs had turned up nothing.

Tyler recalled a picture he had once seen of the three wise monkeys carving at the Tosho-gu shrine. They represented the maxim 'see no evil, hear no evil, speak no evil' that had become synonymous with avoiding malevolence at all costs. That was what everyone was doing. No one could tell him anything because they didn't know or didn't want to know. At least that is what he told himself when he was thinking about it.

CPSU had gone through the scene with a fine tooth comb. "Clear application of arson with an extreme accelerant derivative likely being the source fuel". The line from the report still stood out in Tyler's mind. What it really meant was they didn't know shit. The fire had destroyed any evidence the attackers might have left behind. There were no discernible DNA samples, fingerprints, or other useful physical information. These murderers had destroyed his life and then vanished without a trace. Tyler had tried to picture what they looked like in his mind's eye, but couldn't see a face. Just a type of blankness. A lack of humanity which was more palatable than the alternative. It was easier to think that monsters had done this rather than people.

Lieutenant Alan Rooks had pulled him off the case for admittedly a lack of real evidence. Tyler had hated him even though it was the right call to make. The case was still considered in a state of ongoing investigation, but even those outside the law enforcement community knew that it was a dead end. The media had stopped focusing on Tyler's family and had moved on to other more immediate stories. The general public made his story a footnote in a sea of ongoing tragedies. He had received cards, calls, gifts, and prayers, but none of it would bring back Grace's paintings or a smile from Emily. Prayers did not bring back the dead.

Tyler walked back into the living room and sat down. His head still throbbed, but the pain had crawled towards the back of his skull. He liked to rest out here on the couch, but sleep was never more than a few hours at a time. The dreams he had were fitful and violent. The bedroom reminded Tyler too much of holding Grace late at night. She would creep in with an embarrassed grin, saying she had a bad dream. All three of them would fall asleep together and usually that kept the nightmares away for months.

Tyler could not imagine living in the old apartment now. That was, of course, not an option anyway. The only pictures that he still had were from the office. He had taken those and put them in a cardboard box, sealing the top and bottom with layers of packing tape. Sometimes at night, he could feel the pictures staring at him through the cardboard, and that was when he would leave the apartment for a drink or five.

Tyler stared down at the coffee table in front of him with its dull, chipped finish. Amidst the half empty or completely dry bottles sat his two 40 caliber Glock Model 22's. They were always cold to the touch regardless of the weather. Tyler had been looking at them a lot lately. It was hard to focus on anything else. His mind made his vision a blur.

All other police gear, including his badge, had been boxed up and stored in the closet next to the pictures. He had kept everything out after the case had been reassigned but as time went on it had become meaningless. Eventually he had put all his past belongings away. It was something to do rather than any symbolic sacrifice.

The first 48 to 72 hours were critical for any homicide investigation, with the national clearance rate being between 62 and 66 percent. The longer the time span, the lower the clearance rate dropped. It wasn't because some criminal mastermind had more time to devise an ingenious plan or the officer had to reprioritize the case (though eventually that did happen). The answer was simple: evidence was never discovered, the suspect had fled, or most of the time, people forgot details as their memories dimmed. This was true even for horrific events. It was the brain's defense against traumatic experiences. When you first talked to a witness they could usually describe little nuances that six months later were forgotten. Eventually the horror glazed over and became a terrible story to tell neighbors.

One of the main exceptions was, of course, when the event happened to you. Sometimes the memories could become more acute as the person reflected on them over and over again. Unfortunately, there was no pill to help ease the pain. Tyler had not forgotten a moment of that night no matter how hard he tried.

After the reassignment, Tyler had spent half his time looking into the case on his own and the other half drinking in his apartment. One night he had thrown all of his furniture and several glasses against the walls in fit of rage. Someone had banged on his door, and he had answered with the Glock in hand. Luckily, no one had been there. He was sure his neighbors thought he was insane. Maybe there was some hard truth to that. None of them would meet his eyes except the new tenants and that didn't last for long. He couldn't blame them really.

Tyler pushed all the bottles on the table onto the floor. They landed on the carpet with light clinks or heavy cluggs. Liquor spilled out onto the already stained carpet. The smell of alcohol immediately filled the air and made his throat ache. He regretted his rash move, but it was for the best, the deposit be damned. In front of him on the table sat his two weapons like a simple solution to a complex problem.

Tyler had thought about killing himself every day since the night of the fire. He had held out hope that he would find some vital clue or shred of information that would give him a trail, a source, or even a vague idea of where to go next. At one point, he was convinced he would find some piece of evidence overlooked by everyone else. The last embers of these hopes had died as his nightmares and guilt had become stronger. It was obvious at this point that he would never catch the people responsible. There was no justice in this case. Justice wasn't blind, she was fucking clueless.

Tyler picked up one of his handguns and checked the magazine. He had cleaned both weapons continuously, even when all the other routines of his profession had fallen by the wayside. It gleamed dully in a state of readiness that only a well-maintained weapon could have. The gun felt heavier than normal, but maybe he was paying attention to its feel for the first time in years. Tyler checked the chamber and placed the gun against his temple. It felt very cold but also comforting.

A lot of failed suicides were because of methods that still offered the chance of survival, if the person was found quickly enough. Very few people survive a bullet to the head. Perhaps he would be in Heaven with his family? Maybe Hell for his sins? Maybe nothing at all? It didn't matter. He was already in Hell, and the others would only be improvements.

Tyler's finger touched the trigger and waited for the right moment to end this pointless mockery. There was no safety to worry about. As he waited, he mouthed the words of goodbye that would not be in a note. There was no one left to write to. As he finished his words, he paused and breathed for a moment. Just listening to his lungs breathe in and then breathe out. Breathe in. Breathe out. What was he waiting for? Emily and Grace were dead. His mind debated the pros and cons of living while his finger tapped the trigger. He continued to think as the hours passed by without an acceptable answer.

A booming knock on the front door woke Tyler up. He must have fallen asleep. The taste of gun oil was in his mouth, and the Glock lay in his right hand. What the hell had happened? Had he put the gun in his mouth at one point? He must have but he couldn't remember doing so. He wasn't sure if the knock was real until it came again.

The booming sound echoed again through the living room. Tyler stretched his back, feeling a sense of unreality wash over him. None of this was really happening, was it? The gun began to shake in his hand. He laid the weapon down on the table with great reluctance. Tyler stood up to answer the door.

CHAPTER 7
Rooks and Herrera

THE DOOR OPENED, letting in Lieutenant Rooks, Detective Annabelle Herrera, and a cold wind that seemed to chill the entire apartment. "Hello, Tyler, how have you been?" Rooks said with an offered hand. A laugh almost escaped Tyler's lips. It was like a gathering of old friends for the weekly poker game. He opened the door wider to allow them entrance, ignoring the hand which the Lieutenant dropped as though anticipated. Rooks and Herrera entered the living room and stood near the couch. Tyler kicked a bottle under the table but said nothing.

Alan Rooks was known to be one of the brightest and most hardworking lieutenants in the state, but the recent surge in crime had obviously taken a heavy toll on him. His usual starched white shirt seemed muted amidst the heavy coat, and he stood still, hunched over, as though trying to dodge a bullet. Rooks could be somewhat of a heartless bastard, but despite this, he was well-liked above, by departmental leadership. Tyler could admit that Rooks usually got the results needed. It was rumored he had passed on several promotions, as this was the last level in which he could still take his trademark "hands on" approach. Perhaps he was regretting that decision now.

"Let's go sit in the kitchen." Tyler said as they walked through the living room, dodging bottles and small pools of alcohol like a field of landmines. The small, compact table had three chairs, one on each side, with the fourth side pressed flush against the apartment wall. Tyler's muscular frame barely fit into the groaning chair as he sat on the right side. Rooks sat on the opposite end with Herrera as "mediator" in the middle. This was the first time he had company in the new apartment.

The kitchen was dark despite the hour since no lights were on. The blinds had been closed since the day Tyler had rented the place. No one made any motion to change the lighting. It was odd sitting in the shadows like this. Rooks continued to stare directly at Tyler.

"Suffice to say again, I am very sorry for your loss. We aren't here to rip open wounds that are still healing. I know how intelligent you are, Tyler so I won't waste your time with a lot of fluff and bullshit." Rooks said, "Detective Herrera has made a potential breakthrough in your case. Well, the only case that matters to you right now and I thought you should hear it from her."

Tyler's eyes widened and his thoughts reeled at Rooks's bold proclamation. It was just like the lieutenant's reputation for cutting to the heart of the matter. Had they done it? A link that could bring some new scrap of information or maybe resolution? Rooks might as well have announced that he could walk on water. There was no room for miracles but he dared to hope anyway.

Tyler's eyes snapped to Annabelle Herrera, who still had not spoken a single word. She looked like the top lawyer of a prestigious firm who had won her cases through determination and the belief in what is right. The pressed suit suited her well. All she needed was a suitcase rather than a gun.

Tyler had never worked with her, but Annabelle was known for her quick wit and direct nature which were attributes he could appreciate. She had risen through the ranks of Chicago's police force quickly and was the first Hispanic woman to make Homicide before the age of thirty. He had seen Annabelle many times at the station but never talked with her. She refused to meet Tyler's gaze. The exact opposite of Rooks's approach. All that mattered right now were answers.

Annabelle said, "I don't want to overstate this or make our visit something it isn't, but last night we did a raid on a local Abyss den. They have started to become more common in the last six months since you left. One of our arrests is a regular Abyss junkie by the name of Jesse Polis. Ever heard of him?" Tyler shook his head no, and Annabelle continued. "He is the usual low-level fuckup. Petty charges. Nothing too serious, though he has become one of few long termers for Abyss. Sunken eyes, unhealthy skin, nosebleeds, the works. He also has a healthy dose of paranoia when he's off the stuff. This morning he starts wanting to make a deal for no jail time. No bargaining or time loss, but complete amnesty. In return he says he can tell us the name of….." Annabelle turned to look down at her notepad for the exact quote of what was said. 'The guy who burned that cop's family during the summer. I know the exact bitch you are looking for.'"

Tyler waited to see if she had anything more to say. When nothing else was coming, he turned to look at Rooks. Was this a joke? Rooks shook his head no and said, "We have no idea if this is legitimate or not, Tyler. No one has spoken to Jesse since he offered this information. It has only been a few hours. We've kept him in holding. He has been informed we will be having some discussions, and someone will be talking with him shortly. Detective Herrera came to me with this news less than an hour ago and that is why we are here with you now. You had every right to know, as this is our first potential lead. Even if it is a ghost of a lead at best."

Tyler shifted forward in his chair as both Rooks and Herrera studied him. He kept thinking about Grace's mobile which had become ashes in the flames. He thought of the hummingbird that would never be given to his daughter. He said, "I need one hour to get ready." Rooks held up his hand both in placation and acknowledgement. He looked more like a pleading elementary teacher than a lieutenant of CPD.

The lieutenant said, "No questions? No doubts of legitimacy? It all seems kind of random to me, Detective Morgan. Doesn't it to you?"

Tyler shook his head without hesitation and said, "It doesn't matter. It is a lead. Any lead matters at this point, Lieutenant Rooks. I am not going to question the why right now."

Rooks leaned back in the chair causing it to creak loudly. He said, "Tyler, I know this is something you would want to be involved with personally, but this information comes with a caveat. Do you really think this is a good idea? You have every right to know, but is this something you can handle without emotion getting in the way? Really?" Tyler leaned back in his chair mimicking Rooks and pretended to contemplate the question. His heart raced at the thought of finding his family's killer or killers. He looked at the ceiling and noticed several spider webs that seemed broken. They swayed in the regulated air.

Tyler kept looking at the ceiling and said, "With all due respect Lieutenant, this is exactly why you came here in the first place isn't it? You need one of your lead detectives to break this down, and you know I will get the job done, no matter the circumstances." Tyler held up his hand as Rooks began to protest. "I can tell you now, emotion is going to get in the way, but I don't give a damn and, quite frankly, I don't think you care. You want results and you will get them. Honestly as far as my future in this department goes, how would I ever come back if I didn't take care of this first?"

"You won't, Tyler, I know that." Rooks said, "I also know this is what you need and that it is important, but I know you. I saw that look in your eyes for a second that tells me that this case will either be solved brilliantly or with a lot of bloodshed. I don't want the bloodshed. Everything has to be done by standard protocol, and I want you working as a team with Annabelle. That is my one stipulation for you even being a part of this investigation at all."

"What about Chris?"

"Chris? Chris Wessler? Wessler moved over to Narcotics several months ago. Didn't he tell you?" The question was simple, but the answer was not. Tyler hadn't talked to Chris since the funeral but not for a lack of trying from his former partner. It got to a point where Tyler had started deleting all his voicemails unheard. His phone had constantly beeped. He didn't answer the knock when he heard someone at his door. Chris had tried that route many times too.

The need to talk to others just didn't seem that important, and it hurt to be reminded of any part of his former life. Tyler was sure

Chris was doing well at Narcotics, cracking his lame jokes and wearing some new brown and neon green shirt. In a way it was good that Chris didn't talk with him anymore. It was better to keep tired memories than actual friends who reminded you of the past.

Rooks leaned forward as though trying to anticipate any questions. He said, "Detective Herrera is more than qualified for this case. She could learn from your creativity, and you could learn from her diligence to protocol. A better partnership I can't envision. This could be the finest Homicide team Chicago could have in quite a while if you can keep your act professional. I just need you two to work together, Tyler. I need an emergency switch in this case, and you damn well know why. No holding back and if you get in too deep, you back off. Can you stay within those guidelines, Detective Morgan?"

He seemed disappointed at Tyler's quick nod, but it also was expected. A moment of silence fell over the table. It became an awkward pause. Tyler could tell Annabelle was shifting in her seat impatiently, perhaps regretting wearing the suit.

Tyler began to rise, and all three were up, pushing the chairs in at the same time. It seemed unreal as they walked back to the entrance to the apartment. Tyler held the door open for his guests. Annabelle put on her coat and turned to him as he waited for Rooks to leave. Annabelle spoke for the second time, looking him in the eyes. "I just wanted to say I am genuinely sorry. Your wife and child were beautiful. No one should have to go through what you did." Tyler began to say a casual 'Thank you' dismissal, but he looked into her eyes and saw genuine concern. It was easy to say words but true empathy was far rarer. He nodded his thanks. The lieutenant also had put on his coat and walked over to Tyler. It seemed he had aged twelve years since the last time Tyler had seen him.

Rooks said, "Tyler, I hope this hasn't given you false hopes for some sort of catharsis but.........."

Tyler held up his hand. "I need one hour." Rooks nodded and walked out the door into the cold wind that promised more snow. Annabelle followed without a backwards glance. Tyler shut the door behind them.

Lieutenant Rooks and Detective Herrera walked back to the car without saying a word. They got into Rooks's car, a dark green Honda CR-V, and began to pull out of the complex. Annabelle waited several more minutes for the car to warm up before she took a deep breath. She said, "Lieutenant, I appreciate the trust you have put in me by assigning lead in the case, but do you really think this is a good idea? That man lives with ghosts, and did you see the look in his eyes? That wasn't hope or justice there. It was vengeance I saw. That man looked like one of the dead when he answered the door. I realize that his family's involvement makes the situation unique for him, but isn't this going to make the problem worse? Is this truly the best way to start our investigation?"

Rooks replied, "Honestly, I don't know Annabelle, but I couldn't live with any other decision. Detective Morgan is still a member of our family, and he is hurting. We can't just let the man go on with no closure."

"But at what cost?" Annabelle replied, "No offense, Lieutenant, but are you more concerned with his state of mind or your clearance rate? I know Detective Morgan's credentials are impressive, and it would do wonders for our PR. 'Detective solves family's murder' has a certain ring to it, but is that really the most logical..."

"That is enough, Detective Herrera." Rooks said in a tone of impatience. "You are going to do fine. I am going to do fine. Tyler Morgan is going to do fine. The only people I would worry about are anyone who gets in his way. Those are the ones you need to be concerned with. Watch him every second, Herrera. I mean it."

Annabelle turned to look out her window as she adjusted the shoulder strap for the seatbelt. Just who would benefit from a man like Tyler Morgan being on this case? There didn't seem to be a good answer to that question. She hoped there would be one soon or it would be both their asses on the line.

CHAPTER 8
Annabelle's Decision

TYLER CLOSED THE door and leaned against the doorframe, exhaling all of the air in his body. The maelstrom of emotion wasn't something he was used to, but he would endure anything if it led to some kind of peace. He felt anger and exhilaration swirl about him making his motions seem slow. The turbulence also seemed to give him a type of clarity he had not felt in months.

He walked into the bedroom and began to rifle through his closet. The flimsy storage boxes formed two imbalanced pylons starting at the floor and moving up to the hanger bar. After tossing several aside, he found the one he needed with the scrawled label of 'work' on the side. He ripped off the packaging tape in one movement and dumped out all of his detective equipment onto the bed in a jumbled mass.

Tyler sorted everything on the bed into more organized piles before getting ready to take a shower. He didn't wait for the water to warm up as he jumped in, the cold hit him causing his limbs to shiver. By the time he was done using the soap and shampoo, the water was boiling as it tried to wash away a week of grime. It almost felt like washing away his past sins. Almost.

Stepping out of the hot water, Tyler wiped away the steam from the mirror to shave his thin beard. The face that stared back at him was different than it had been a couple of hours ago. It was hard to identify, and Tyler could not figure out exactly what it was but something had changed. The hard edge was more pronounced than ever, but he looked energized, for lack of a better word. He knew the why already. He had a purpose for life again, at least at this moment.

Tyler's smile became a grimace at these thoughts. He shook them away and turned from the mirror. He didn't have time for in-depth analysis of his character or the subliminal connotations of recent tragedy. What he had was an hour, and even that seemed like far too much time. He finished getting ready as quickly as he could, and fifteen minutes later put on his holster and badge. Out of the closet came his black leather jacket still encased in waterproof sealant. Emily had always teased that it was not a winter coat, no matter how much he wanted it to be. It creaked with familiarity as he put it on. Grace had loved the smell of it. She would hold up the sleeves to her nose and breathe deeply. More thoughts of his daughter propelled him across the apartment, and without a backward glance, Tyler opened the front door leading out into the cold.

The Mustang waited in the parking spot, always ready like a horse of the Apocalypse. Tyler jumped into the car which sagged under his weight, but not as much as it used to. Tyler noticed this for the first time as he put the gear stick into reverse. It was like his anger had gradually eaten his body. Gnawing tissue away in order to feed a rage that grew with every breath.

He could have driven the route blindfolded, and his mind began to think about the interview as the car took the twists and turns of the Chicago streets it knew so well. The snow fell in slow, fat flakes that clung to his windshield. Winter had arrived in that chaotic way it always did. Each year Chicago became a beautiful city during the spring that rivaled any other, but it never lasted. Winters were cruel and deadly. Mother Nature could be a whimsical, magical personification of beauty, but she could also be a real bitch when she wanted. Especially to the residents of his home city.

The streets downtown had turned to an icy slush under the constant tread of salt-crusted tires pressing down with the urgency of those already late for work. Those unfortunates having forgotten the golden rule of adding a half an hour for Chicago light snow traffic were paying for it now. Finding a parking spot was always a fun challenge if you didn't use a taxi or had a good pair of boots.

Tyler arrived at the police station, and, for a moment, it felt like putting on his old jacket. It was familiar and something he knew so well that it had become part of his nature. There were twenty-five stations in Chicago not including the Marine Unit Station in the harbor. This particular district's station was newer than most since the mayor had remodeled the entire building four years ago. The previous architecture had been dying since the 1950s and the remodeling had upgraded not only the infrastructure, but also the entire feel of the building. It was cold and sleek like the inside of an airport rather than a centralized hub of the Chicago police department.

Tyler saw a few new faces and a lot of old ones who seemed to pause as he walked by. Tyler hoped it was obvious he was not here to chat, though one officer whose name was Michael raised his hand in greeting as he walked by. He waved back but kept walking. There were a few scattered whispers, but most of the focus was on running the department rather than a returning police detective. It was strange and comforting at the same time. Far better than the lingering gazes and tear-wrapped eyes of his last visit.

When he arrived at the lieutenant's office, Rooks was talking on the phone with the door open. The lieutenant had obviously come straight back and gone to work without missing a beat. Rooks stood at a large mahogany desk with a cup of coffee and several manila folders lying open in front of him. The stories of the dead, thought Tyler, as his superior beckoned for him to take a seat. The chairs were toughened leather. It was like sitting on the back of a crocodile. The room was filled with paperwork and files, but there was still a sense of organization and order. The lieutenant owned the room, not the other way around.

Bookcases contained works on criminal psychology, law, and

medicine. Tyler noticed a copy of Othello had managed to pry its way in-between Forensic journals. Some things never changed. The file that sat centermost on Rooks's desk was open. Tyler saw his own picture from when he was a rookie in the upper left corner of the page. The lieutenant had done his homework to gain some perspective before coming to see him. Tyler would give anything to go back to the rookie patrol officer in the picture and warn him of what was to come. Hindsight was always twenty-twenty whether you wanted it to be or not.

"I don't care what the press is saying; I want it taken care of now." Rooks spoke into the phone in a calm voice that hid his pacing behind the desk. "Give me an SU report in two hours and keep me posted of any changes. Also let Herrera know I want her back in my office right away." He put the phone down by the files on the desk and looked at Tyler and nodded. "You know, Tyler, I still remember that profile you put together on the Street Strangler. You remember that? Your list of probable targets, habits, and hell, even the description of the psychological mindset was dead on. Greg Lark was exactly how you described him. The meticulous care of the house and the fact that he smoked that goddamned pipe like he was out of a Sidney Paget illustration. He was laughing when we caught him with the dead boy in his basement. Did you know that? He hadn't even dumped the body yet, and Lord knows we would be searching for another one right now, if it wasn't for you."

"What point are you trying to make, Lieutenant?"

Alan Rooks ignored the question and continued, "Summa cum laude GPA at University of Chicago, excellent marks in physical endurance and marksmanship, as well as a recommendation from Sergeant Bridges. Hell, that couldn't have been easy. You really have to earn that man's respect. Aptitude in psychology including familiarity with MMPI, CPI, and TAT as well."

"Yes, I know all that Lieutenant. What is the reason behind going through this now? We are wasting time."

"I'm sure you know, Tyler, that with your background and excellent PDT scores you could have been in FBI, DEA, ATF, or possibly the Department of Treasury. You could have gone almost anywhere. But instead you chose here where the high homicide rate means that it is not a matter of if you will burn out, but when. You chose here because, ultimately, it is where you belong." Tyler was silent.

"You are a damn good cop, Detective Morgan. That is why I am giving you a chance with this, but I see that look on your face. You are out for blood, and I honestly don't know if I can blame you."

Rooks seemed to realize he was still standing and sat down in a chair much more formal than the ones in Tyler's kitchen. He said, "I can only imagine what it is like to lose everything in one night, let alone to evil bastards that are still out and walking around our city. But it is important to remember we are on the side of the law which means you complete this case with the same standard protocols you would if it weren't your family. You can't make it personal. Modus operandi, post mortem, Corpus Delicti, surveillance, forensics, all of it. Anything you think, say, or do should be displayed on my monitor or on the top of my inbox all the time. Let me also reiterate that Herrera is involved in this every step of the way. Do you understand what I am trying to say, Detective Morgan?"

Rooks's eyes drifted behind him to the doorway, and Tyler knew that Herrera had arrived. He turned to see her trying to stay out of earshot beyond the doorframe. She didn't quite make it. "I understand what you are saying, Lieutenant." Tyler said, and Rooks's eyes snapped back to look at him. He stared at Tyler for several more seconds trying to gauge his soul. Tyler knew he didn't have a prayer if Rooks could read his inner thoughts but the point was moot. Rooks finally nodded and shut Tyler's file with unsubtle meaning. The lieutenant turned back to his computer as though no one else was in the room with him.

Tyler stood up and began to walk toward the doorframe. He stopped without turning around and said, "Every case is personal to somebody, Lieutenant. Always." The sound of typing stopped for a second but then resumed without further comment. The sun shone through the blinds, but there was more shadow than light in the room. The darkness seemed to have spread in the few minutes he had been sitting in the office. Tyler closed the door behind him. It clicked shut with a sense of finality.

Annabelle Herrera had stepped forward to meet him. She looked at Tyler and said, "Well, that could have gone a little more diplomatically."

"With all due respect, Detective Herrera, if we are going to work together on this case, the one thing you should know is that I am not in this for standard protocol or diplomacy." Tyler said, "I am here to track down the murderers of my family by any means necessary. Where is Jesse Polis?"

"I had him moved into Interrogation Room 3." They both began to walk towards the area. Tyler knew the path well.

"Lawyer?"

"Actually since he is trying to cut a deal with us, he has declined his right to an attorney. Trying to sweeten the deal might be a better phrase, I think. Maybe it's just the drugs that have addled his brain. Either way he doesn't have legal counsel at this time."

"Good, that is all we need." Tyler said. Herrera stumbled slightly as they continued their path toward Interrogation. The hallway narrowed as several patrol officers walked past them, having already been through their daily briefing. They were just beginning their shift for the day. There were over 12,000 sworn officers at any given time, so schedules were constantly in flux. It must have been a bitch for administration.

"All we need for what, Detective Morgan?"

"I am going to interview him by myself. I need you to stand watch outside the room for me."

Annabelle stopped walking and turned to face Tyler. Tyler stopped as well. Here it comes, he thought as she frowned at him. She looked like she didn't know whether to be confused or furious. She said, "What the hell are you planning on doing? Remember we are to close this case following all the normal and, more importantly, legal procedures. Nothing further. You know why? If we don't follow procedure, not only do we lower our level of performance, but there is also a chance for some of these scumballs walking. Especially if they have a semi-co-herent lawyer on their side. It helps out the criminals and looks bad for us. That's what I call a no-win situation, Detective Morgan."

"I am going to lay it all out on the table, Herrera, point blank. I know Lieutenant Rooks wants this situation closed, and we both know I can do it. You know why you are here, and that is to keep me in line. I know your reputation as an intuitive police detective. You are also known for not deviating from protocol, which is great in most cases. This is not one of those cases, and I am not here primarily as a detective. I am here for my family. They are dead. I am not." Annabelle stepped back at his words but Tyler pressed on. "I have to ensure the people who are responsible are finished, by any means necessary. That is why I came back. Now I am going to need your help, but I can also tell you that we are going to have to bend or even break some rules. We will get the job done, but in the way it needs to be done. Not what is laid out in a textbook. Can you deal with that, Detective Herrera?"

The look she gave him was so filled with conflicted feeling that in another life it would have torn his heart to see a woman look like that. A lot of emotions had seemed muted to Tyler for the last six months and for once he was grateful for it. She continued to look into his eyes, weighing what he said, as Tyler looked back, waiting. No other words would help her decision.

Annabelle closed her eyes with a sigh and exhaled. She said, "Look Tyler, I know you have been through a lot, but we can't break rules. We both know it. I don't even know what the hell you mean by that, but I don't like the implications. I am going with the Lieutenant's decision on this, but I am starting to think it is a bad one. We have to do things according to protocol, and that is that. Agreed?"

Tyler said nothing, and a silence fell between them for several moments while the office buzzed with the daily operations. Finally Annabelle nodded, not saying anything further; they continued the walk in silence.

It took another five minutes to arrive to their interrogation room. Both detectives walked up to the see-through glass where they could see Polis sitting at a small aluminum table.

Tyler asked, "Any info on him I should know?" Annabelle opened the file she had been carrying. "Ummm, let's see. Jesse did some time on a possession charge, though he did get early release for good behavior. Also there was an attempted rape charge filed by the family of a fourteen year old girl, but it was later dropped due to a lack of evidence. Another rape charge from a fifteen year old girl, but that was also dropped by the family. Weird."

Tyler snorted. It wasn't weird at all. He said, "Probably intimidation. I am surprised it worked, looking at this guy. "

Tyler walked up to the glass to get a better view. Jesse squirmed in his seat as though he could not sit still for more than two minutes. He had no idea he was the most important person in Tyler's world right now.

Stained clothes clinging to his body like he was a scarecrow. Jesse looked like one of those people that had lost too much weight too quickly. His skin hung on his face as loosely as his clothes, and the bloodshot eyes spoke more volumes than any confession he could give. The occasional twitch made the sleeves of his too long shirt flutter in an imaginary wind, like a flag in a storm of nerves. Tyler thought he looked like some deranged diet survivor whose strange obsession with a lack of food was starving him to death faster than any drug addiction.

He said, "So what we have here is a child rapist with an addiction to a drug that isn't completely understood but is known to cause the user to lose their sense of reality through extended sense distortion. It really is amazing he hasn't been shot by someone this month or even this week. I get nervous just looking at him."

Most police interrogation rooms are set up so that either the camera is positioned in the upper corners of the room or behind a see-through glass wall. This particular district's cameras were setup behind the glass, for which Tyler was grateful. A tripod had been mounted to the floor with the lens firmly positioned to capture the breadth of the area. He reached over and shut the camera off. It powered down without a sound.

"Tyler! What did we just talk about?!"

"This isn't going to be a formal interview, Herrera, so there is nothing for you to stay aligned with, right? Just a quick discussion between him and me. For the official record, an interview with you will take place later today. You are going to get the same information

I will. It is just going to be a little more pleasant for him the second time around."

Tyler could tell his new partner wanted to talk about it further by her scowl. Any delay would only cause greater hesitation on her part. He pushed forward and said, "Can you please keep an eye out while I am in there? Knock on the window if you think there are going to be any problems." He turned and walked toward the interrogation room door.

"Tyler?"

"Yeah?"

"You're not going to hurt him are you?"

Tyler walked into the interrogation room. The door swung shut behind him, not giving her the chance to say anything else. Annabelle growled in frustration as she turned to look into the hallway. Crazy police detectives, strung out junkies, and civil rights violations. This was not going to be a good day.

CHAPTER 9
Information from a Bullet

Tyler walked across the room and sat down opposite Jesse. The chairs were aluminum with no padding. The room was devoid of furnishings except for the table and two chairs. This was intentional so that the suspect or witness was uncomfortable with nothing to divert his or her attention away from the interview. The dull hum of air flowing through the ducts added a layer of monotony to the environment. The walls were painted a dull beige that did nothing to attract the eye. Tyler had just walked in and already wanted to leave. Sitting here for hours could be a kind of agony all by itself. The jumbled nature of boredom gnawed on Jesse as he waited for something to happen. Tyler could see it on his face.

Tyler stared at the potential informant who seemed absorbed in staring at his worn sneakers. The twitching man's face already had the beginnings of a smirk that said, "See? I can play ball with you. See? You are going to get me out of here. All because I have something you want, you fuck. See?" There was more hilarity in that smirk than if Jesse had actually laughed out loud. Tyler couldn't believe the arrogance. He felt like he was wasting time.

Tyler thumbed his Kydex holster that held the Glock handgun and pulled the weapon out into his right hand. Jesse jumped back in the chair, and his hands curled into claws in front of his face. It looked as though he meant to catch the bullet. "Shit! What the fuck! What the hell are you doing? I am CO-operating!" The emphasis on the beginning part of the word sounded like an entirely different phrase. Co. Operating.

Tyler shook his head. He ejected the Glock's magazine and held it up for Jesse to see. The Abyss junkie stared at him as though he was trying to decipher the Rosetta Stone.

"What the fuck am I looking at?"

Tyler laid the magazine on the table and slid it over to Jesse. He said, "Pick it up." Jesse stared down at the table as though it were a poisonous snake. He leaned as far back in the chair as he could with arms anchored to the seat. Tyler repeated his words. "Pick it up".

Jesse raised his eyes to Tyler. "What is this?"

"Pick up it up right now goddamnit!"

Jesse hesitated then reached down and picked the magazine up. He handled it like an explosive and looked into the chamber. It was fully loaded. Tyler nodded and said, "Good, now slide it back to me." Jesse laid the piece of metal down and slid it back to Tyler with his fingertips. Tyler ejected the round in the chamber and caught the bullet, putting it in his pocket like an amateur magician. He slammed the magazine back into the Glock before holding up the gun for Jesse to see. "Now you know the gun is loaded. There are no empty magazines or rubber bullets." He slammed down the gun on the table with a bang that echoed throughout the room. Jesse cringed in spite of his earlier bravado.

"Do we have an understanding?"

"What the fuck are you talking about, you crazy-ass cop?"

"I am not talking about anything. I am showing you something. My name is Tyler Morgan, and my family is dead. You have information about that, which is why we are sitting across from each other right now. What I am showing you is my will. That's all. It is my will to solve this case, so I can put my family to rest. Right now they aren't at peace, and it is because of pieces of shit like you or the pieces of shit you know. You see, this problem is the center of my world and now it is the center of yours."

"The one thing I have learned in my years of police work is that scum like you don't appreciate subtleties. You don't care about diplomacy or amelioration of the soul. You don't care about the concept of greater good or Aquinas's cardinal virtues any more than anyone else in this building. All you care about is your next piece of high or your next piece of pussy. You care about your own ass, and everything else is a pathetic joke. I see all of that, and I don't even know you. You are either going to help me right now, or I am going to put a bullet in your skull." Tyler's finger pointed to Jesse's right. "Your blood will paint that wall right behind you."

Jesse Polis had gone a shade of pale that would have made his face invisible had he been standing near the dull paint. He opened his mouth to speak, but only a dry croak came out. He shut his mouth though his eyes were open as wide as the sockets allowed. He looked like the dead frog Tyler had dissected back in his distant high school years. He wondered if Annabelle had gone to get backup yet, while he waited for Jesse to get his shit together.

Finally a shade of color returned to Jesse's face and with it a slight flicker of the earlier arrogance. He looked around the room to reassure himself he was in a police station. Tyler could almost read Jesse's thoughts. They said I am safe here. Those thoughts were wrong.

"Look, as I told the other officers, I want to make a deal. It is the best for everyone cause you guys eventually get....."

Tyler jumped out of his chair before the informant could finish the sentence. He circled the table and kicked the chair out from under Jesse Polis's stick-like frame. The Abyss user's head fell forward to land with a hard thud on the table. It sounded like the turning of a key in a rusty lock. Jesse bit off a small piece of his tongue as his teeth clicked shut by the impact. He slid off the table onto the floor and sat there staring up at Tyler. He spat into his cupped hands and stared at the drops of blood speckled on smooth skin. He wore a look of disbelief and fear.

The door to the interrogation room creaked open. Tyler raised his hand and made a quick chopping gesture. He was in control. The door swung shut without any further sound. Jesse was too busy staring down in anger to even notice.

"You son of a biwch! Tha's my fucking tongue! I will sue you and thiw department!"

"No, no, you won't. You see now, the next step is I take the barrel of my gun here and place it firmly against your right kneecap." Tyler picked up the Glock off the desk and leaned down over Jesse placing the weapon against his leg. Jesse didn't move an inch. He looked like a rabbit caught in a trap, his eyes darting back and forth, looking for an escape route.

"Do you know why knee gunshot wounds hurt so much?" Tyler asked, "There are a lot of nerve cells traveling through a narrow space which all carry messages to the brain. Messages of pain." Tyler gestured down at Jesse's leg. "Of course, at this range the bullet will shatter your right patella. Probably damage the vastus medialis as well, but it is hard to tell from this perspective. What that means, is that you will never walk the same again. That is, of course, assuming you get through the extreme agony and loss of blood from the bullet. You can live a long time with a leg wound. I bet it sure hurts like a bitch though."

"You won't do thau! You're a goddamn cop!"

Tyler smiled. "That's true, Jesse, but you are missing the important fact that I have nothing to lose right now except time. Time which you are wasting. Tick tock. We don't have weeks, waiting to see if you can get a few days off your prison sentence. Instead of testing whether or not I plan on shooting you, why not tell me the information you were going to give up anyway? Give me the name! Now!"

The shout caused Jesse to jump. He looked up into Tyler's eyes and stared without blinking. Tyler let him see the reality of who he was. He had nothing to hide at this point, and he had spoken the truth. There really was nothing left to lose. After what seemed like fifteen minutes, Jesse looked away. He glanced down at the floor, studying his hands lying flat on the cold concrete floor. He muttered something into the ground.

"What?"

"Hiwth name ith Harrith. Harrith Dell."

"Harris Dell?"

Jesse nodded. Tyler knew he was going to get all the information he wanted. Body language said more than any words could. Words could be changed or could be outright lies, but it was harder to hide what your body felt. Bloody tongue or not, Jesse Polis had become his new best friend in the world. It didn't really give either of them any comfort.

Twenty minutes later, Tyler walked out of the interrogation room to see Annabelle standing outside the door. She glanced around and went to grab his forearm, but apparently thought better of it, which made Tyler smile. She said, "Can I talk to you about this privately, Detective Morgan?"

"Whatever you want to talk about we can say right here, Annabelle. No one around and nothing to hide."

"Are you out of your fucking mind, or just trying to ruin the department? I think I lost count of the violations to standard procedure around twelve. What exactly were you trying to accomplish? You turned off all recording equipment, assaulted an informant, put a gun to his leg, and coerced information that we would have eventually gotten anyway!"

"Anything else?"

"Anything else?! No, there isn't another damn thing I can think of! Isn't that enough, you fucking psycho? Were you going to kill him?"

Tyler smiled again. He said, "Annabelle, the key part of what you just said was 'information that we would have *eventually* gotten,'. By the time we negotiate a deal with him, work out all the legalities, and agree on the offer, we would have wasted weeks. Let alone the fact that we are dealing with a rapist."

"Alleged rapist."

"You know as well as I do that multiple cases don't pile up like that without some inherent truth. I highly doubt all these young, teenage girls conspired secretly to point the finger at someone they don't even know. Finally, Jesse Polis is not going to cause this department any disruption because one, he still has a deal on the table, and two, did you hear the final words in the conversation?"

"No. You said something to him, but I think I was too busy wondering how to write up my letter of resignation. Why?"

"Let's just say he is aware that if the information slows us down in any way, he will need all the police protection he can get."

Annabelle shrugged her shoulders and sighed. It was usually a gesture of defeat, but Tyler didn't think that was the case here. Annabelle didn't seem the type. She looked up at him and said, "Tyler, this isn't how the Chicago Police Department or any police department operates. You know that. If anyone finds out, you will be fired for what you did today. The law applies to everyone."

Tyler nodded in agreement. "You are absolutely right, but I am not about the law right now. I am about something else completely. I am only here because of my family. Nothing else comes before that. Now we still have a lot to do before Tuesday, so tonight I want you to think about all this. Then come talk to me tomorrow. If you are still uncomfortable, then we can separate as partners. I won't let you be a scapegoat for any of my actions. Just let me know. Turn me in to Rooks if you need to."

Tyler began to walk away but stopped when he heard a whisper.

"Did you say something Herrera?"

"You didn't answer me when I asked if you were going to kill Jesse." Annabelle said, "I think you were in control, but would you really have shot him in the knee if he didn't give you the information?"

Tyler looked her straight in the eyes and Annabelle flinched in spite of herself.

"What do you think?"

CHAPTER 10
Fire from the Sky

TYLER STOOD ON the lawn outside of the old apartment complex. The sun shone down and beat a trail of light on his back. The grass had a withered look due to the summer heat. It crumbled like parchment under the heavy steps of his shoes. He stared up into the hollow window of his former home. Glass had fallen like pieces of razor on the night of his family's death, raining debris down on the front entrance. He was certain he could still find tiny shards buried in the sidewalk cracks or amidst the dirt of the lawn.

Tyler wanted to go into the building, and go upstairs. To see the room where Grace had slept or the spot where Emily and he had laid down every night. He wanted to go inside to see where his family had been and maybe cry. Cry out some of the pain as a type of catharsis. Tyler had no illusions. He knew he had no tears to shed. They were gone just like the laughter of his daughter. He turned away from the view and began to walk back to the Mustang.

"Tyler?"

Tyler's foot stopped in mid-air as comically as a cartoon character, but it wasn't humor that caused the pause. The sound of his name had all the syllables of pure joy. It was better than any drug, and he turned around. At the top of the entrance stairs stood one of two people he thought he would never see again. His wife's long brown hair had been bound into a carefree ponytail that lay on the shoulder of the white dress that she wore on weekends. Tyler's breath would not come to him. He reached arms out for her, but could not make his legs work. He gasped and croaked, but no words came from his throat. He finally managed a whisper.

"Emily."

She smiled and walked down the steps with a dignity that he could never hope to match. Light steps carried Emily within a few feet of him. He stared at his wife, looking for a flaw or a trick of the light, she was real, perfect for him in every way. The dress swayed in the warm air. Tyler had always loved that dress as it made her look like a bride all over again. The fabric kissed the ground in a glide of movement. His feet would not move to close the gap. He had to use all of his concentration to voice two utterly simple words.

"How? What?"

Emily Morgan closed the gap between them and held up a finger to his lips. She said, "Shhhh. We can talk about how and what later. I just need you to hold me, Tyler. I have missed you so much. I have been so lonely without you."

Tyler's body broke the paralysis. He grabbed Emily and kissed his wife as hard as he could. Her lips were warm and soft. His arms wrapped around her in an embrace that was six months of relief. He breathed in the scent of the perfume she always wore. It was the smell of jasmine. Emily kissed him back and held onto him. He could feel tears trailing down his face to fall and mix with his wife's.

He pulled Emily away to look into her eyes. She smiled up at him as a shadow darkened her face. Tyler looked up into the previously clear sky to see a cloud of darkness begin to gather overhead. His wife moaned softly in his arms as the cloud spread, blotting the midday light into the deadest of nights. It was like looking into a growing abyss. Tyler could barely make out the outline of his wife's white dress in front of him.

"Tyler, I….." Emily's words were drowned out in a roar of flame that crossed through the sky illuminating them in a light more akin to the fires of Hell than a Chicago summer. Suddenly Tyler knew. He knew what was happening and what was going to happen next. The flames of the sky roared down in a blaze that seemed to burn brighter. It was fueled by the very air itself, growing to become an inferno. A tower of death descending down on top of them.

Tyler grabbed his wife's hand and ran for the vestibule of the apartment. The few scant steps seemed a mile and he knew they weren't going to make it. Not a chance.

He looked up in time to see the flames as they crashed down with a force that his body could not possibly withstand. The impact knocked Tyler to the ground as though he were made of straw. He felt the intense heat surround and bury him. No pain entered his skin. Tyler held up his hands to see that they were untouched. None of this made sense.

"Emily!"

He turned to grab his wife, but the heat fought back, beating him down into submission. Emily stretched her hand towards him, but recoiled in agony as smooth skin bubbled and blistered. Her long hair caught fire and emitted a sickening, sweet smell unlike anything he had experienced before. Emily shouted at Tyler, but the words were drowned out by the roar of the fire. She began to writhe as her body blackened and took on the form of ash. Her cries were mercifully cut short as the flames consumed skin and bone. She was gone. Tyler began to scream.

Tyler sat up in bed trying to kill the sound that had begun to grow inside his throat. His heart beat like a train out of control, barreling down a set of broken tracks. He stared at the ceiling trying to find a center, trying to find any strength. A gasp that was more akin to the sound of dead leaves than a man in the prime of life finally came. After the forced breath, he began to cough in rapid uneven bursts. His body took several minutes to adjust and smoothed out the erratic breathing.

Tyler looked down to see hands that had become claws buried into the comforter of the bed. He unclenched, feeling the joints pop as they relaxed. He reached up to feel around his eyes, cheeks, and nose. There were no salty tears drying on cheeks. No tracks of wetness to show signs of grief. Tyler had nothing left to give. Even for his dreams. Even for his nightmares.

CHAPTER 11
Baxter's Visit

HARRIS DELL WOKE up to a pounding crash that he wasn't sure was in his head, or coming from the other side of his apartment wall. God, he couldn't stand those damn neighbors. The cheap linoleum matting of his kitchen floor swam into focus. He knew it was the floor because he could see the random peeling, and the roach that he had killed in the corner. He had smashed the shit out of it weeks ago. He noticed one of the legs of the table he used for breakfast was bending like that tower in London or wherever it was. His vision blurred for a second and then burned as a drop of sweat fell into his left eye. Harris cursed and rubbed his vision when the sound of the pounding came again. This time it was definitely real which meant Harris needed to do something. The noise was coming from his apartment door, and it sounded insistent.

He got up on his hands and knees. They ached and moaned inside his body. Harris felt like he was over a hundred years old, rather than twenty eight. His muscles screamed at the effort and his bones felt like they could break with the slightest twinge. Under normal circumstances, he would be wondering what the hell was wrong with him, but he knew. Oh yes, Harris had begun to recognize when he needed more

Abyss. His body told him quite clearly, and then made him feel like he was dying. It was funny because when he was on the stuff, he never felt more alive. Taken hostage by withdrawal.

I just need one more shot of it and then I am done, he thought. No more of that poison. Make no mistake, it was poison and he knew it. Poison that made your bones grind together in heat and made your skin turn against you. But the reward was like being God. God for a few minutes then dead for a day.

Harris tried not to think about it, unaware that he kept licking his lips. He crossed the chasm of the kitchen, and through Herculean effort managed to pull himself up onto his feet. His legs felt like steel rods had been driven through the bone. His feet stumbled once as he walked into the living room. He almost made it halfway across when his legs betrayed him, and he tripped over a lamp cord, landing face first into the paper-thin carpet. Harris pulled himself up to his knees and began to cry. The tears of a pussy. He tried to control himself, but the sobs erupted from a part of him that was weak. He was still wondering what was happening when the door exploded.

Harris ducked as a shower of splinters and locks burst into the living room. The door might as well have been made of balsa wood. Maybe it was. None of this felt real.

When Harris was sure it was safe, he put his arms down and looked up into the smiling face of Baxter. He had never met Robert Baxter, but Harris was sure it was him all the same. He was dressed in black with silver trim, which made the man look like he would be more at home in a corporate boardroom. That was until you saw his face. It was the face of a grinning devil from those old horror movies.

Baxter said, "Hello, Harris, you rude son of a bitch. We need to talk." He stepped into the room stomping the top of the door, which groaned and splintered further under the weight of the tall man. Only then, did Harris even notice Will, who walked in like some shadow trailing its owner. Harris wondered if his neighbors had heard the noises and then realized, even if they had, no one would help him. Especially not those fuckers. He was alone in this. Some things never changed.

Harris tried to think of a weapon he could use as he wiped the tears from his chin. He had sold his guns for Abyss about a month ago, and nothing else seemed a good defense. The only thing Harris had left was a Stanley hammer on his kitchen table. His father had given it to him as his first and only tool. He had used it to knock the table leg back into place or smash roaches; still a tool was better than nothing. He was going to die here otherwise. He almost fell again but managed to stand up facing the two men with his back to the kitchen. His feet took several steps backwards to allow them to come in further.

"Hello, Will, and you must be Mr. Baxter," Harris said with a black tooth smile that made Baxter's grin widen. "Come in. I thought I heard a noise, but I was asleep. Let me grab us some beers, and we can hash this out." He began to step back towards the kitchen. Harris wanted to turn around and run, but his eyes wouldn't let him look away. His body betrayed him again, and this time he couldn't blame it on any drug except fear.

Robert looked at Will and nodded. Will began picking up the shambles of the door and placed the pieces back in the frame as best he could. It was an exercise in futility. Harris stumbled back into the kitchen with a still smiling Robert Baxter right by his side. The man moved almost silently.

"So Baxter, can I ask you something?" Harris felt like an idiot as soon as he said the words. This was not a guy to fuck around with casual conversation but it might buy him time.

Robert Baxter's smile again widened. "Sure, Harris, we're all friends here. What's on your small mind?"

"How did you find me?"

Baxter leaned his head back and roared with laughter. Harris jumped in spite of himself. Damn him for being so fucking intimidating. He chuckled for a good minute and then the sound disappeared. Harris wondered if it had really happened at all. Baxter said, "An Abyss junkie, whose sole supply happens to be me, wonders how I managed to track him down? Please Harris, stop and think for the only time in your short life. Any dealer you talk to comes through me.

Any pusher, salesmen, user, or junkie has to be connected to me. Do you know how much your life is worth out there? Nothing, Harris. Absolutely nothing. Nothing but what I say it is worth. My hand is on the scale. You never want to irritate someone in that position. Never."

Harris brushed his back against the table and his fingers scrambled like a spider. He faced Baxter while Will still stood in the living room. Harris's fingers tapped the neck and head of the hammer and within seconds he had the handle. It was the best feeling in his entire life as his body blocked Baxter's line of sight to the victory.

Now just let him come a little closer. God please let me get one chance to bash this fucker's brains out. Harris prayed to whomever or whatever was listening. It was the feverish prayer of a desperate man, but sometimes even a sliver of hope was better than a mountain of logic. He wondered if either Baxter or Will had a gun. So far he hadn't seen either of them pull one. The small kitchen space meant that if Baxter took even one step closer he would be in striking range. So far the bastard hadn't moved. Was it precognition or fate?

Harris said, "So where do we go from here?" His tongue felt thick and the words incoherent. Baxter seemed to understand and shrugged his shoulders like a man with no particular place to be.

He replied, "Well, I always believe in being honest with people, Harris. I can't stand the human race as a whole, but there is such a thing as honor, no matter how outdated it is. I came here to kill you, and make no mistake, friend, you are going to die today. Here and now. You have caused enough chaos to get me out here, which was mistake number one. Then mistake number two was when I arrived, you didn't answer the door. Now I am going to have to leave here rather quickly, so that is the only silver lining you are going to get. Hopefully it is enough for you; I am going to make this quick and painless."

"So what is the deal? Money? Drugs? You want me to shoot someone? How do we get out of you killing me?" Harris's hand grasped the hammer in a grip so tight he could feel the grooves of the rubber handle.

Baxter shrugged again and said, "You don't. I didn't come here so that you could plead a new deal. You asked a question, and dead men don't deserve taking a trip to Hell without having their facts straight. Now that we have settled the matter..."

Baxter stepped forward and Harris brought the hammer up to swing as hard as he could at the smiling man's face. He screamed as Baxter moved like a snake and twisted his body so the impact struck a glancing blow off collarbone instead of mashing muscle and breaking bone. Harris wondered how a man could move like that. The impact knocked Baxter backward. The taller man hissed in pain, but he recovered and charged forward. Baxter wrenched the hammer out of his hand, and then a fist made Harris's face explode in pain.

He stumbled back against the table and grabbed the edge to keep from falling down. Harris struggled to keep alert, but the world was blurred and out of focus. Baxter brought the hammer up in an arc over his head. He reversed the grip in a move that made it hard to follow. Baxter brought the claw end of the hammer down on Harris's hand. The metallic teeth punched through tendons and tissue to embed themselves into the table. Harris cried out and fell to his knees which made the pain erupt in a second wave of torture. He kept screaming as he felt the breath of Baxter right above him.

Baxter pulled a Beretta 92 out of his black coat and laid it flush against his side. He pulled the hammer back. The movement seemed to be about making a point, rather than any threat. He looked down on Harris and said in a soft voice, "Stand up."

Harris tried to look through tears at his attacker. His eyes met Baxter's and there he saw a glint of respect. The grinning man nodded and said, "I admire a man who will try to kill his enemies with anything he can get his hands on. Whimpering at fate only gets you a coward's death. Even Jesus himself used carpentry tools like that humble hammer. I have newfound respect for you, Harris, and that says a lot. It takes real courage. Your personal Valhalla is coming, so stand up."

Harris tried to pull himself up using the table. His hand was wrapped in pins of pain and his stomach was trying to claw its way out. He felt like he was eating cotton. None of his thoughts made any sense. When his head was above the tabletop, Baxter put the gun to his temple and pulled the trigger.

Baxter and Will left soon after Harris died. Not a single person looked out into the hallway to see what was going on. Most were seasoned veterans of the building so they knew better. It was the third gunshot disturbance in less than three months. Several people were frantically dialing 911 at the moment. It was far too late, as Baxter and Will left the building in less than a minute. Forty-five seconds later their car pulled away from the front parking spot. Five minutes later, sirens reached the ears of the apartment tenants. Some breathed a little easier, while others rushed to hide their own sins. The sun had not yet begun to appear on the horizon, and the air was already gritty to the taste.

CHAPTER 12
Loose Ends and New Walls

Tyler Morgan stepped through the perimeter tape and walked up the steps with snow clinging to the soles of his shoes. He had arrived at Harris's apartment a few minutes ago. The look of the place was as dead as their suspect. The string of buildings had supposedly been erected during the fifties city expansion. Each piece of architecture mirrored its neighbor in silent defeat. The style was plain to the point of nonexistence. The complex owner seemed to encourage that mindset since it was obvious no renovations had occurred in decades. The paint was a drab russet that meshed well with several dying cars in the area. This was a place for people who needed to hide.

Tyler's breath had just ceased to be visible when Annabelle came running up behind him with an apologetic wave of her hand. Her own breaths came out even and controlled which told him she was a runner. Her step was light and she moved through the snow as though it did not exist.

Once inside, both detectives were careful to remove any speck of snow. They ascended the steps two at a time, but the activity left Tyler enough time to hear Annabelle question why crime scenes she investigated were never on the first floor. He nodded to show he had heard, but his attention was fixed on seeing Harris Dell, or what was left of him. They passed several officers performing advance interviews of the neighbors until they reached the apartment. Harris's door represented the death of Tyler's last lead. It was in shambles and the larger pieces were propped up outside the frame. A heap of dead wood for a dead case.

Tyler stepped inside the apartment. It was exactly what he expected. The hygienic habits of the individual died once Abyss was introduced. It was like a collective hive where each comb showed the same sloppiness and degradation as the last. A white couch sat at the center of the room with multiple stains all over the fabric. Tyler had thought it was an odd pattern of maroon and varying shades of yellow at first glance. He bet if an ME lifted up the cushions, they would find a used needle or strand of rubber.

Fast food wrappers lay on the floor in little piles. They overrode the iron scent of blood that was coming from the back of the apartment. Tyler had once seen an apartment where the suspect would literally shit himself, then use the cheeseburger wrappers as toilet paper since the toilet was broken. He would toss the wrappers into piles for future disposal, but they were forgotten until his death.

Well at least that isn't the case today, there's my silver lining, Tyler thought with a grimace.

Several agents were working on gathering evidence samples as the flash of the camera digitally recorded the minutiae of Harris's life. The forensics team took the Locard Exchange Principle to heart in every case they addressed. All physical evidence had to be documented, recorded, and in most cases, removed. Each piece discovered was stored separately to avoid any type of contamination. The team was gathering the most fragile samples first, looking for blood, hair, clothing fibers, and of course, latent fingerprints. Most of them gave Tyler a wide berth as he worked his way to the kitchen.

There lay his last link in the case, broken beyond belief. Broken was the only word to describe Harris Dell now. He hung to a table by one hand, impaled by a hammer. Harris's body leaned forward in a way looked unnatural. It looked as if the dead man was fighting to stand up but just couldn't make it. A scarecrow held up by a single nail. Tyler thought it looked like he could sway in the wind if there were any moving air in this dead place. Depressing as hell.

Tyler said, "Annabelle, make sure they focus on looking for prints and fibers on the upper body. There had to have been some sort of struggle which is when I am guessing the hammer blow occurred. Also the bullet was fired at table height, not the victim's, if it hasn't already been found."

Annabelle bent down, putting her hands on her knees. She glanced up, brushed a strand of hair back into place and said, "What makes you sure that the hand impalement wasn't done postmortem? Some sort of message or symbol?" Tyler leaned over her shoulder in thought and shook his head.

"No, this whole scene screams pragmatic rather than symbolic or emotional." He said, "One gunshot to the head with no other distinguishing shots fired unless forensics turns up something that I am not seeing. According to the call log received from 911 there was only one shot heard by multiple callers. I am surprised anyone even called it in. It looks like the hammer strike was to incapacitate Harris, not to vent any frustration, though there was a lot of force behind the swing."

Tyler stopped talking for a second and stared at the hammer until he could feel Annabelle's questioning gaze. He shook his head again. "No, this was quick and well thought out. My guess is we won't turn up any evidence unless the killer was wearing some sort of rare clothing or shoe type. The snow tracks from all the tenants melted in the hall so distinguishable footprints are going to be damn near impossible to find. I would bet my paycheck we won't find a usable print that isn't the vic's, though we still have to make sure. Whomever did this got to the point and got out."

Annabelle stood up and gestured around her. Her frustration flowed through the gesture more than she was aware. "All this and you think we will get nothing? Well, I hope you are wrong, Tyler. What the hell does that leave us? Where do we go from here?"

Annabelle turned to look at him and arched her eyebrows, waiting. Tyler felt more calm right now than any other moment in recent memory. This was his element and something he could understand. He couldn't give in to rage right now, or he would lose any chance of future leads. It was sad that a crime scene was the place where he found his logical side, but that was the way he worked. He had a reason, and now he needed to apply his deductive abilities to wade through the bullets and bloodstains. Forensics wasn't going to give him a name on this one, so he had to look toward the next step.

"Annabelle, are you familiar with Louis Jolliet and Jacques Marquette?"

She looked as surprised by his calm words as the unusual question. "Sure, the explorers who mapped a lot of the Mississippi River. What's the point?"

"They also visited the Chicago River in 1673. A lot of explorers followed the rivers to document and map their discoveries. We are at the mouth of the river, Annabelle. But we need to find the source, which means we need to move upstream regardless of the resistance we get along the way."

"Ok, so how do we get to the source?"

"We start by looking for the flow. Let's see if any of the people in this building can tell us who Harris's dealer was, assuming he had one."

Forensics initiated their final sweep as they walled off the crime scene in plastic. One officer began to unroll yellow tape, stretching it out to canvas the doorframe. It is like we are preparing to wrap another present, Tyler thought as he walked out of the kitchen and wove his way towards the exit. They still had a lot of work to do.

They went door to door talking with the neighbors, most of whom wore expressions of suspicion. Tyler caught several looks of relief as they closed each interview, having answered all questions with a "no" or an "I don't know". It was one thing to call the police for help when gunshots rang out, but quite another to have them in your apartment. They were invited in once, which was probably due more to Annabelle than anything else. The man let them in with an almost shy expression as though he felt special that she had knocked on his door. The shy expression turned to one of business when he glanced at Tyler's face. Like all the others, he didn't know Harris Dell or anything about him, though he did recognize the name, which put him above the rest of the building.

Their questioning failed to yield any new information, and by the end Annabelle was muttering to herself as she checked her cell for new emails. Tyler had expected this result, but would not have been able to sleep until he had exhausted the interviews. They walked out of the building amidst the perimeter officers and sawhorses which all said the same thing "Police Line Do Not Cross" with the smaller words of "Chicago Police Department" etched subtly underneath. The onsite officers had more effect than any words in keeping onlookers or pseudo reporters out of the building until everything had been documented or removed.

Tyler walked out to his car with slumped shoulders and the taste of defeat in his mouth. A cold wind bit into exposed cheeks, and he wondered how much hell the temperature would play with determining time of death for any murders that were committed outside. Typically a corpse would lose 1.5 degrees an hour until it reached the same temperature as the environment in which it was located. The ME also had to take into account any external aspects such as age, weight, clothing, and the external temperature. Luckily being indoors helped alleviate some of these factors so in their case, it was much easier. The corpse hadn't even entered rigor mortis yet, if they had needed to establish any type of timeframe. He shook his head at the thoughts. He realized he was trying to avoid going back to an apartment that would never be his home.

He started walking towards his car when a voice shouted out. "Hey, Detective Morgan!" Tyler turned around and Annabelle was standing by the entryway of the building. The snow seemed to swirl around her in an aura of ice that could not penetrate her warmth. She looked beautiful, but then she always did.

"Care for a drink?" His partner had begun moving towards him before his head could finish shaking no. She walked over to him and looked up defiantly into his eyes. Annabelle had known the answer before she asked. She smiled and said, "Come on, I don't bite. I hardly know anything about you other than what your file says. Well, that and the fact that you are driven beyond rational thought. If I am going to at least try to keep you in line, I should know you a little better."

Tyler shook his head. It felt like an odd time for her to ask him this. Maybe it was just her way of dealing with tension? Guaranteed Lieutenant Rooks had briefed her before they had begun the investigation. He couldn't fault either of them for that. She needed to know what she was getting into. He asked, "What does my file say about me? I have never read it."

"It says that you are brilliant, but you already know that. What I want to know is the person behind the badge." She said with a sigh. "I don't expect your life story tonight or anything you don't want to talk about, but at least something. I can even spend the first hour or two talking about myself if you want. My ex-boyfriend said I was always good at that." Annabelle said the words with a sincere smile. Tyler knew it was a selfless offer of building a friendship. Her kindness reminded him of Emily. Unfortunately, Tyler couldn't focus on anything but Harris Dell right now. His family demanded nothing less, even if they had no words to vocalize their needs anymore.

Annabelle nodded as though she could read his thoughts. "Ok. Stubborn ass." She said, "Everyone can use a friend once in a while, you know. Even a borderline psychotic detective." Annabelle cushioned the words with another smile showing that the offer still stood.

Tyler nodded his thanks. "Goodnight, Detective Herrera," he said, turning towards the car, but she stopped him by tapping his shoulder.

"Tyler, that river analogy you mentioned earlier. Where do we need to go next?"

"Next, we have to head upstream to where the current flows faster and the water is deeper. That is where we will find more information."

"What type of place would that be?"

"A place of importance, Annabelle. A place of blood."

CHAPTER 13
Blood Ties

THE AIR WAS cold and crisp to the workers of downtown Chicago as they walked to their vehicles. Many of them went into office buildings where they would spend the next eight to ten hours earning a paycheck. It was still dark enough that Tyler had his headlights on when he arrived at the police station. This would grow more common as Illinois moved into the depths of winter. He had spent the night hours working on his sit reps that were due to Lieutenant Rooks today. Forensics would be pleased or annoyed to find his emails already there inquiring about the different components of the case. Components was such an interesting word to use for the pieces of someone's life, even someone like Harris Dell.

Tyler brushed the thoughts away like ethereal cobwebs. The last few days, his mind seemed to be wandering a lot, which was due more to sleep deprivation than anything else. He had slept about forty-five minutes last night, give or take twenty minutes. Several hours were spent staring at the ceiling while the clock glowed an angry red, beating into his eyes. He had finally gotten up and pulled its plug out of the wall. If there were truly no rest for the wicked, what did that make him?

Most of the police force had not yet arrived, and his footsteps sounded like mortar rounds in the hallway. Tyler arrived at his desk to find a white, stoneware mug sitting in front of the computer filled to the brim with coffee. Thin wisps of steam rose from the cup. It wasn't his mug and it wasn't his coffee. He could tell by the smell it was an Arabica dark roast. He took off his coat and laid it on the chair before taking a tentative sip. It was a perfect cup of coffee in every way. An experienced brewer had created this masterpiece. Only Annabelle would have done this for him. He could already hear the sound of her light steps behind him, her mild perfume mixing well with the coffee bean.

He turned and Annabelle smiled. "I thought you might need that. Consider it a 'start on the right foot' offering for today. From the flurry of emails I see in my inbox, it is obvious you were quite the night owl. Now a morning person too, from the looks of it. I don't know how you do it."

"It beats lying in bed staring at a wall for hours. Thanks for the coffee, Annabelle."

Her smile widened for a second, and then Annabelle held up a thin manila folder as though she were a public speaker anticipating the audience's next request. She said, "I haven't been here too long, but I read your email and did some digging on Harris's family. He wasn't married and he is the only tenant listed on the apartment contract. Parents are both deceased and just the one sister, Stacy. I know you tried to get a hold of her last night."

Tyler nodded. "I called and stopped by, but she didn't answer. It was a borderline insane hour so she may have just been asleep. I left my number, but so far I haven't gotten any callbacks. Any extended family to be aware of?"

"No other relatives living in this area or even within the state. Harris has a cousin out in Brooklyn. Seems he was flying solo for quite some time. It isn't likely there is anyone else who could be a lead."

Tyler leaned back and took another sip of the coffee. The warm beverage was turning out to be the highlight of his morning. He said, "Did you find any information about the sister?"

Annabelle opened the file and started to flip through the documents. "Well, it is pretty limited. She doesn't have a record, so she isn't listed in the National Crime Information Center. If it doesn't have anything on her, then there is little chance of any known criminal ties. All the information I could find was from DMV which gave the address and phone number you used. I also printed the digital copy of her driver's license picture for you."

She pulled the image out of the folder for Tyler to see. The face that looked back at him was a plain woman with brown hair and a blank look on her face. The eyes seemed sad, speaking of a mediocrity that she didn't quite believe in. This was a person who hung up too many slogans in her house like "Dream on" or "Happiness is a journey". Annabelle handed him the rest of the file which he scanned. She was right; there really wasn't much else.

Tyler put the picture back in the folder and laid the file on his desk so he could put his coat back on. He took a large gulp of the coffee before regretfully setting it down. He said, "Want to go see if Ms. Dell is awake and ready to talk?" Annabelle turned and went back to her desk to grab her coat without a word. It was time to have a conversation with Stacy Dell.

THE DRIVE TO Stacy Dell's apartment was quick and ended before there was a chance for any type of awkward silence to set in. The Mustang handled the snow as well as could be expected. Tyler had thrown several bags of rock salt into the trunk. If the weather got any worse, he would probably have to drive his other car. Emily had driven a Toyota Camry for several years until her death. Tyler had sold it three months ago. It would always be her car and not his. She had even nicknamed the car "Trooper" since the vehicle never had any real problems. Even cars had liked Emily. He had bought an older Ford Explorer to help offset the impeding bad weather but just couldn't bring himself to use it. Tyler had received a large chunk of money after he had paid the funeral costs so there hadn't been any serious financial concerns yet. Emily had always believed in life insurance a lot more than he did. His wife had always been focused on coverage, 401Ks, and rainy day funds.

It didn't matter, no amount of money would bring him peace or give him a good night's sleep. Those things couldn't be bought regardless of any pill, pamphlet, or promise. Those concepts were dead to him now. They were treasures for other people.

Stacy seemed to be doing ok for herself. The apartment building was off of North Damen Avenue in Bucktown and had the usual middle class look to it. The building was old but well kept, with little paint or visible structural deterioration. Stacy's call button was the only one without a name listed on it. Maybe she did have something to hide, or rather was hiding from someone? Her brother might have something to do with it. Some people just wanted to be left alone. It was a shame they couldn't do just that right now.

A nervous voice answered the call once Tyler identified who he was through the speaker. Annabelle walked through the door before he could put his hand down. They stomped the residual snow from their shoes before proceeding into the main reception area. The inside of the building matched the exterior. It was nothing special, but safe and well-maintained. That was all anyone can really ask for, Tyler thought. Stacy was on the main floor so they were in front of her door within seconds.

Tyler took out his Glock 22 from the holster, pulled the hammer back, and put it in his coat pocket as Annabelle raised her hand to knock on the door. She looked at him with a silent question. Tyler said, "Herrera, we are going to question the sister of an Abyss user who was murdered and pinned to a table. We have to be ready for anything."

Annabelle arched her eyebrows and replied, "In this neighborhood? These people look normal to me!"

Tyler smiled. "Those are the ones I don't trust the most. They will smile to your face and hit you with a shovel when you aren't looking. At least the crazy ones wear their warning signs openly."

Annabelle shrugged and knocked on the door. The door opened less than an inch and part of a woman's face moved into the gap to gaze out into the hallway. She stared at them both for several seconds. Her visible eye was more like that of a timid deer than the sister of a hardcore Abyss addict.

Tyler said, "Police, Ms. Dell. We called about your brother. I'm Detective Morgan, and this is Detective Herrera." The voice from behind the door said, "Can I see some identification please?" Annabelle and Tyler both held out their badges in front of the narrow opening for several seconds before the eye seemed to nod in acceptance.

The door opened to reveal a woman with thin brown hair and an even more slender frame. She would have been somewhat attractive, if not for the tic of nervousness that was accompanied by overly clasped hands and quick tilts of the head. Tyler thought she was the type that might have a breakdown if she got stuck in traffic more than once, or if the grocery store stopped carrying her favorite kind of soap. It must have been hell to deal with her brother.

The apartment was neatly kept and exactly what he would have expected slogans included. This was not a woman who used highly experimental variants of Heroin or carried wads of cash in a plastic clip. She led them into the living room where they sat on a couch facing the television. Stacy herself sat in a La-Z-Boy recliner that looked to be the oldest piece of furniture in the room. Her shoulders slumped forward in a release of tension as she eased back into the chair. The apartment was warm and felt safe.

Stacy said, "If you are here to tell me about my brother, don't bother. I already heard the news from another officer. There isn't anything else to say. It isn't like I am going to inherit any money or anything."

Annabelle looked somewhat shocked at this proclamation, but Tyler nodded his head. He said, "Ms. Dell, you don't seem particularly broken up about the news. It sounds like he was your last close relative. Your last blood tie. At least around here, right?"

Stacy shrugged and settled back further into the recliner. She said, "Harris was my brother, but he was also a piece of shit that would put a gun in my face if it could give him another high. My parents gave up on him years ago, but I guess I was a late learner."

"Did he ever threaten you?"

"No, but not because he loved me or anything." She said, "I was Harris's only friend in a way. If people like my brother have any friends. I was the only person he didn't owe money to, and not from a lack of trying on his part. I wouldn't give him cash, but I would listen if he needed to talk. It didn't happen often, but sometimes I would get a phone call at some insane hour with him high on some crazy shit or 'getting the shakes'. He would start talking about whatever mess he had gotten into until he felt he had said enough. Then he would hang up, and I wouldn't hear from him in months. No goodbyes but that was Harris."

"Did he talk about any illegal activities?"

"Constantly. Harris didn't seem to have any fear that I would rat on him. Honestly who could I rat on him to?" Stacy laughed for a second and it echoed in the apartment. She looked away before continuing. "I think I knew more about his drug dealer than he did about our family. He was always paranoid, especially about getting some 'shit junk', as he would put it. He was afraid someone would water down his supply with fertilizer or rat poison. In the end, I guess that isn't something he has to worry about anymore, is it?"

Tyler waited for a moment as Stacy stared off into space. The small woman seemed to rock back and forth without being aware of the movement. He reached over and put a hand on her knee. She jumped but seemed to focus and become calm. He said gently. "You mentioned a dealer?"

"Yeah, as soon as I said that, I knew you would come back to it. His name was Marco Brent, though that could be a fake name. Harris never described him or anything. I think the only reason he even told me the name so many times was in case something really did happen to him. Looks like even junkie losers can be right once in a while." Stacy turned and wiped a tear from her cheek. She shook a little but no sobs came out. Tyler squeezed her knee in support. He didn't understand, but he was listening.

Stacy nodded in appreciation but then pushed the hand away. Tyler looked over at Annabelle. Had she ever heard of Marco Brent? Annabelle shook her head no. Another loose end in a series of dead leads. They always seemed to be one step behind. Tyler was going to have to put a stop to this. Annabelle asked a few more probing questions but it was obvious Stacy knew very little else of use. Tyler asked if there was anything else she wanted to say.

"Look, my brother was scum." Stacy said, "I hate to say that, especially of my own blood and also because he is dead, but it's true. Even when he was little, he always had an excuse for himself. Knives, guns, drugs, violence, and on and on. He only cared about me at all because he knew I would help him in whatever way I could. Not because he loved me. I doubt he really loved anyone. I can't say there was a lot of decency in him, but the people who killed him are just as bad. Can you promise me you will try to put an end to this violence? At least let me know that the people involved won't hurt anyone else. Please?"

Tyler stood up with his eyes never leaving Stacy's face until she looked away. The waning morning shadows deepened the sockets of his eyes, and the hard look he wore like his own skin became magnified. Stacy thought he looked like an aged skull. He said, "I promise you this much, Ms. Dell. It will end and not well for the people involved. That is all I can promise. This case will not end up in a forgotten file or locked away as a memory. We will put it to rest one way or another."

The answer seemed to satisfy Stacy, and as if it was choreographed, both women stood up at the same time to join Tyler. Stacy led them back to the door seeming to know there was nothing else to talk about and that the interview was over. The meeting had taken twenty minutes at best. Tyler and Annabelle walked out into the hall as Stacy held the door open. She said, "Be careful, Detectives. I think a part of me was tainted by hearing all of Harris's rants. Dealing with that kind of black poison leaves a mark on people that doesn't go away. It's damnation."

"Ms. Dell, I am damned already. Have a good day."

Stacy shut the door behind them as the detectives began to walk down the hallway. If they had stayed a few more seconds, they would have heard three separate locks being clicked into place with a deadbolt being last. There wasn't time to waste as there was still more work to attend to, and the temperature was dropping outside. The wind clawed at Tyler's face as they walked outside into the light.

CHAPTER 14
The Whereabouts of Marco Brent

Tyler put the Mustang into drive as Annabelle began to type on her cell phone, her fingers working the small keys with precision. From the amount of clicks, there was no doubt she would run out of characters and move on to the next text message. "Just giving a quick summary to Lieutenant Rooks, since I have a feeling we are not going back to the station any time soon." The words were said with a casual tone but Tyler knew it was a question.

"No, we are not." he agreed. "Can you try to get a hold of someone from Vice? Maybe Casey, if he is around."

Annabelle turned to look at him. Tyler wanted to look back but he had to stay focused on driving. The roads were already an icy slush. Annabelle said, "Didn't you have a partner that is now in Vice? Wessler right? Why not reach out to him?" It was a good question. His partner was a part of his former life, and the pain he wanted to forget. Tyler shook his head and said, "Whoever you can find that knows anything about Marco Brent. I don't care, but see if you can get an address."

In most cases, a drug dealer was pretty easy to locate once you had a name. There was no hidden location with bodyguards armed to the teeth. Usually the dealer would be more destitute than his customers, especially if he was a user as well. A lot of Vice and DEA used CIs to find an address or area. Once you had a line into a particular neighborhood, it was fairly simplistic to locate a seller of whatever product was being sold. Abyss was an exception since there was one supplier who had proven more than willing to eliminate anything or anyone tied to the product. The supply chain was long which made it harder to trace. The Chicago Police had found little luck in this area and it was a sore spot with the department.

Annabelle made a phone call and was soon nodding her head after asking a couple of questions. She finally said, "Ok." and held out the small device into the haze of his peripheral vision. "Here, it's for you."

Tyler shook his head and said, "Just get the address please." Annabelle then shook her head mimicking his movement. "He says he wants to give it to you."

He took the outstretched phone and said, "Hello?"

A baritone and amused voice spoke into the phone. "Tyler, you don't call. You don't write either. Of course, your handwriting sucks ass so maybe that is for the best."

"Hello, Chris."

"So, Rooks has you working on your own family's case now?" Tyler could hear the wonder in Chris's voice. Tyler's lack of a response seemed to be all the answer he needed. "Jesus Christ. Rooks may have thought he was doing you a favor, but he really has no idea what he has turned loose, does he?"

Tyler said, "Lieutenant Rooks knows I am suited for this case, and my clearance rate alone qualifies me for any assignment period."

"Yeah, but he really doesn't know you like I do." Chris laughed out loud this time. It was friendly and sarcastic at the same time. "Now that you are back in the game, you are like a goddamned machine. You aren't going to let any of it go until the case is closed, or everyone is dead. Does Annabelle have any idea how you handled the Stockler murders?"

"It is there for anyone to read. You know everything is saved in the reports just like I do. Besides that, it was within police protocol. No one got killed and that was before......." A heavy pause filled the space between the phones. Tyler didn't know how to break it, but Chris punctured the pause for them.

"Yeah, Tyler, before Grace and Emily. I know." Chris said, "You know if you would just return a phone call once in a while or…"

"So I hear you have an address for me?"

Chris laughed into the phone again. Tyler could almost hear him leaning back in his chair in amusement. He said, "All right Detective Morgan, we will play it your way. I know you would just get the information out of some other part of Vice anyway. Probably would be on the phone again before our call was completely disconnected, too. Marco Brent has become somewhat of a big fish so several of us have had our eyes on him. What's sad is that we haven't caught him doing anything of substance yet. We certainly haven't caught him distributing Abyss. Just don't rough him up too much. We may need Marco down the road."

Chris gave the address which he repeated out loud for Annabelle to copy down. Tyler asked him to repeat it to make sure the street number was correct. Annabelle entered the information into her phone's GPS. Once he was sure they were set, he said, "Thanks, Chris, I appreciate the help on this one. I also appreciate all the support that I didn't deserve. It is all a part of my past.....I just can't deal with it right now." The words felt awkward and fake to Tyler.

The smile returned in Chris's reply. "I know that you are trying to get through this bullshit, but don't give up on the human race just yet." Chris laughed again. "I almost pity Marco Brent and any other bastards you are heading towards. But you reap what you sow on both sides of the law."

Tyler shook his head in silent agreement with his former partner. The line had gone dead and he handed the phone back to Annabelle. She opened her lips slightly as if to say something but then seemed to reconsider. The car wobbled to the right as his foot pressed the pedal to a higher speed. Both of them were silent and the sound of Steve

Winwood's "The Finer Things" echoed through the car until they arrived at Marco's apartment.

Chicago is known for some of the finest architecture and beautiful apartments that money can buy. This was not one of those places. The building seemed to sag towards the right side as if in pain. Tyler wondered how it would hold up to a safety inspection. Graffiti marred the outside in random scribble marks denoting those who could not truly identify themselves as artists. It was completely different than some of the murals that were painted downtown. One window was punctured with what appeared to be a bullet hole. It had been covered by cardboard warped by earlier rains and made stiff by the intense cold. The same cold kept all but the most diehard travelers off the sidewalks. Tyler saw Annabelle's breath become visible as they exited the car and walked up the front steps.

The door into the building was hanging onto the hinges by two screws and a prayer. Tyler wondered if they would have to pick the handle off the floor as they entered. Marco's apartment was five flights up from the entranceway, with each stair making a different grunt or moan as they marched upwards.

When they reached the fifth floor, the air throbbed to the bass beat of someone's stereo who was either deaf or pretending to be home as a security feature. The music could not be discerned as any particular album or artist, but it sounded like a machine gun in a microwave. Whatever the song was, it put Tyler in a bad mood.

Several people were standing outside their apartment doors, but the hallway cleared before they had gone five steps. "It's not like they can see our badges already," Annabelle muttered in a growl. Tyler replied, "They can tell that we don't belong here. Either we are here to arrest someone or kill someone else. All these people care about is getting away from us." Another door slammed shut as if in agreement.

When they reached Marco's apartment, Tyler thumbed the holster release on his Glock and Annabelle glanced at him in mock amusement. She said, "Do you always do that?" Tyler nodded his head and her smirk evaporated when she realized he was serious. Tyler made his large hand into a fist and banged on the door as hard as he could. The sound was like thunder in the tight hallway. He knew that they would have Marco's undivided attention.

Tyler could hear the steps to the door and a voice barked behind the wall. "Who is it?"

Tyler spoke loudly, "Marco Brent, this is Detectives Morgan and Herrera. We need to talk to you." The door opened to reveal Marco Brent standing in a black pseudo-silk shirt and maroon pants. The absence of tacky jewelry was really the only difference from countless others Tyler had met. It was a relief in a way.

Tyler stared into red ringed eyes and asked, "Marco Brent?"

"Who the fuck are you?" Marco snarled, "Just who the fuck are you and why are you bothering me? Are you two doggies sniffing for snacks? Fuck off. It isn't my payday, so it won't be yours anytime soon either." He went to slam the door in their faces. Tyler rammed his knuckles into the flimsy door which shuddered under the assault. The frame looked like it had probably been kicked in several times already. Marco's eyes widened as he tried to shut it again, but the door didn't budge as Tyler locked his arm.

Tyler said, "See, the problem with dealing and using cocaine is that you start to lose track of the little details. I am sure you check your nostrils and the front of your clothing but sooner or later you are going to miss something you shouldn't have." He pointed towards Marco's shoulder which was dotted in white powder highlighted at the top seam of the black fabric. Marco turned his neck to glance down and Tyler punched him in the stomach. The dealer doubled over in pain as Tyler grabbed him by the shoulders and shoved him back into the apartment. Marco stumbled backwards and fell onto a woven rug where he lay in the fetal position.

Annabelle shook her head before stepping through the entrance. Tyler shut the door behind them, closing all three in Marco's apartment. The living room would have been more at home in a high-rise condo than this building. Leather plush couches faced a new big screen television with a dark wood coffee table filling the gap between them. Video game consoles that Grace would have loved were stacked next to

Bose speakers. The room had a surround sound system unlike any he had seen. Several end tables and wood cabinets crowded the room as if Marco was unsure what exactly the furniture was used for, but wanted as much of it as possible.

Marco crawled onto the largest couch groaning in pain. Annabelle sat down on another smaller couch while Tyler sat on the other end. He wanted to be close to the whining man. Marco lifted his head still groaning and said, "Fuck you! This is police brutality. You can't just come in here like that without a search warrant or some shit. I know my rights. I will kill you and this cunt for…." Tyler held up a hand and Marco cringed.

The classic bully mentality of harassing those who were presumed weak, but remaining subservient to strength. It made Tyler feel sick to his stomach. Marco probably took out his aggression on coked-up addicts and prostitutes. Anyone who couldn't fight back or turn to the police was fair game for this asshole. His mouth felt gritty in disgust.

"Have you heard of probable cause, Marco?" Tyler asked, "Normally, we do need a search warrant, but when you have cocaine plastered all over your shoulders like some amazing case of dandruff, it nullifies the need for one. See you have already broken the law, and you are wearing the goddamn evidence." Marco glanced at his shirt again as though hoping the drug had disappeared. No line of junkies was going to snort away his problems. The white dust was still there, more pronounced under the living room light.

"Perhaps we can cut some sort of deal on your jail time, depending on how informative you are for us. We aren't here for you, though I really wish we were." Tyler said, "We are looking for someone else right now. You sell drugs on the street which is bad, but we want those that are selling drugs to the entire city. You get it? We want one of your suppliers, and I think you can help us."

"I don't sell drugs." Marco muttered the words more into the couch than to anyone else.

He looked with pleading eyes at Annabelle who said, "Bullshit". Marco then glanced at Tyler who replied with a hard stare. He felt a flood of rage at the man who peddled dangerous drugs to poison the people of the city. Why did Marco have the right to do things like this while his daughter would never go to a prom?

Marco looked up at the ceiling while Tyler continued, "I am not even answering that, as Detective Herrera has addressed your statement. You can file a formal complaint later. Now what can you tell us about Abyss?"

Marco's eyes widened. "I don't know nothing about that voodoo shit. High-priced stuff. You fuckers caught me, ok? I sell pot every now and then, but that is it. Arrest me and book me for that. I will be out in no time."

Tyler smiled which made Marco flinch again. "Ok, so now we can add lying to a police officer. You do realize that we can search your apartment now that we are here, right? Is there anything else you want to say before we get started?"

Despite the depths of winter that chilled the air outside, Marco's face was completely drenched in sweat. The silent pause grew longer and longer as they waited for an answer.

Marco started to rise. "I need to go to the bathroom. I'll be right back." Tyler said, "Sit down Marco. You can go in a minute. Answer the question first. What can you tell us about Abyss?" Annabelle stiffened as Marco stood up. Tyler yelled, "Sit down!"

Marco repeated, "I need to go to the bathroom. Hang on one minute."

As Tyler and Annabelle began to rise, Marco jumped sideways, bashing his leg on the table. He ran towards the back of the apartment. Tyler and Annabelle drew their guns, but they were already staring at empty space. The bastard was clumsy but quick. A loud bang echoed in the confined space. It was the sound of a doorknob hitting the wall. He had heard that same noise several times when Grace would burst into a room trying to surprise him. The fear of jail could turn people into professional athletes. Tyler felt Annabelle flinch and his own breathing quickened. The grip on the Glock cut into his fingers. He whispered,

"Annabelle, call for backup and stay here. I am getting him. Cover the exit."

Annabelle shook her head no as she stood in the modern Weavers stance covering the hallway. She whispered back, "Why don't I go after him while you cover the exit?"

"Because if you get killed, there will be a lot of sad people. Now stay here." Tyler started to creep forward.

Annabelle hissed, "Tyler!" but he was halfway down the cramped hallway. The bathroom faced him with the door open and the light on. The mildewed shower curtain had been pushed to the wall. Marco wasn't in there, unless he was hiding in the bottom of the tub. Another step forward confirmed that it was empty. There was no sound except his heart. Tyler could almost feel the silence as it wrapped around his ear canals. He could now lean over to look into what was presumably the bedroom. The familiar sound of a magazine being slammed into a firearm made him wince.

Tyler forced himself to take even, deep breaths as he remained still. One important aspect of surviving any potential gunfight was to remain calm. It wasn't about who was faster or had the best weapon, most of the time. Adrenalin and fear made people terrible shots. The most crucial component was that you stayed focused. You needed to aim and put a bullet into your target while everyone else was shooting at the ceiling or into a sofa.

"Come on, you fuckers!" Marco screamed. "I will kill you, Morgan, then I'm gonna fuck that bitch cop until she bleeds! Come on!!!"

Tyler was crouching down on his hands and knees when Marco opened fire with a string of bullets that slammed into the hallway wall. The bastard had some sort of machinegun in there. The weapon roared in the confined space. There was already a faint smell of smoke in the air. Where the hell did people get weapons like that?

Tyler lay prone on the thin carpet. It reeked of urine and sweat. He inched forward until he could look into the bedroom at floor level. Inside there was portion of a tan mattress held up by a wheeled frame. He couldn't see anything else and forced himself to wait. Time was working against Marco and it was obvious the drug dealer knew it. The gunshots would escalate the call-ins for the building. Tyler again slowed his breathing and held the Glock's heavy grip with both hands.

"Let me go! I have coke, money, whatever you want, just let me go! I can walk and you can take it all!" Marco sounded on the verge of hysterics. "Let me go!"

"Drop the gun, Marco!" Tyler yelled. There was movement underneath the mattress frame. Marco was crouched somewhere behind the bed. He waited for the dealer to make his move. When you are silent, every sound is magnified and time slows down until a minute seems like an hour. He hugged the floor holding the gun in front of him staring down the sight for any indication of where the drug dealer was.

"Fuck this!" Chaos erupted as Marco stood up and began firing. The air hummed with thunder, but Tyler concentrated on visible movement. There. He squeezed the trigger three times in rapid succession and jumped up. He ran into the bedroom pumping bullet after bullet into the room aiming towards the mattress. He continued firing, emptying the Glock's magazine to keep Marco ducking for cover.

Tyler moved around the bed to find Marco lying on the floor, holding onto his leg with one hand and grasping blindly with the other towards the bed. He stomped on the seeking hand, pivoted and kicked Marco into the wall. His wounded attacker grunted in pain but continued to hold onto his leg. Tyler's eyes caught the black gloss of an AK 107 laying at Marco's feet. It was nowhere near where the drug dealer had been reaching, but he kicked the gun across the room anyway. No sense in taking any risks.

One of the bullets had hit Marco right above the ankle, more than likely shattering the tibia. There was a lot of blood spreading onto the floor. It was almost impossible to tell how badly the wounded man was injured. Tyler pointed his gun down into the tear-stained face of Marco Brent who quieted but continued to moan in pain.

Fear etched the criminal's face in a way that was better than truth serum. Tyler kept his eyes locked onto Marco's face. He lifted his right foot and held it over the wounded man's leg. He said, "Listen to me and answer clearly. What do you know about my family? Emily and Grace Morgan." Marco's hand lifted in a silent plea for mercy. It was the same hand that had been reaching for the assault weapon seconds ago.

"I. I. I. don't know who you're......talking about"

Tyler stomped his foot down onto the remains of Marco's leg.

AAAAAAHHHH!

The loud scream echoed in the small room. Marco cried and cursed nonsensically at the same time. Finally he said, "I don't know! I don't know! Please!" Tyler could see the truth behind the desperation of the words. The man didn't know about his family.

"Ok, I believe you. Next and last question. Where did you get the Abyss? Give me a name or a location or you are going to suffer some more." A small part of Tyler cringed on the inside as he said the words. He quelled the feeling, drowning it in the anger he felt oozing beneath the surface. It had become a festering wound. Tyler raised his foot once again and Marco began to turn onto his side. "It's either my foot or another bullet." Marco stopped turning and whimpered. He would pass out soon and would be useless. "Tell me, right now!"

The words he needed to hear were muffled in a cloud of saliva and blood loss. Tyler said, "What? Say it again!"

"Anton. Anton Lynd."

"Thank you, Marco. You give that information only to me, you understand?" Tyler pointed the gun directly at Marco's leg and the dealer cringed before shaking his head in agreement. "Tell anyone else, and I will cripple you for life."

An unfamiliar voice startled Tyler as it shouted, "Put the gun down!" Tyler turned to see a police officer he didn't know and Annabelle Herrera staring at him. Both of them were pointing guns directly at his head.

CHAPTER 15
Going Rogue

TYLER REALIZED HE still had his gun pointed at Marco Brent, and lowered it to his side. The police officer looked to be about twenty-three years old with eyes so wide they seemed ready to fall out of their sockets. It was a skeletal look that would have been comical in other circumstances. The officer's stance was off, and Tyler doubted he would be able to hit anything with that slight shake that comes from disbelief and fear. Annabelle, however, could easily put a bullet through his skull at this range. Her face also wore the lines of disbelief, but it wouldn't affect her professional habits that came from years of practice. She wouldn't hesitate to stop him if he continued to hurt the criminal lying on the floor. Marco started to sob in a pool of pain and broken bone.

Tyler held up his free hand and holstered the Glock. Annabelle nodded as he began to reach down. He pulled up the AK 107 by the stock and walked over to the officer, being careful not to let his hands stray near the trigger guard area. Bullets had killed people for less, and there was still much to do. The officer let out a large breath and holstered his gun. He took the AK from Tyler like it was a live bomb.

Tyler pointed to the weapon and said, "You won't be able to trace it.

See, the serial numbers have been filed off. My guess is illegal import, though I would also check local dealers with similar merchandise." The officer stammered, "What about fingerprints? You touched the gun."

Tyler shook his head. Maybe it was the rookie's first day. "Look around you. You have all the evidence you need, officer. I'd get the paramedics to him as quickly as I could though." He turned to look at Annabelle. She holstered her gun without saying a word.

They walked out of the room and left the apartment as several more officers rushed to the door. One looked like he was ready to ask questions, but Annabelle said, "Not yet." Nothing further was needed. They walked outside to a flurry of snow punctuated by the blue and red lights of several police cars. Already a crowd was beginning to gather, and Annabelle had to shout to tell several gawkers to move back before turning to Tyler. They were alone for the moment. Surrounded by people, but cut off by the howling wind.

"Tyler, what the hell happened?" Annabelle said. Worry lines creased her face in a way he didn't like. Snow gathered in her hair like wisps of white cotton. "What did I just see?"

"Just how much did you and the new rank see?"

Annabelle sighed. "Enough, Tyler, enough. You can't do things like that. You know that, and now there will be an investigation. You could lose everything, let alone the fact that you will definitely be suspended. Why did you do that? He was just some lowlife dealer."

Tyler's tone hardened as he replied, "Just some lowlife dealer who has information that will help us find the people who killed my family, Annabelle. You know how long Marco would have toyed with the department, let alone the courts? That is assuming he would have even given us any real information! All of that just to find another fucking link in the fucking chain. You ask me why I did 'that' but let me ask you a question. Would you have done anything differently if it was your family? If your family was brutally murdered and then burned to ash? Burned until you couldn't recognize their eyes or their hair. Couldn't recognize that it was even someone you loved?" Tyler struggled to keep from shouting at her. He should have stopped a long time ago.

"I don't know the answer to that, Tyler." Annabelle said, "All I do know is that what you just did was wrong. We swore an oath! Preserve the dignity? Protect the rights of all individuals? Any of that mean anything to you?"

"Not right now it doesn't, to be honest with you. I'm sorry."

Annabelle looked down at the ground. Tyler thought she might be crying, but when she looked up again her eyes were dry. He could see so much strength in her beauty. It almost hurt to look at her. She said, "Ok, so what now?"

"Now? This is where we have to go different directions." Tyler said, "You are right, I will probably be suspended pending an investigation. I can't afford to lose my badge and gun just yet. The gun isn't a huge problem; I have others, but the badge is a key. It will help me dig out the information I need from some people who wouldn't talk otherwise. Annabelle, I need you to stall Rooks. If you can give me a little bit of time, I will answer for everything, but I can't do much good on a leave of absence. I am going to lose our intel already, but I can't lose my credibility as a police detective right now. I need your help. I'll be honest; my chances of solving this go down dramatically without you."

Annabelle brushed a strand of her hair back and sighed. She stared off into the distant Chicago skyline, not speaking for a moment as the snow fell. "Well, I won't do anything illegal, but I can gather all the evidence and statements accordingly. I'll have to be very thorough before presenting it to Rooks anyway, but you know that won't buy you much time. Maybe a few days at the most."

"Thank you, Annabelle I really appreciate the help, especially under the circumstances."

"Hold on. I want something in return, Tyler. I know you have been through more than most people can imagine. I see those dark circles under your eyes. They look more like bruises than sleep deprivation. I want to know what really happened to you......or as much as you can share. I want to help you, but I also want to understand. You have to help me understand."

Now it was Tyler's turn to look at the skyline for several moments.

He said, "Really? You have to know that? It isn't really worth talking about. It is just another sad story in an ocean of sad stories. Rooks probably gave you all the details anyway."

The silence that greeted the statement gave him time to think. Annabelle stared at him. She had him and they both knew it. In the end, it was not a hard decision. He needed her more than she needed him. Logic could be such a bitch.

"Ok, if you are willing to help, then it is the least I can do. It will have to be in a few days. Fair enough?" He pulled out a small notebook and jotted down some information as she waited. "Here is my personal email address. Can you send any updates you have about the case to me? Until I am considered suspended, consider it a request from a fellow detective. Just give me some time, then look into the info yourself. By that point, I will either have something, or I will be done."

There was nothing else to say. Annabelle hesitated before holding out her hand which he shook. He could tell she wanted to say some sort of goodbye, so he looked away and nodded. Nothing else was needed right now. He turned towards the street leaving a few footprints in the slush. His feet became soaked as Tyler made his way back.

The car started in a comforting way that told him it would get through the snow. He clicked the seatbelt and put his hand on the gear shift when he heard a knock on the window. Annabelle was staring at Tyler as he rolled the window down. Her eyes showed emotions he wasn't sure he could interpret. She said, "Good luck, Detective Morgan. I don't know you that well, but for some reason I do believe in you. Don't make me regret that." She turned and walked away without another word.

He whispered, "Thank you, Annabelle." into the howling wind but his words were snatched away. Tyler rolled up the window and put the car into reverse. He drove off without looking back.

THE AIR INSIDE the bank was warm though the floor was damp from today's business. Tyler remembered when he had opened Grace's college fund the month after she had been born. Right at this very branch of the bank. Emily had insisted on it even with how tight money had been during those days, and Tyler had agreed. It had been so important at the time. The money he had received from the insurance company after his wife and daughter's deaths had joined the funds they had hoped to use for Grace's future. It was too much to think about.

The carpeting stretched on like a road leading to a proverbial pot of gold and a bank teller Tyler was sure he had met before. ABC's "The Look of Love, Part One" was playing softly on the speakers somewhere overhead. It was the last business hour of the day, and there were few people around him since it wasn't a payday. He should have enough time. He was greeted warmly by the teller who smiled for the hundredth time today. It looked fake and was something he probably wouldn't have even noticed a year ago.

"I'd like to make a withdrawal."

"Certainly sir, let me get some information and look up your account. How much would you like to withdraw today?"

"All of it."

CHAPTER 16
Richol's

Will knew Robert Baxter was annoyed by the way he laid the Beretta 92 down on the cheap-looking table before sitting down. Usually when Baxter was angry, it didn't end well for anyone. Will had no idea what any of this was about. He had gotten a call a half an hour ago and had jumped out of bed before he even realized it was four in the morning. The Uber drive over had been tedious, but short due to a lack of awake Chicago drivers. Will had no trouble finding the restaurant. Now he was starting to regret not being stuck in traffic.

They were in some sort of kitchen in a recently closed-down restaurant called Richol's. Richol's had been a trendy Italian and Greek restaurant that tried catering to two entirely different demographics. Instead of cutting some sort of new niche market, it had ended up constantly in the red and finally bankrupt. The name had not been a good fit, and now neither was the restaurant. Will had never eaten here so it was unfamiliar to him. Apparently some unknown contact had arranged this, or Baxter had resources that Will hadn't seen yet.

He had found his boss sitting in the back of the kitchen after weaving through the main dining area. It was a depressing setting with knocked over chairs and exaggerated hanging hooks. The single table resembled a butcher's block. Even sitting, Robert Baxter seemed tall. Will found himself wanting to shrink and hide in the pantry behind them.

Baxter said, "Ok, Will, here is the deal. In about fifteen minutes, we are going to meet with a Mr. Nick Garza who apparently has enough support to warrant this little discussion. He has ties to a cartel in the south, and is scouting north to see if he can get a foothold here. He has heard good things about our product and is looking to cut himself a slice of the pie. Garza is coming alone except for his bodyguard as a sign of good faith. How is that for a one minute summary?"

"Who's the bodyguard?"

Baxter stared at him until Will felt an overwhelming desire to swallow, but he couldn't. "You aren't paying attention, and I don't have patience for stupidity this early in the morning. It doesn't matter who the fucking bodyguard is. He is a meat shield. They are coming alone as a sign of good faith, but faith and good will only go so far. They will be armed I guarantee it, so be on your guard. They want to be business partners with us, but quite honestly I don't think Garza is going to offer much in return. That means today could be a bad day for peace and prosperity."

Will dared to ask one more question even though he knew this wasn't the time. He said, "Why don't we just take them out or buy them off then? Doesn't sound like a good business plan to me."

Baxter leaned back in his chair and smiled. "Yes Will, you're right. Unfortunately Nick Garza is one of those flies that will keep buzzing around no matter how hard you try to swat the little bastard. You have to get the fly to land in one place long enough to crush him with the palm of your hand. We need to act interested to get the man to stop buzzing around. If he has something, great, but if not, then at least we are ready to raise our hand. Got it?"

"We should have brought more men."

Baxter replied, "More men would only ensure we have a problem.

If you showed up to a meeting with one guy and saw the other side had seven, what would you do? "

"Good point."

They were both silent as they waited for Nick Garza to show up. Will wished he hadn't worn a watch. He could hear it ticking the seconds away, which made time slow to a crawl. He just needed to get rid of the stupid thing since he used his cell phone for checking the time anyway. All the ticking told him was that he was waiting to make a deal. Of course, he might also be waiting to get shot. Life was funny.

The far kitchen door opened with a groan. A man dressed in white, whom Will assumed was the body guard, stepped in first. He took an opposite stance across the table. The grizzled bodyguard was taller and had the face of a professional killer. Will thought of the proverbial shark hunting for traces of blood or the next easy meal. Why the hell did he always associate people with animals?

Nick Garza entered the room next, and he didn't look at all the part of a major player with Cartel ties. Maybe that was the point. The rotund man was maybe five foot four on his toes. He wore a dull gray shirt and brown jacket. Garza looked more the part of a bumbling night clerk, but when Will saw his eyes and the set of his mouth; he knew this was a man who usually got what he wanted.

"Hello, Mr. Baxter and associate." Nick Garza's chin nodded to Will, but his eyes never left Baxter. Baxter said nothing but indicated for the larger man to take a seat, which was gratefully taken. He could feel the chair sink an inch into the floor, as impossible as it sounded. Despite the weather outside, Garza's forehead was lightly beaded in sweat which made Will feel nervous. The perspiration was probably due to the fact that Robert Baxter's gun sat on the table in plain sight. It was a glaring topic that Will wished to avoid. Apparently Garza had other ideas.

"Is the gun really necessary?" Garza said pointing a finger the size of a sausage, "We are all friends here, and I am not armed." Baxter continued to say nothing, but looked up at the bodyguard as a question.

Garza shrugged and said, "Well, he is armed, but we already agreed not to deceive each other."

The tone was apologetic, but Will was sure Garza was armed just like his white garbed silent friend. If one could be friends with a shark anyway. The air grew still until it swelled to an aura of discomfort. It felt like a showdown already, which was probably exactly what Baxter wanted.

Garza cleared his throat and continued. "Mr. Baxter, I can tell you are a man that doesn't waste time, so I will speak plainly. We both have something the other wants. You are in a unique situation of solely controlling a new product. I am in a position to offer both protection and, more importantly, expansion. You have done an amazing job distributing your product in the Midwest already, but what about the future? New York, Miami, Los Angeles, and so forth. I am sure you are very capable, but even you cannot do this venture alone." Garza gestured with his hands in a casual way indicating such was the way of things. "You need a partner with ties, my friend. That is what I bring to the table."

The large man looked like he wanted to say more, but Baxter started tapping his finger on the table in a rhythmic pattern. Up. Down. Tick. Tick. Tick. It sounded like drops of blood splashing onto the heavy wood. Baxter smiled at the silence the sound caused. Tick. Tick. Tick. The evil son of a bitch was enjoying this.

Will wanted a cigarette so badly, but he didn't dare to make any sudden moves. His stomach was in knots. He prayed his body wouldn't make any noises in the uncomfortable ghost restaurant setting. An upset stomach getting you shot was a great way to ruin the day. Finally the smiling man spoke.

"How much do you want?"

"Perhaps I should go into detail a little more first." Garza's words were slurred in surprise. The large jowls moved uneasily as he labored to urge the words out. "If we merged with your operation....."

"How much do you want?"

"Mr. Baxter please let's......"

"How much do you want?"

"Sixty percent."

"Sixty percent? Of what? Overall revenue? Profit? A division of the Midwest?" Baxter laughed into the silence of his questions. "What part of the balance sheet are we talking about here, Garza? Sixty percent is a pretty vague number to fuck with."

"Sixty percent overall with shared expenses and profit. In return you get…"

"Don't sell me, Garza, I know what we get. I wouldn't have come to this meeting if I didn't do some digging first." Baxter said, "I spoke with some of your ties and weighed what you could bring to the table."

Baxter stopped talking and let another silence envelope the room. This time Will could swear he saw discomfort even in Garza's silent guard. He is going to try to shoot me first, Will thought. The room seemed to swell and beads of sweat popped on Garza's forehead as the large man stared at Baxter. Will could feel sweat on his own face now, and his shirt felt sticky on his back. He wished he were home watching television and drinking beer. He would even settle for water right now.

"Sixty percent overall with shared expenses and profit is fair. I think we have a deal, Mr. Garza." Baxter smiled and the room shrank back to normal size. Will struggled so he wouldn't let out a sigh of relief. Garza smiled and his bodyguard seemed to nod in affirmation. He wanted to give them both a high five.

They now had a new partnership that would benefit everyone in the long-term. Robert Baxter was more intelligent than anyone Will had ever met, but he was unpredictable on the best of days. This was one of those cases where he hadn't been sure if Baxter would do what was best for everyone or what amused him. Every day was a flip of a blood-etched coin.

Both Garza and Baxter stood up almost simultaneously as they shook hands from across the table. The meeting had lasted about six minutes. The large man rumbled in approval and said, "Excellent, Mr. Baxter. We can begin as early as tomorrow, and my associate here will setup another meeting for details. Once we have secured our arrangement, we can begin tying up any loose ends you may have." The four men walked out of the kitchen with the nameless bodyguard in the lead. Garza followed showing his back as a sign of trust as they walked down the hallway. Each step an echo of wood and cheap labor.

Before they had reached the main dining area, Garza began talking about the expansion and this is when Baxter raised the Beretta and began to pull the trigger. Each shot boomed down the hall, a bullet ripped a piece out of Nick Garza's back, tearing bits of flesh, blood and ichor to splatter on the walls and ceiling. Before Will had his gun out, Baxter had shot Garza four times and grabbed onto him. He rammed the obese dying man forward, and Will could feel the body slam into the bodyguard who cried out in fear. The surprised man fell forward like a domino and hit the floor. He scrambled to turn himself over from underneath the two hundred and fifty pound dead weight, when Baxter shot him in the head. Blood splattered onto the floor and crawled towards their feet. Will hadn't even fired a shot as he stared in disbelief. He took three steps back then took two more.

"What the fuck, Baxter?!"

Robert Baxter's eyes never left the two bodies, but he sliced his hand in a downward motion that made it clear for Will to shut up. They could both hear a broken wheeze coming from Garza. Will felt his eyes widen at the sight of the shaking drug dealer. He was grateful Baxter's height blocked some of his vision. Baxter had to shuffle somewhat to the side, and he leaned over to roll Garza onto his back. The dying man could no longer do any harm. The wheezing sound coming from Garza was awful to hear, and it gurgled on for a few seconds. Will could feel a scream beginning to build in his throat. That sound was fucking horrible.

"You're fucked….Baxxx……"

Amazingly the man's words were clear enough for Will to hear. They were a death rattle turned to a whisper. Baxter reached into his jacket and pulled out a large roll of cash that he dropped onto Garza's face, where it rolled off to land on the floor.

"I sent fifty of these to your connections in Guadalajara almost two weeks ago. They agreed to a much more hands-off approach and definitely not sixty percent. Matter of fact, as long as I keep sending these hefty payments, they have to do very little as there is no real vested interest in micromanagement." Baxter smiled. "The only loose end was one fat fuck who couldn't get it through his head that he wasn't going to become the next heroin kingpin of Chicago."

"Fucking…..lying….."

Baxter smiled at the words. "Garza, I would lie to all the virgins and holy men of this world if it allowed me to put an easy bullet in your back rather than spending months in a costly war. History is written by those who aren't too busy dying on the floor in a goddamn restaurant."

Garza opened his lips to say something else. A bubble of blood filled his mouth and popped into a fine mist which smothered the wheezing sound. Baxter waited for a few seconds listening. He then reached down into the dead man's wound on the left side of his ribs, making a fist in the gore. He pulled out his hand and held it up for Will to see. His face was curled into a snarl, but his words came out in a cold tone that made Will take another step back.

"Never make noises like that Will, and don't ever question my actions. If you hesitate in any way again, I will kill you myself." Baxter stretched out his fingers like a puppeteer. The blood fell from his hand like thick honey landing one drop after another on the floor. The meaning was perfectly clear. "If you blink even for a second, you are the loser. The other man will kill you with protests still in your lungs. It won't matter if you are a stone cold killer or a student at Tiananmen Square. You will be dead and going to whatever hell you believe in. I am not a man who blinks, Will. Not for one second."

CHAPTER 17
Ashes of the Living

TYLER MORGAN LET out a breath that he had been holding for at least a minute. He had given up the last semblance of his former life now that he was in danger of losing his badge. He had sacrificed the last thing he held sacred for a name, and, more importantly, a little bit of time. Tyler could see a clock tower in his mind that loomed over him and darkened the sky with its shadow. It counted each second with a tumultuous click. Herrera would help him as much as she could within the confines of the law, but that wasn't much. He didn't really expect any other help from this point forward.

Tyler had used the Chicago Police database to look up any and all information CPD had on Anton Lynd. Lynd apparently didn't have a criminal record. That was a rarity for the people that he usually had to investigate. It also made the search harder since the only reference point was the DMV information. He printed out Anton's picture and address from their records and memorized the man's features. While he was still searching, Annabelle sent him a message saying that they had taken Marco Brent to the hospital where he was in stable condition. She also mentioned Marco hadn't talked to her or any other police officers yet. At least the name of Anton Lynd hadn't been given out to anyone else for the moment. It was the first hint of good luck all day.

Tyler regretted not being able to respond to Annabelle, but he hoped she would understand. He shut down the laptop knowing that his access would be put on hold relatively soon. Then he would only have access to the CLEAR system. The Citizen Law Enforcement Analysis and Reporting system could be useful, but it was more limiting than what he was used to. Tyler's information trail was slowly dying with each hour. Rooks or anyone from IA could also feasibly look at his search history to determine the research into Anton Lynd. It would not take an entire police force to figure out where to look next. By that time, if Tyler hadn't found out how the man was connected to this, he never would.

He had withdrawn all of his savings since electronic payments could also be tracked through debit activity. It was a large sum of cash so conversion was needed. He had purchased several prepaid credit cards, and the rest of the cash was put into a Nike duffel bag. The money didn't matter anymore, but it was necessary to serve his needs for the rest of the investigation. He was carrying around his family's former hopes and dreams in a nylon sack next to a stuffed suitcase. He had picked clothing that Emily or Grace had bought for him. Tyler could feel his sanity slipping staring at a black button down shirt Grace had given him for Father's Day. It was impossible to throw away any of their gifts no matter how unhealthy it seemed.

Tyler locked the front door of his pseudo-home after doing a final look around in case he had missed anything he would need. He had placed three months' rent into an envelope for his apartment which was deposited into the central drop box on the way out. He felt nothing as he pulled out of the complex. It had never been home to him.

The sky darkened, growling with the late hour. Tyler had trouble seeing as he drove through the streets looking for a hotel. You could find a room downtown even past midnight, but you would pay a high price for it. The first place Tyler stopped was called the Monarch Hotel, guaranteeing some money would leave the duffel bag. The entrance arched over him as he walked through the double doors pulling out a wad of cash like a 1950s gangster.

It was possible, however unlikely, that Anton was not involved in this. Tyler believed Marco's information, or at least he wanted to. He still needed to appear at a normal hour like a normal detective making normal cursory rounds of interviewing. That meant sleep or at least trying to, no matter how much of a pain it was to toss and turn.

The clerk at the front desk was far too awake for Tyler, probably due to either caffeine or the enthusiasm of a rookie employee. Tyler preferred the ones who didn't look at you twice, and didn't care if you had a nice night or not. He glanced at his keycard and shuffled towards a glass elevator.

The room was on the eighth floor and looked suitably expensive, considering the ridiculous price of it all. Tyler dropped the duffel bag and suitcase by the door and then fell onto the bed. He reached over and set the alarm clock for six, even though he wouldn't need it. Since Emily and Grace had gone, insomnia had become a close friend of his. Tyler had discovered he could go several days with little sleep, but the price was a night of heavy and dream-ridden tossing and turning. He didn't want to go to bed at all, but his body had demands of its own.

Tyler lay on the bed facing the ceiling as he kicked off his shoes and placed the Glock on the nightstand. He had to turn slightly to take out both wallets. One had all the traditional information, and the other held his badge that was currently being warred upon. Most detectives carried two wallets as the badge would not fit properly in a standard size case. A custom-made, additional, or police issue was usually needed. Tyler opened his and held up the piece of metal that symbolized the last shred of a normal life. It felt dull and lifeless and he laid it down next to the gun. No magic talisman was going to make this night any easier.

Tyler stared at the ceiling and focused on his hate. It was a dark block of rage that he could feel in his chest. It beat in time with his heart, telling him to go to Anton Lynd's house and put a gun to the man's head right now. Hatred had kept him going since the death of his family, but now it felt stronger since he had found a purpose. He could feel the anger throb through thin veins with each pulse beat. It kept up with the time that was slipping through his hands faster than any sand.

There was a law of diminishing return when dealing with a homicide, especially in the first forty-eight hours. So what had that return become when it had been over half a year? It was best not to think about such things. He had a tenuous thread of a lead which was better than nothing. At least there was still hope for tomorrow.

Tyler focused on a dot in the stucco ceiling. He stared at it, listening to his heartbeat and the time flowing around him. His eyes strained on that single speck, and he sent his whirlwind of thoughts forth. He sent all the anger and sadness into the tiny space to be confined for the evening. Emotions kept returning to his body despite the effort. His mind's eye could see the dot even as his thoughts betrayed him and drifted back into memories. Memories that he didn't want to revisit.......

TYLER WALKED INTO the CPD morgue as quietly as he could. It was a grim and drab area that smelled of formaldehyde and old blood. The bright overhead lights made it almost painful to look at the white tiled floors. The cold faucets that arched over the sinks were easily twice the size of a standard bathroom set. It had been four days since his family had died, and he didn't want to be here. CPD had found the dead bodies of Emily and Grace too badly burned for any type of facial or body recognition. They had used dental records to identify each corpse. A body had to be exposed to temperatures around 1,500 degrees Fahrenheit or higher to become bone. The intensity of the fire was not enough to stop the identification process, but had made his family unrecognizable to look upon.

Tyler walked toward the reception area, if it could be called that, where a short red-haired man was working at a Dell computer over a large coal slab table. He wore the typical trappings of a mortician down to the clean but faded white lab coat. He turned as Tyler approached and said, "Detective Morgan?" The tone was solemn and conveyed just a hint of disbelief that he was here.

Lieutenant Rooks had urged him not to come. Identifying the bodies wasn't necessary from a protocol perspective. The point of identifying a corpse had become more of a formality rather than a necessity due to forensic science. In cases like this, it was not considered relevant to anyone but Tyler. Why exactly was he here? Tyler wanted to turn around and leave. He wanted to go home and drown himself in Scotch. An ocean of hard liquor crashing down on his senses. He wanted to enter a coma sleep for as long as he could.

The truth was that he had to see what had been done to Emily and Grace. A small part of his mind was still in denial, regardless of all the evidence he had gone through. Tyler's thoughts kept repeating the same cruel lies; Emily and Grace weren't dead but had gotten out at the last moment. They were wandering the streets of Chicago in a state of amnesia trying to find their lives again. They were kidnapped and tied up in someone's basement. The false possibilities were endless.

These thoughts had the enticement of the illogical and delusional, but they gave him the slightest ray of hope. Now, here he was ready to shred the last thin threads of denial. Tyler knew why he was here, but sometimes knowing the answer was the worst kind of cure. It would kill the last bit of warmth he had.

Tyler realized he had been standing there for several moments as he watched a furrow of wrinkles crease the mortician's forehead, waiting for an answer. It was comical and sad at the same time. He said, "Yes, I am Detective Morgan." The mortician nodded as though he had police in to identify their dead families every day. "Please follow me."

The walk down the hall was at a brisk pace and the man in the white lab coat said nothing to him. Tyler was grateful for the lack of small talk or pseudo-sympathies, but he found himself dragging his feet across the floor. The mortician turned back to look at him several times before compensating in step. At the far end of the hallway lay a door painted in bright cadmium, a stark contrast to all the white entranceways that lined the hallway. The color was absurd to his eyes. Tyler thought it resembled jaundiced skin. He knew this was where they were going. Any room that contained the deceased was denoted clearly to keep any mistaken entries at bay. It was a warning for both the living and the dead.

They reached the door and the mortician turned toward Tyler who noticed his nametag said Jenkins. Tyler knew he would remember this man's last name for the rest of his life.

"They are in there, Detective Morgan. Take all the time you need. I will be up front if you need me."

This statement uttered, the mortician nodded in respect and walked back down the hall. Tyler was alone in front of the door. He put his hand on the handle expecting to feel some sort of cold that usually emanated from areas of the ME field, but he felt nothing. He stared at the scars on the back of his hand. Funny how he couldn't recall where they had all come from. Tyler looked away from his hand and the door, feeling a nausea creeping into his stomach. He eased his arm down to his side, feeling warm and ill. His mind was trying not to think of Emily or Grace, but it was so hard. Too hard for him anyway.

This is what you are here to do, Tyler thought. Lay your family to rest in your mind. Go in, look, and say goodbye. Maybe you will feel better. This isn't for them, this is for you. So get it over with or you will be back here tomorrow. Say goodbye, Tyler. Say goodbye.

He didn't want to say goodbye and he sure as hell didn't want to be in a morgue looking at his eight year old daughter's burned corpse. Tyler's anger swelled inside of him like a balloon being rapidly filled with helium. He welcomed it. He wanted to feel anything but the sadness that emanated from the door. He wanted to find the people responsible for this and make them suffer. He wanted to burn their flesh and take away everything they cared about. He wanted them to feel how he felt right now. His hate was a blackened screw turning within his heart.

Tyler rubbed his eyes trying to clear them of terrible visions. These thoughts were not what Emily and Grace would have wanted from him right now. He needed to see his family for the last time and not have his mind clouded by anger. Tyler wanted to think of all the good memories, but that was worse because he knew there would be no more. He needed to gain some sort of closure even if it was just the murder of self-denial.

He stared at the floor and wondered how long had passed since the mortician walked away. One minute? Ten? An hour? How long before he would walk through the door or turn around and run down the hall screaming? Enough was enough as the saying went.

Tyler pushed the door open. It closed behind his back without a sound as he stepped through. His heart hammered against his ribcage as he walked into the large room. Overhead lights glared down on black slab tabletops and several laptops in screen-saver mode. A Kilotech hanging dial scale and several digital scales were next to a steel basin. A gauge of organ weight was mapped out next to a chart of human anatomy that reminded Tyler more of the Vitruvian Man than anything else.

The far side of the room had a steel-latched door where all the bodies were stored for preservation, and in front of the door lay two gurney beds covered in white sheets. Lieutenant Rooks must have said something to have the MEs bring his family out in case Tyler did come. He was absurdly grateful for the gesture, but he still stood by the doorway. He willed himself to step forward closer to the beds. The room was eerily quiet. He could feel the lack of sound envelop his ears in a barrier of silence. His footsteps sounded like gunshots on the tiled floor as he moved toward the two sheets.

Sweat began to slide down his forehead despite the cold temperature of the climate-controlled area. He could now see that the bed on his left was only filled to the mid-section. This is Grace, he thought. This is my daughter.

Tyler had been attacked by criminals, in accidents, had been shot at, but this was the most horrifying experience he had ever been through. The two beds were separated by a little over four feet. He stood in the gap at the foot of the gurneys staring down at the sheets. In a complete sense of unreality, Tyler stepped between the two beds, his breath coming in ragged gasps. Nothing moved except for his lungs trying desperately to pump oxygen through his body.

Tyler reached down to the sheet on the right. Emily. The body of Emily, he mentally corrected himself. It is just her body, not HER. His fingers plucked at the cold linen as he drew it down all the way to the bottom of the bed.

He rammed a hand into his mouth to murder a scream that threatened to erupt. The blistered body in front of him was a patchwork of burned, residual tissue and scorched bone. The face looked more like a blackened skull than the flawed beauty he had fallen in love with so quickly. Charred teeth screamed out at him.

The salt of tears touched his lips as his vision blurred. Tyler struggled to breathe as he thought of all the phone calls and sympathetic talk, speaking of his family being in a better place. There was no better place here.

Tyler reached over and pulled back the other sheet to see the smaller and equally burned body of his daughter. The shell of his little girl was curled into a cocoon, as though trying to hide from the flames. It made him sick to see his daughter wrapped up in death and pain at the age of eight years old. He thought of her morning pounce wrapped in giggles and how soft her thin hand was in his own.

"You didn't deserve this….." Tyler said, "We didn't deserve this!" His voice echoed in the room. The words came back to his ears with no answer. He wanted to say something else to them, but any eloquence he possessed had fled in the wrath of this violence.

Tyler collapsed to his knees between the two beds moaning. It was a sickening feeling to realize that no one could recognize who they were. It was like they had never existed. Most of the pictures and videos had burned up in the fire, forbidding him to replay their happy memories. The only ones he had were in his head and they hurt too much to recall.

For the first time since childhood, Tyler sobbed uncontrollably. He struggled to get up on his knees and took the blackened hands of his wife and child in each of his own. The feel of them was like paper and held nothing of their humanity. Memories flashed through his mind as he thought of his wedding day and the time Grace had tried to make spaghetti. His tears continued to fall making tracks down his face. Sobs racked his body and he could not control the spasms.

Tyler realized that his eyes were closed and he was unsure how long he had been kneeling. "I'm sorry. I failed you. I should have been there. I should have stopped this. I only pray you find it in your hearts to forgive me and know that I love you more than anything. Please........ forgive me."

Tyler stood up to look down on them for the last time. He pulled the sheets over the bodies to fully cover them again.

Tyler held up his hands in front of his face. They were covered in bits of ash and the remains of his family's life. He could feel his own essence coalesce and mix with the ashes on his fingertips. Inside, the once constant warmth was replaced with dark anger and other emotions he couldn't identify. All of them felt demonic and malevolent, like a fiery hand had grabbed his soul and crushed it in undead strength. He was alive but felt muted, as though seeing the end of his family had put the final twist of pain into a dying soul. Tyler turned away from the remains of his burned life. The smile on his face resembled a snarl that Emily would not have recognized. It was a mixture of hatred and cruelty.

The dull throbs of anger focused him as he wiped the tears away with the back of his hand. Tyler walked out of the room, not looking back, as his footsteps echoed down the confines of the hallway. The red haired mortician with the nametag of Jenkins was standing at the end of the hallway jotting down notes on a portable table. He glanced at Tyler and then glanced again, before stepping aside as quickly as he could. Sweat dripped down from the smaller man's forehead as he continued to back away, stammering at whatever he saw. Tyler ignored the man and walked out the door into the night.

CHAPTER 18
Amalgamation

TYLER STRUGGLED TO open his eyes as he realized he had fallen asleep thinking of the past. He struggled through the layers of fatigue that had taken a toll on his body, burying them in the depths of his bones. He was tired but had not been plagued by nightmares. That was a plus, at least.

Tyler stretched and got up, walking over to the blinds of the room's large window. It was seven in the morning and still somewhat dark. The snow had begun to pile up as flakes drifted through the air outside. Sometimes you could feel the Chicago winter wind battering at the windows in rage, but today it seemed calm. He prayed there would be no traffic issues. It was time to talk to Anton Lynd, and he didn't want to waste any time.

Tyler selected a blue button-up shirt and khakis from his makeshift closet, also known as a suitcase. He laid the clothes onto the bed and set his duffel bag next to them. The money inside would buy him the supplies he needed to get through this. Tyler couldn't help but think about how it used to represent his family's future. This money was for house payments and college funds. He had planned on buying Grace an old car, which was an unnecessary luxury in Chicago, because he had wanted to teach her how to drive like his father had. Taking her out to an old parking lot and letting her get used to the brakes and the slight, exaggerated motions of turning the wheel. Tyler smiled at the thought of his own excursion. He had bashed the hell out of that car but learned quickly. His smile faded.

Tyler found a miniature gym downstairs and lifted weights for almost an hour. The pressure on his arms and chest helped work out the stress. Then he went back to the room and took a shower as hot as the faucet would allow. He let the water beat down on him, thinking on his next move.

Since Anton Lynd was a civilian with no record, he would have to be more subtle. All he had was the word of a man who had shot at him. Tyler was glad of the steam on the mirror as he turned off the water. He didn't want to see the dead look in his eyes. He walked into the bedroom and slumped down onto the thick mattress.

Tyler turned on the television. The news promised snow, ice, and cold permeating the air. There was no mention of Abyss, which was a miracle or deliberate censorship. Tyler dressed and put on his holster. He adjusted his belt so that his badge was visible. Who knew if it was even valid at this point? Walking away from a crime scene which he was directly involved with would almost guarantee a reprimand. He simply could not afford to be tied up in red tape right now. Each day that went by erased a little more of his chances, and Tyler was grateful for Herrera's assistance. The executioner's axe was coming but he had a little more time.

He went downstairs to grab some toast and coffee from the morning buffet. It would have looked more at home in a chic breakfast nook than an overpriced hotel. Piles of crackling bacon and cinnamon-dusted French toast sat next to glasses of iced orange juice and a carafe of milk. Tyler had to force himself to eat food anymore. He chewed the toast mechanically and swallowed bites as quickly as he could without choking. Tyler focused on the motion of his jaw grinding up the food to not let his thoughts wander. He needed to keep his strength up, but food was there for sustenance rather than pleasure. It seemed the only things that still tasted good were caffeine and alcohol. Not even bacon was appealing, and that had always been a favorite.

When Tyler was done eating, he went to the front desk where a different clerk with a pseudo smile took his money. He set up another night's reservation and paid cash. He needed to go to a different hotel soon, but didn't want to spend the time looking one up. There was, after all, lifesavings to burn through in the next few weeks. Lifesavings was an interesting term when your life was beyond saving. The parking lot was connected to the hotel through the basement level. He took the elevator down and was shielded from the bitter cold outside. His car started with a purr.

The drive to Anton Lynd's apartment was brisk, and Tyler enjoyed driving on the streets as traffic was a lot lighter than normal. His thoughts drifted to Annabelle. How was she doing? Tyler smiled at the thought of having a partner like him and all the headaches that came with it. She must think he was crazy, and maybe that wasn't far from the truth. It was a completely different relationship than when he had worked with Chris Wessler a lifetime ago. Chris had been considered more of the wildcard and Tyler the voice of logic. Tyler's slight smile turned into a smirk at the thought. Chris had gone on to further his career, and Tyler had hit a dead-end with his. Destiny was a schemer and Tyler could feel its cold claws grabbing his throat ready to squeeze. Annabelle had already stuck out her neck for him in their short time as partners. He was grateful to have a person to depend on.

Anton Lynd's apartment resembled a steel fortress more than a condominium. He had arrived earlier than anticipated and took a second to stare up at the grandiose structure. Tyler idly wondered what Anton's job title was. Independent Consultant? Efficiency Analyst? Client Manager? Some kind of job where it would be harder to track revenue sources, and also one that would require few hours of being physically present. Appearances were all that mattered in a case like this.

The term "lamb" had been used for people like Anton Lynd for quite some time now. A lamb was a drug dealer with no prior criminal history. They were usually not in the business for long, as the reputation of the individual would be used up quickly. It was this same "clean" reputation that offered protection for their brief career. No record with the police, no discernible recognition in the criminal element, and most importantly, no claims for bigger pieces of the profit. The only benefit to this profession was an obvious large amount of cash. The smartest lambs were the ones that operated for a short period of time and then opted out. Most of them were not that intelligent and were arrested or killed by the end of their tenure.

Tyler hoped Anton Lynd was a lamb for another reason. If Anton was inexperienced with law enforcement, he would roll over thus becoming an asset. Tyler would then have an active lamb who could lead him to the manufacturers. That was, of course, assuming cooperation, Tyler thought wryly. His worries were trivial, since he was, more than likely, a suspended detective getting ready to interrogate a civilian with no real probable cause. The lines he was crossing were painful but necessary; at least he hoped so.

The inside reception area smelled of too much money and not enough taste. Tyler was surprised there wasn't a doorman. The irony of not being able to afford a place like this, while a heroin drug dealer could, was not lost on him. He pressed the call button below a neatly labeled scrolled plate saying Lynd. A voice answered almost immediately, it was a voice of faux culture.

"Yes?"

Tyler said, "Mr. Lynd? My name is Detective Morgan. I was wondering if I could come up and speak to you?"

"Yes, of course." The immediate reply gave no hint of urgency or nervousness, but Tyler noticed there was no question about what he wanted either. The buzzer echoed and was absorbed into the overly thick carpet. Elevators and stairs were both easily accessible and conveniently placed. Tyler took the stairs. Let Lynd sweat a little, while he got a small dose of exercise.

The stairs were steep, which Tyler liked, as he climbed his way to the sixth floor. He and Emily used to go hiking once a year, and his favorite part had been the climb up the long trails. Two years ago, they had gone to Pokagon in Indiana. Emily had wanted to stay close to Illinois where Grace was being watched by Emily's parents. Tyler had gotten a card recently from his in-laws but hadn't written back. He didn't know what to say.

The sixth floor hallway stretched toward Anton's apartment with the same exaggerated style as the building's reception area. Tyler reached the apartment number listed on the call button and knocked with his knuckles. The door swung open and Anton Lynd stood before him, reaching a height of 5'5 or 5'6 at the most. He was dressed in a dark blue button up shirt that looked rumpled, like it had just been picked up from the bedroom floor.

"Detective Morgan?"

"Mr. Lynd, may I please come in and speak with you?"

"What is this in regards to? Is everything all right?" You should have asked that earlier Anton, thought Tyler as he shook his head. "No, everything is not all right, Mr. Lynd. I need to speak to you about a serious accusation that has occurred in one of my investigations. May I come in? I would prefer not to do this in the hallway if possible."

"May I see some identification please?" The clipped sentence was as cursory as the glance he gave Tyler's badge when it was brought out. Anton nodded as though it was all part of their customary greeting and gestured for Tyler to come in. Tyler walked past Anton but kept the smaller man in his peripheral vision. The inside of Anton's apartment was a relief compared to the exterior. A white and black theme followed them from the foyer into the living room. The furnishings were stark glass and synthetic wood. Anton sat down on a black leather couch while Tyler took an overstuffed chair.

"How rude of me, would you like something to drink?" Anton asked.

"No, thank you, Mr. Lynd." Tyler said, "I don't want to waste your time, so I am going to get to the point. A man by the name of Marco Brent was recently arrested. Is he an acquaintance of yours?"

Anton Lynd sat back, muttering the name to himself as though in deep thought. Tyler already knew the answer. He wasn't at all disappointed.

"No, I cannot recall a Marco Brent." Anton pronounced the name with a hint of confusion. "I deal with a broad range of clients in my line of work, but they are more concerned with their trust funds than interacting with the Chicago Police Department."

"Well, Mr. Lynd, that is funny because after I shot Marco in the leg, I asked him about his supplier. All he could do was scream your name over and over. This was before we carried him out of his apartment on a gurney because of his blood loss. He is probably unconscious right now, but I am betting, when he wakes up, his answer will be the same."

Anton Lynd's face flushed but then he smiled like it was a small joke between them. The man was good. Tyler had dealt with a few lambs before, and most collapsed at the mere mention of jail time or violence. Anton was calm and collected which probably served him well dealing with heroin junkies. Right now, it was also a sign of guilt. He was too collected to be innocent. Innocent people accused of a crime wore expressions of shock or confusion with telltale shaking hands or short uneven breaths. It could be faked, but only by those who knew what signs to exhibit and which ones to repress.

"Detective Morgan, I have graciously allowed you into my home, and I will cooperate in any way I can with the police. I feel they are one of our city's most underrated assets, but this is absurd." Anton raised his hands out in a questioning gesture. "Are you accusing me of something? What exactly? Some criminal says my name after a significant amount of blood loss, and you rush over here spouting inane nonsense. I really don't understand this conversation. Now, if there is anything else, please be quick, I have a lot to do today."

"What do you know about Abyss?" Tyler asked without waiting. There was a slight shift of the eyes to the right as he watched Anton. The man's voice was pure reason but his body movements were becoming more of a tell than he realized.

"Nothing really, other than what is on the news and in blogs." Anton replied, "It is a spreading blight in our city. Some sort of new form of heroin. A growing problem that faces a lot of our youth today, which saddens me, but what else is new?" The spread of hands in a gesture of disdained helplessness accompanied his words but it was hollow. Tyler noticed a bead of sweat had begun to coalesce on the side of Anton's face. It spoke more to Tyler than any of the words he was hearing.

"I think you know a lot more about Abyss than you are letting on Mr. Lynd, and I am getting some answers today." Tyler said, "This isn't a Machiavellian play or something you can dismiss."

Anton Lynd rose in a motion of pseudo-rage and shook his fist in Tyler's face. "That is enough, Detective Morgan! I want you to......" Then Tyler made his move. He jumped forward and tackled Anton onto the couch. The smaller man squirmed, trying to escape from his hold, clawing at Tyler's face. He punched at Tyler and landed a hit on his shoulder. Tyler threw a punch at Anton's face, and it landed on jawbone with a loud crack. Anton's eyes glazed in pain, and Tyler threw him face first into the carpet. He planted his knee on the stunned man's back to keep him pinned and grabbed both arms. He brought them behind Anton's back and held them with one hand while he pulled out his handcuffs. The click of each cuff seemed to wake Anton, and he moaned in agony as Tyler stood up.

"You can't do this! This is barbaric. Animal!" Anton roared, "I am filing a lawsuit against the Chicago Police Department for this. Enjoy this moment. Soon I will have your badge, Detective Morgan!"

"Not if someone else gets it first." He muttered as he started to look around the living room. Anton started to rise. Tyler said, "Stay right where you are. I don't want to add anything onto attempted assault of a police officer." Anton murmured to himself so faintly Tyler couldn't hear it.

"What did you say?"

"You are dead."

"Now why would you want to say something like that?" Tyler asked "In addition to attempted assault, we can add death threats. Anything else you want to say? "

Anton stopped moving and Tyler began opening end table drawers and the enclosed shelves of an entertainment center. It seemed ridiculous that any seller of illegal substances would have them in such common places, but some lambs became overconfident and sloppy. Tyler had once found four pounds of methamphetamine stuffed under the cushion of a futon. There was nothing quite so obvious here unfortunately.

Tyler grabbed Anton by the links of the handcuffs and hauled him to his feet. He led the shocked man through the apartment, until he found a large bathroom. Tyler pushed back the shower curtain and made Anton step over the tub wall, until he was kneeling by the faucet handle. His knees covered the drain.

"You will stay in here and not move." Tyler stated, "If I see you step out of the bathroom, you will suffer more barbarism than you have ever experienced. Do we have an agreement?"

Anton muttered something along the lines of "Fuck you" but Tyler couldn't quite make it out. Whatever it was didn't resonate with the cultured voice that had spoken a few minutes ago. He opened the drawers, the closet, under the sink, and even the toilet tank to confirm that there was nothing hidden in the bathroom before shutting the door. If Anton tried to leave, Tyler would know about it.

Tyler started searching in the room to his right which turned out to be the master bedroom. The closet revealed nothing but Armani and Stefano Ricci. Some of the shirts and jackets cost more than Tyler's rent. Nothing in the drawers more dangerous than a vibrator which Tyler had no intention of touching or wondering about.

He moved on to the other bedroom which yielded no results. Tyler began to breathe faster as he moved towards a hallway closet. Where were the drugs? For the first moment since he had entered the apartment, he felt a stain of doubt seep into his mind. What if Marco Brent had sent him on a wild chase and was smiling in his cell? Tyler felt he had become good at seeing through the many false statements he had heard over the years, but the problem with lies was sooner or later you ended up falling for one of them.

By the time he reached the kitchen, he felt like a desperate thief as he began to throw pots and pans out onto the marble tiling. They clanged on the floor like a gavel pronouncing innocence in the face of accused guilt. The freezer held nothing more than old TV dinners and freezer burned ice cream. He even opened a pint just to be sure. Tyler stopped looking as he tried to catch his breath. Despite the weather outside and the cool air of the apartment, he wiped sweat from his forehead and then at the temples. He mentally rewound through the frantic search and went back to turn through the places he wanted to examine more thoroughly.

Tyler knew he had crossed the proverbial "line" that all policemen and politicians spoke of, which was the division between law and chaos. He had probably lost sight of it the day he had said goodbye to his family. But had he dropped so far so quickly that he had just assaulted an innocent man and ransacked his home?

He thought of the badge in his wallet and wondered if a slight hint of tarnish had entered the center of the metal, creeping into the letters that said 'Urbs in Horto' which stood for "City in a Garden". It had been the motto of the city of Chicago since 1837 and had been the first Latin phrase Tyler had ever learned. Would those letters blacken as he strayed further? Tyler wanted to take his badge out to look, but it was an insane thought. The shake of his head was the only denial sound he would make. It was time to talk to Anton again.

The bathroom door opened showing that the handcuffed man had not moved since he had been placed in the tub. Tyler reached down and pulled him out in an effort of strained muscles. They walked back into the living room with Anton leaning on Tyler as if intoxicated. The supposed drug dealer slumped onto the couch and lay on his side for a moment before sitting up. Tyler watched as Anton rearranged his face back into the composed facade he had seen earlier. It was disgusting to watch.

"Now that you have trashed my apartment and abused my civil rights, I suggest you let me free, Detective Morgan." Anton said, "I cannot deny that I am considering a lawsuit, but perhaps if you let me go and leave now, we can forget this whole atrocity. I know it is stressful being a police detective and…." The words died on Anton's lips as he looked up and their gazes locked. Tyler could literally feel his vision reach out and pin Anton to the smooth leather beneath him.

"No Mr. Lynd, I don't think I will be letting you go just yet. There are two simple facts that tell me, despite appearances, that I am in the right place." Tyler replied holding up a finger, "One, the fact that Marco Brent said your name specifically means a lot. This is the same man who shot at me, cursed at me, and then was tortured by me. Acts of desperation can sometimes yield truths you want hidden."

Tyler raised a second finger. "Two, the fact that you are able to be as calm as you are is pretty damning. It means you have something to hide and I don't mean your damn sex toys. Now, I am going to pull out this gun" Tyler pulled out the Glock 22 and rested it against the side of his leg. "and I am going to expect some answers. Either you provide them expediently or we reach a more uncomfortable understanding."

Anton Lynd tried to raise his arms, but they were still handcuffed behind his back. The gesture looked odd, rather than sympathetic. He said, "I don't believe you. You are a member of the police and it is your duty to protect the innocent."

"You aren't innocent."

"I am innocent! I am innocent of everything. You don't have any proof of anything at all. You have nothing…"

Tyler raised his leg back and kicked the glass coffee table in front of Anton Lynd as hard as he could. The force of the kick ripped through the table as shards of glass flew out in an umbrella of tiny shrapnel. Anton crouched down and cried out in fear. He started murmuring sounds that sounded like words but not from any language Tyler had ever heard. It was weak and wormlike. More like the mewling of an injured cat than a human being. He almost felt pity for the man who was obviously beyond his depth, but there wasn't a place for pity right now. Not one bit.

Tyler picked up Anton and dropped him into the destroyed coffee table. The handcuffed man fell into the broken glass and landed with a yelp. Tyler could almost feel the shards inch their way into the drug supplier's nose. Anton tried to turn his head to see what Tyler was doing, but all he could manage was a sideways glance. Tyler took his foot and put it on Anton's back. The man began to shiver uncontrollably. Tears mixed with glass, synthesizing a new formula for sorrow.

"You can't....."

"You attempted assault, remember?"

The small idea his mind had created a few minutes ago began to grow inside Tyler's head. What if the man truly was innocent? What would his daughter think if she found her father standing over a man in a pool of glass and pain? If Anton was innocent, then Tyler was just as guilty as the people he was after. Would he destroy someone's family to get what he wanted?

"Right corner...bedroom..."

He leaned down to hear the words more clearly as his weight drove Anton's body deeper into the makeshift shrapnel. Another grunt of pain. Tyler asked, "What did you say? Say it again, Anton."

"The BEDROOM! Right corner.....Dresser."

"Stay right there."

Tyler forced himself to a brisk walk back to the bedroom and the dresser. He had already looked through the entire room so what was he missing? He looked through all the drawers again but still nothing. He felt the sides and back looking for any hidden caches or false components, but there were none.

Finally, he stepped back and studied the front of the dresser itself. It was a Verona piece, and Tyler noticed the only furniture in the entire apartment that was on wheels. The low drawers and squat nature of the furniture had almost hid the fact that it was mobile. It looked custom made and out of place. It stood out from the rest of the apartment in a way that he should have noticed before. He pushed the dresser to the left and out of the corner.

Tyler studied the floor but saw nothing out of the ordinary. He knelt down and began to feel the carpet with his hands. Along the far right corner, the carpeting rose to the touch. There was definitely something there. He grabbed the edge of the thick carpet and pulled.

The fiber covering gave and came out with a more forceful tug. Tyler peeled it back, and saw an oak panel that meshed with the rest of the floor. The thickness of the wood had caused the slight rise, unnoticeable to the eye. A notch in the corner was the only handle, and Tyler pulled with the tips of his fingers. He set the piece of wood to the side and looked into the gaping hole beneath.

The dimensions of the design were extremely precise, but Tyler was more focused on the contents. Inside Anton's secret compartment was a .50 AE Desert Eagle, two kilos of marijuana, one kilo of cocaine, a bag filled with bundled money, and a black briefcase, all lying on insulated fabric. A fucking goldmine for any dealer in Chicago.

Tyler pulled it out and held up the large handgun. It had the serial numbers filed off which was the only mar to the gold plated finish. It was gaudy and unwieldy as he examined it in the light. Tyler thought the weapon suited Anton since it was expensive and more for show than substance.

He laid the gun down on the floor and ignored the drugs and money inside the compartment. He grabbed the briefcase by the handle and was surprised at its weight. It came out with a struggle. The suitcase seemed custom-made as well, indicated by the fact that it appeared to have no locks. The handle felt like snakeskin in his hand.

Tyler stood up with the suitcase and walked over to set it down on the bed. The grooved latches clicked open with a sound like pencils snapping. He lifted the lid and looked down on why he had come here. The five plastic wrapped kilos of Abyss were a fortune. This suitcase held more of the drug than he had ever seen since it had surfaced on the market. The sheen was an almost maroon black color that was the trademark for which thousands would steal and kill. He had found it.

Tyler sat down on the floor in a slump like a marionette with the strings cut. His mind reeled at the find and the implications. He could turn all of this over to Lieutenant Rooks right now and be the hero cop of the hour. Sure, there would have to be some explanations and he may receive some sort of provisionary slap on the wrist. But who would fire the cop that had singlehandedly confiscated the largest bust of Abyss in history? He could use that newfound momentum and interest to catapult a reopening of his family's investigation. Maybe the police had overlooked a clue. Maybe a new witness would step into the light. Maybe. Maybe. Maybe.

Tyler wanted to laugh at the ephemeral daydream, waving away wisps of false hope and naive feelings. He was the only one who hadn't closed the case, and the only one who cared. Anyone who had known the specifics was either dead or not talking. There was only one thing to do, and there was little time to waste on fool's dreams. He could dream when he was dead.

In the moment's silence, he heard the scratchy sound of broken glass in the other room as Anton shifted on the floor. He needed to get up before the drug supplier decided to try to roll onto his side. He reached down and picked up the Desert Eagle again. He ejected the chambered bullet and took out the magazine. Both of these went into his pocket as Tyler stood up and took the bag of money out of the compartment. He was able to fit some of it in the suitcase and then filled his pockets with as much as possible. The rest of the money fell onto the carpet. The pile still looked like a fortune.

The suitcase was much harder to shut now, and felt incredibly heavy as he carried it out of the bedroom. Anton had managed to roll onto his side. The glass had made little cuts that appeared as specks of blood on his arms and face. Anton's eyes shifted to the suitcase. His tear-stained squint made him look more akin to a mole than any human ideal of culture.

"What are you going to do with that?"

Tyler set the suitcase on the floor. He pushed Anton down slightly before unlocking one of the cuffs. He locked the open handcuff to the underpinning steel framework of the couch. It was far too large to fit down the bedroom hallway. The crouching man would not get far linked to the bulky frame. Anton's shoulder drooped as he struggled to sit up and move away from what used to be his coffee table.

"I know what you are going to ask me. You won't believe me when I tell you, and then I know you are going to hurt me. I know this, but I swear I am telling the truth." Anton licked his lips and tried to stop the quivering of his chin. "I don't know the man who brings the Abyss. I don't have a number. He calls me from a payphone or some disposable cell or something because it is always a different number. Sometimes I run out of supply, and I still hear nothing. I have to wait. All I have is a name."

"How do I know you are telling the truth?"

Anton looked up at the ceiling. He would not look into Tyler's eyes. The supplier whispered, "Because I am scared of you, and I think you would kill me if I lied to you. I won't lie, but please don't kill me. Please don't."

"What's the name?"

"Will. That's it. I don't have a last name."

"What does he look like?"

"White. Brown Hair. He is taller than me but not as tall as you. Uhhhh he wore normal clothes......Nothing else I can think of............"

"What about eye color? Scars? Tattoos?"

"I.....I don't know his eye color and I don't think he had any scars. He wore normal clothing, and he looked just......normal except you could tell he was rough. Kind of like you, but not as hard. He always looked dead too. You know, no real expressions. He never laughed or anything. He would do business and leave. He talked like a fucking robot."

"How would you do business?"

"He'd call and ask if I was home." Anton said, "I made sure I was, and he would stop by carrying a suitcase with the product. Always the same amount for the same price. He would trade me for the money and then leave without saying a word."

"He wouldn't count it? He trusted you to be honest?"

Anton shook his head in bewilderment. "What am I going to do? Steal from the only supplier of Abyss? Who the hell would back me up on that? They would come back that day and shoot me. No one is going to protect me from the supplier. I take exactly what is owed and not a dollar more. Anything else is suicide."

Tyler nodded in silent agreement as he considered the information. He debated what his next move would be even though he already knew the outcome. Since the supplier only used one way contact, the best move from a police perspective would be to have Anton continue business as usual until he was contacted by 'Will' again. They could then setup monitoring equipment and arrest the supplier when he arrived with the heroin.

How long would that be though? Weeks? Months? Probably several months at the bare minimum judging by how much of the designer drug Anton currently had. Since Tyler was not exactly a police detective at this point, he didn't have the luxury of time, nor could he sit with Anton for months on the possibility of meeting his contact. It was too obvious, risky, and the contact could discover what was going on and become a ghost. Especially if the police were involved at this point. Even an excellent police force had a few morally challenged individuals who might give up the information for the right price. No, this was something he had to do on his own and let the chips fall where they may. The police could afford to take a shot with Anton and miss, but he couldn't.

"Stay here. When the police arrive, you tell them what you told me about your contacts, but I wouldn't mention the Abyss." Tyler said, "You are already facing serious jail time. Wouldn't want to add anything else that will enrage the judge, and Abyss is definitely a factor for that. Did you read the article last week calling it Chicago's new Angel of Death? Definitely wouldn't add any pity points. Besides you still have enough evidence in that room to sink your case as it is."

Anton rolled over to his other side in pain. He moaned softly. He looked toward Tyler and said, "What does it matter? I am probably dead anyway, right? What good is a clean image once you don't have it anymore? I am dead!" He glanced at Tyler looking for some sort of confirmation of safety. Everyone wants safety in a world full of danger. "I am dead, right?"

"Maybe."

Tyler bent down and picked up the suitcase. He turned to walk away.

"Maybe?! That is your consolation? That is how you are going to help me feel safe in police protection? Maybe! So you are saying I am dead, right? Shit! Why are you taking the Abyss? What the hell kind of detective are you?"

Tyler walked out of the room and closed the apartment door behind him. He muttered, "Who said I was a detective?" as he reached out to push the elevator button.

TYLER WAS IN his car and driving away from Anton's apartment before he called Annabelle. He told her everything about Anton including the Abyss. It was now on the passenger's side nestled snugly on the floor mat in the car. It was hard to believe so much money and power was all wrapped up in a suitcase without even a lock.

"Tyler, what are you doing?" Annabelle asked, "So, basically you entered a drug supplier's apartment based off a name given to you. You searched his apartment, destroyed his property, rubbed glass in his face, and then stole what is probably over a million dollars street value of cash and Abyss, right? Did I miss anything?"

"He is handcuffed and waiting for you at the apartment. You have more than enough to hold him. He attempted to assault and threaten me as well."

"How much of that is exaggerated?"

"Not much."

"But somewhat, right?" Her sigh was exasperation. But more than that, it conveyed she knew there would be no going back to the station anytime soon. He doubted it was even an option.

Annabelle said, "Rooks is trying to get a hold of you. You may have a day at best. I'll do what I can, but it won't be very effective. You really need to give him a call. My hands are really tied from here on out."

"Thanks, Annabelle."

"Don't thank me just yet, asshole. Remember I still want to talk to you about….all that has happened."

"What about tonight?"

"Tonight, really? Is that enough time for you?"

"No. But there won't ever be enough time. I might as well talk to you now rather than later."

"Ok, if you are comfortable with that. I will try to coordinate with a patrol officer to get out to Anton's apartment." Annabelle said, "You may be taking some heat for this one, but at this point, I don't think you even care about the charges. You will have to get in here at some point for your statement and sit rep."

"I know. I'll send you a text where to meet. Thanks, Annabelle."

He hit the button on his cell phone, ending the call. There was some time to kill, so Tyler headed back to the hotel. He needed to change his clothes and ensure he wasn't walking around with glass in his feet. He could almost feel the particles ingrained in the bottom of his shoes. It was easy to imagine them working their way through the tough soles to cut through his socks and into soft flesh. It would be fitting considering what he had done but he felt no pity for Anton Lynd. The man had ruined more lives than Tyler could even imagine. It was important not to think too far along those lines. After all, he had just become a major supplier of Abyss looking to link up with the manufacturer. A drug supplier with a conscience was not a drug supplier for very long.

CHAPTER 19
No Matter

THE BAR WAS secluded since it was off the main streets of downtown. Tyler had almost walked past it from the sidewalk. It was called Shriver's, a generic name for a generic place. The tables wobbled and he thought the chair would collapse under his not-insignificant musculature. There were a few people scattered here and there huddled in small pockets of resistance dedicated to stopping the bankruptcy of their watering hole at all costs.

Tyler had ordered a Guinness and glanced through what was supposed to be a menu. The list of alcohol was extensive and the food choices almost nonexistent. He could get something, but it wasn't worth the time or energy. Not even the waitress knew what the special was. He wondered if anyone else in the bar even knew there were food choices.

He had received a message from Annabelle suggesting this place, and was grateful. It was later than he had thought she would want to meet. Anything to keep the mind active and not in a REM state was fine by him. He sat in the chair focused on the condensation building on the outside of the bottle. It crept onto his hand like liquid tentacles.

The first half of the beer had gone down smoothly, but then he had lost his taste for it. Tyler focused on the cold feel of glass and the drips of water that began to flow onto his knuckles. Trying not to think about the suitcase filled with money and custom heroin. The same heroin that had somehow taken form and killed his family in a red storm of bullet holes and flames.

Annabelle entered the bar like a local patron who had been here a hundred times, and maybe she had. She saw him at the table and smiled with a warmth that Tyler envied. He caught several customers pause for a second to watch her go by with subtle or definitive glances that showed their intent. Annabelle ignored this as she probably had her whole life making a direct path to him. She made the simple motion of easing into the chair as graceful as a ballet dance step. Before she removed her coat, she ordered two more Guinnesses and brushed off the few flakes of snow drying in her hair. It wasn't braided today, and flowed down her shoulders in a cascade.

"Well, Rooks is starting to call for your head finally. Did you email him?" She asked as a greeting, not wasting a moment.

Tyler pushed a folder across the table to her. "Here is my report. I had to save it onto a memory stick and print it at Kinko's. That should buy me an hour."

Annabelle smiled and shook her head. "Not even that, Tyler. He says you aren't answering your phone. Do you have any idea how suspicious that makes you look? We have Anton in custody and he is talking, but there doesn't seem to be much to tell. He is more worried about looking for a deal than any repercussions against you." The waitress brought their beers and Annabelle took a sip before continuing. "I mentioned the assault charges as well as the usual bullet points. That Desert Eagle must have cost a few bucks and the street value of the drugs is significant, though I'm guessing, not compared to what you took. I think Anton will stick with discussing our findings, but after he consults legal counsel he may feel otherwise. This guy is not a criminal mastermind, but he isn't stupid either. I doubt you are going to come out of this completely clear."

"It doesn't matter. I just need time right now." Tyler said, "Six months from now a court of law can decide to pronounce him guilty or declare him a candidate for mayor of Chicago. I am focused on today."

Annabelle leaned forward on the table. Tyler could see his features in the soft, brown eyes. The faint smell of jasmine reminded him of summer days long past. She spoke softly enough that Tyler strained to hear the words. "So what you are saying is no tomorrow, is that right? Your actions are certainly showing it. I see a top notch police detective burning through his credibility at an alarming rate. Even his partner is not sure if he is going to be on the side of the law tomorrow. Hell, even breathing by the end of the week! I know you have been through a lot, but can you honestly say you are making your family proud?"

"I wouldn't know, would I?"

"I can't pretend to understand how you feel. I can't even...." Annabelle paused as she leaned back and took a deep breath. She took another sip of beer and winced either in distaste or unease. "Look, all I do know is that your family would not want you to do this to yourself. They are dead, Tyler, but they would want you to live. I know that much."

Tyler replied, "Annabelle, you came to hear about my past, but quite honestly there isn't a story to tell. I came home from work to find my apartment in flames. My wife and daughter were both shot once in the head. Later on, despite the knowledge being blocked, I found out that from the body's positioning my wife was probably raped before both she and Grace were killed."

"Tyler, I…"

"Do you know what men desire more than anything in this world, Annabelle?"

"A variety of things. Love. Money. Power. Pleasure. It probably depends on....."

"Immortality." Tyler interrupted, "We want to live forever in some way or another. Some people build monuments to themselves while others go to kneel on a pew every week hoping to reach a better place. Musicians compose scores wanting to be remembered after their epitaphs have worn away. Kids carve initials on the trunks of oak trees or spray paint their symbols on the side of a building. Everyone wants their name to be remembered somehow. Do you know the most common form of immortality? "Tyler continued without waiting for an answer. "Children. They carry you inside of them. No matter how good or how bad they turn out to be, a part of your life is passed on to the next generation. You do the best you can with your children to try to make their lives better than your own. You teach them about the mistakes you made and the successes you had. My immortality is gone. My child will not outlive me. In fact, her last moments of life were probably lying on the floor watching the rape of her mother before getting shot in the head."

Annabelle winced and Tyler tried to stop talking but he had opened a door deep inside. A heavy, metallic gate that was too wide to close again. It had flown open with a force that was greater than all of his strength. All of his demons clawed, stabbed, or chewed their way out and refused to go back inside. They wanted to rip his throat out.

"The fire erased a lot of the story. Maybe they were beaten, or maybe Emily was raped multiple times, all the while having our daughter in the same room watching some strange man hurt her mother in unspeakable ways. Then they were consumed in flames."

Tyler struggled to control the volume of his voice "We couldn't even have an open casket, because no one would want to see their burned flesh. Who would? Who would want to see that? All it would have done was made people uncomfortable. The bodies were burned beyond recognition. You know we try so hard to make death emulate sleep. That's why the eyes are closed when you have a funeral. You can't do that when the dead are a mass of ashes and bone. They didn't have any eyes to close. What's funny though is when I close my eyes, I can feel them staring at me in confusion. Even without eyes. Wondering where I was and why I wasn't there to stop it from happening."

Annabelle reached across the table and put her hand on top of his own. It was warm with a compassion that he did not deserve. She said, "Tyler, it wasn't your fault. There was no way you could have known what was going to happen." He moved his hand away from the warmth.

Tyler said, "Could I have known that some hitman or group of fucked up junkies were going to pick that night and kill my family? No, but I did know that Emily was meeting a contact who had information about Abyss. It was going to be a major story for her. Did I stay with her to make sure she was safe? No. That one action. That single misstep damned my family to flames."

"What about her contact?"

"She never met him. Probably dead. I spent a lot of time looking at associated murder cases but there was nothing from that timeframe. It was almost too perfect circumstantially."

"Did the bartender even…"

"I investigated them all. Hell, I even looked into a lot of families of potential witnesses. I verified the verification. Even checked the phone records and traced all numbers to cell phones, pay phones, etc. Nothing. No evidence at our……at the crime scene. Fingerprints. Fiber strands. DNA. All eaten by the flames. No witnesses. All because I was too wrapped up in my job to take an evening to watch over my wife and child."

Tyler was unaware of it, but his voice had changed while he was talking. It had taken on the hint of a different man. Annabelle thought he sounded like a man who could have been a father who played with his daughter on weekends and a husband who joked with his wife over dinner. A different kind of person than the man she saw in front of her. She looked deep into his eyes to see more of that man. Just for one second she thought she saw a glimmer, but then it was gone. Tyler killed the ghost of his former life like he had turned off a light switch.

When he spoke again it had the edge of a new box cutter. "Now you know, Detective Herrera. At least a little. I owed you a brief explanation and you have it. I didn't meet you because I want to reopen wounds. I did it because I need your help. Will you help me……… please? One more time?"

"I will help you as much as I can Tyler, but I don't think I can walk your path. There is only so far I can go before I can't help you anymore. I need to keep part of my conscience. We have already blurred that

134

line, and I don't know why." She pushed her beer away without even looking at it. She said, "You understand what I mean? I don't know if you are going to help us catch the scum who ruined you, or if you want them in the ground. I will help you on the legal side, but I won't help you become a murderer. I think you should think more about what your family would actually want you to do. You should be the man that they would want you to be."

Tyler rose and said, "I'm not that man anymore, Annabelle." The finality of his tone let them both know the conversation was over. Tyler held out his hand which Annabelle shook, and they both let go like a solemn vow had been taken. "Thank you for all your help. I know you are doing everything you can to help me, and I appreciate it. No matter what happens, I want you to know that. I wish we had been partners longer."

"No matter what happens, Tyler? What does that even mean? Are you talking about murder? Do you really think killing whoever did this will bring them back?"

Tyler did not answer the question but instead turned and walked away. He crossed through the bar without another word. The door slammed shut behind him as a strong draft of winter ushered in several solitary snowflakes from outside. Annabelle sat staring at the beer, lost in her own thoughts. Before she knew it, she had ordered another one. Several men watched her with hungry eyes while she drank half the bottle in a single gulp. "No matter what happens….." Annabelle said to the floor as she dug out her purse. It was going to be an expensive night at the bar.

CHAPTER 20
Druglord of Chicago

THE SNOW THAT was piled along the sidewalk had taken on a dark, gritty texture that came from hundreds of footsteps trudging through the area. Tyler added his own grime as he made his way down the street. He had gone home from Shriver's trying not to think about what Annabelle said. Sleep had come quickly, though only a few hours worth. He was thankful for the lack of remembered dreams. They had become an almost daily occurrence. It was hard to remember what it felt like to not wake up exhausted or covered in sweat. His footsteps weighed heavily on his body. All that drove him forward was caffeine and anger. In his right pocket, he carried a sandwich sized bag of Abyss. All of the rest of the heroin and cash was safe back in his hotel room with a do not disturb sign guarding the door. So many pieces of his plan hindered on so many variables of chance.

His thoughts kept returning to Annabelle, and Tyler hoped he would not need to work with her at all going forward. It had been bad to meet even though he owed her far more than a paltry beer and sob story. She had been right in saying he was going down a path she couldn't follow. He didn't want her to follow. If he ended up being dragged down any further than he was right now, she would not survive with her image intact. Tyler didn't give a damn about his own standing, but Herrera didn't deserve to fall.

The apartment he stopped in front of looked more akin to a condemned bomb shelter than a place that people came home to after a hard day's work. Of course, it was likely no one in this building worked, unless you included selling drugs or fucking for money and disease. Tyler could see the desperation in the stonework and debris accumulating on the front steps. The sight would depress anyone, let alone someone looking for one last refuge from the chilled air outside.

He had come here for Alvin Keth. "Big Al" Keth had been a scumbag piece of shit all his life, and he aspired to nothing greater. Tyler was unsure whether the nickname was in mockery of the short man or because of some other factor he didn't want to know about. All Tyler knew was that Al was one of the few CIs he had left from his early days, and that said a lot. Alvin was an addict of the worst kind, wanting anything from marijuana mixed with coke to Abyss. He would snort bleach if it gave some sort of buzz.

Alvin also happened to be giving more tips to the police department than they knew what to do with. It was a celebration of criminal information all day, every day. Most informants were cautious due to the extreme danger they put themselves in, but Alvin had either not thought it through or just didn't care. Almost all of his tips turned out to be accurate, though a lot of it could be trivial as well.

Tyler didn't care at this point; he just needed Alvin for one task alone, which is why he walked up the stairs to the second floor of the dying apartment. He made no announcement walking down the hall, but several doors slammed shut automatically as though the renters had telepathy with one another, warning that a police officer was coming. The joke was on them, Tyler thought with a smirk. He walked down the hall, making his footfalls stomp hard into the cheap wood floor. It was an old habit to keep everyone aware of where he was. It made the tenants less trigger-happy since they knew he wasn't standing in front of their door. It also gave everyone else a chance to shut the door if they didn't happen to be part of the hive mind. Same type of thoughts, different building.

Tyler recognized the apartment more by the rust on the number three than any numeric assignation. Alvin had helped him numerous times in the past, though never in the capacity he had come for today. His fist made the number rattle as he pounded on the door. The immediate sound of a deadbolt being turned told him that Alvin had heard him before he was halfway down the hallway. The short man opened the door all the way and Tyler walked in without a word.

Alvin shut the door, trapping Tyler in a place that could only be described as a psychedelic nightmare. A myriad of colors adorned the walls in the careless strokes of a continually stoned painter. The room was a puddle of chaos. It was just how Tyler remembered it from the first time he had been here. He had come to arrest Alvin, but the CPD had decided to use him to catch bigger fish instead. Usually Tyler and Alvin would meet somewhere else, but this was an unscheduled visit which clearly worried Alvin all the way up to the lines gathering on his forehead.

Alvin tugged on a t-shirt and said, "W-w-w-what is going on, man? This is kinda unexpected. I know you are the man and all that, but a phone call does wonders, you know?"

"Sorry, Alvin, I didn't have time to call a tweaked out user, giving him my itinerary for the day."

"It is Big Al, asshole. I hate when you call me that."

This was the man in whose hands Tyler was putting his life. He looked like Jesus, if Jesus wore a tie-dye Chicago Bears t-shirt barely covering a bulging stomach and frayed sweatpants. Despite the unwashed hair and enough untrimmed facial hair to cover a child's head, "Big" Al had more connections than anyone Tyler knew. Maybe it was because of his disarming appearance or the fact that he had experimented with everything and still somehow managed to put together coherent sentences. Tyler wasn't sure. All he did know was that if there was anyone who could reach out and find the manufacturer of this stuff it would be Alvin. When Emily and Grace had died he had tried to find something through the CI, but that had been more in line of finding their killers. Now he had another reason, and another way to get the results he needed.

"You seem to be doing ok for yourself, Alvin. I haven't heard anything on the scanners about you for a while. Even now I can tell you are on some shit I don't even want to know about. You still have enough brain cells to help me out?"

"Shit, man, that's harsh." Alvin smoothed his long hair over his shoulders and lowered his eyes to look at a strand of fabric from the seam of his sweatpants. "I've helped you with all kinds of fucked up stuff. I've never let the CPD down yet, have I?"

"No, which is why we turn a blind eye to some of your less scrupulous behavior. Come on, Alvin, you have a sweet deal and you know it. Now, have we wasted enough time with the pleasantries?"

"Fuck, man, stop calling me Alvin." Alvin sat down on a chair that looked like the color of vomit. Maybe that had been an intentional choice when it was purchased, but Tyler still looked for recent stains when he sat down on its twin. The room was jarring to anyone who wasn't eating homegrown mushrooms or coming down from an eight hour acid trip. If there were an actual avatar of chaos, Tyler believed it would live in Alvin Keth's apartment.

"So what brings you to my humble den of 'less scrupulous' behavior?"

Tyler pulled out the bag of Abyss and tossed it to Alvin. The junkie jumped as if he had been handed a bomb and almost dropped the drug onto the floor. He held up the plastic inspecting it as though it took all his concentration to discern the contents. A look crossed his face that made Tyler regret giving him the bag so quickly. Alvin's eyes never left the Abyss, but he spoke as though his words could not come out fast enough.

"Where did you get this shit? Is this what I think it is?"

"It's everything you think it is, Alvin. 100% Abyss uncut."

"Jesus Christ do you have any idea how ex..."

"I do. I also know where to get a lot more of this."

"Where?" The question was innocent enough, but Tyler stared at Alvin until the junkie swallowed and nodded. He huddled over the Abyss, and Tyler was reminded of a story he had read when he was a child, the J.R.R. Tolkien character of Gollum. Alvin said, "Ok, stupid question. I guess a better question is why are you giving this to me?"

"It's proof." Tyler said, "Proof that you want to do business with the manufacturer. Proof that you have moved up in the world and you want a bigger slice of the profits."

"You are a detective. They are never going to buy that stupid shit."

"Which is why I said you."

"What the hell, man? What are you...?" Tyler waited, watching thoughts crawl across Alvin's face. Confusion warred with disbelief until they emerged as a multitude of new wrinkles on his forehead. Alvin said, "You want me to be your seller? I can't sell this stuff back to the maker. You are crazy. You are batshit crazy! Even if I could find them, I would be dead in one minute tops. You know how this shit goes down. There is some sort of chain that keeps the maker safe. They cut the links faster than anyone can trace them. I'd be....You know.... Fuck I'd....."

The junkie gestured wildly in his chair. He stood up whirling like a mad dervish or a top on an uneven table. Tyler waited until he collapsed, using all his energy in a two minute storm of bewilderment. Alvin took a deep breath which turned into a cough. He wheezed, "No way, man. Not happening."

"I think the only problem we've got with that statement is that I'm not asking you, Alvin. I'm telling you. Let me pose you one question before you make your 'not happening' statement again. How long do you think a CI would last in prison? Especially in a prison where people you have helped put away have been sitting for years getting fucked in the showers or wondering if they will get shanked while they sleep day after day? Think about it."

Alvin stared at him defiantly. Tyler thought the CI might jump up and punch him. Alvin's voice was almost a yell. "Yeah, because you guys made me do it! Fuckers. You made me rat them out, not because I wanted to." Tyler held up his hands in disbelief. "We made you? We made you turn your home into a crack house? We made you start distributing drugs to minors? Jesus Christ, I remember when you were trying to push to a nine year old girl!" Alvin tried to interrupt but Tyler continued. "I suppose we made you take that fucking immunity you bargained for too, right? Yeah, Alvin, you are a goddamn saint. What was I thinking?"

Alvin lowered his head in immediate defeat and Tyler felt a slight twinge of something. He wasn't sure what it was. Disgust? Pity? The sight of seeing someone fallen so far was nothing new to him. Tyler said, "Alvin, you will be safe. You will be bringing me along as 'protection' too."

"A bodyguard?"

"Exactly. Really, once we are at that point of a meet and greet, you can relax. I need you as a contact to reach out to these people and just bullshit with them. Nothing too extravagant. You don't have to be a tough guy. Just someone who wants to get in on a good deal. Does that make sense?"

"That's it? After that we are done, right? One meeting?"

"One. Maybe two at the most, depending on how the first one goes. Just to be honest and upfront. I need to find out how to establish contact and build a level of trust. Then you can go home."

Alvin sighed in what was supposed to be deep thought as though his life depended on this decision. In a way it could, and Tyler felt another twinge. They both knew it was a dangerous situation, but Tyler understood it was more dangerous than Alvin realized. They were alone in this endeavor with no backup. That was the piece Tyler had neglected to say. I should let Annabelle know about this, he thought while Alvin weighed his options. He would need some sort of backup, but if he put her in a situation where she would have to report it to the police........ Then what? What exactly was he planning if he didn't want his team there? Murder? The word inside his head didn't sound that bad.

"Ok, I will do it."

Tyler smiled inwardly but did not let any emotion show on his face. It was the reason he enjoyed playing poker. He kept his voice even as he said, "Good. Now what you need to do first is to reach out to anyone who would be a supplier that you know of. Don't just talk with random tweakers or cokeheads. They can't help you and, for a good chunk of Abyss, a lot of them would kill you first anyway."

"Fuck, man, I'm not stupid. I only deal with the pros."

"Of course. You just mention that you know how to get a good chunk of Abyss and are looking to partner up. Speaking of which." Tyler reached over and grabbed the bag out of Alvin's hands.

The junkie almost shivered with withdrawal as he moaned with his arms outstretched. "What the hell, man?"

Tyler said, "Sorry, I am not leaving all of this with you. Just enough for show."

Alvin frowned. "Then why did you bring it at all?"

Tyler shook his head. "Would you believe a cop that came in here wanting to sell Abyss without any proof?" Alvin crossed his arms and grumbled to himself. Tyler reached over and put his hand on Alvin's shoulder. It felt like touching a rattlesnake, but he needed to reassure his CI for this.

He said, "Don't worry, Alvin. It will be fine, and you are actually doing some good today. Do you have anything to cut this with and store it in?" Alvin got up and walked to the kitchen. He brought back a long piece of worn plastic whose original purpose was unfathomable. Tyler cut out a small portion of the Abyss which Alvin would use to disperse into some plastic baggies that he assuredly had somewhere inside the apartment.

"When do you want me to get started on this 'good' you want done so damn badly?"

"When else?"

"Now?!?! Seriously?"

Tyler had already stood up to his full height and waved his arm to indicate he would let himself out. The heavy footfalls echoed and left a few drops of residual snow on the carpet. The door shut a few seconds later, and Alvin was alone in his apartment. He immediately got up to go for some stress relief. His hands shook as he pushed aside the beaded curtain that marked the bedroom doorway. Maybe this would be a good day to restart his coke habit.

CHAPTER 21
With Teeth

TYLER KNEW HE must be dreaming before he even saw Emily and Grace. Usually the sense of unreality that accompanied his dreams didn't occur until after it was over, but this time it was different. He was in their apartment before it had burned into nothing. His vision was washed with a muted pallet of colors. Tyler knew it couldn't be real, and that was all right. He walked into the bedroom where the bed was made and their clothes had been folded into two separate stacks of 'his' and 'hers'. It must be Emily's turn, Tyler thought as he looked for his wife and daughter. Even in this dream (and it must be a dream), Tyler felt a sense of urgency as he glanced into the bathroom to see they were not there either.

He had walked out into the narrow hallway before he realized he had begun yelling their names. His voice wavered in the confined space. I am dreaming, he thought to himself. I can make anything happen I want. The living room opened up before him, and he stopped dead in his tracks.

"Emily. Grace."

His daughter and wife stood staring out the large window that looked onto the parking lot outside the apartment. Emily had always joked that Tyler wanted them in 'stealth mode' and usually opened the blinds as soon as she got home. He said their names in a whisper, but he was positive they heard him. Neither turned around to greet him or even acknowledge his presence with the sound of their voices. Emily reached out and took Grace's hand as they stood there wearing the matching cornflower blue dresses he had bought them for Mother's Day.

"Emily? Grace?"

Tyler took another tentative step forward. Their dresses swayed slightly as though a breeze was moving through the apartment. They still did not turn around to greet him. Were they mad at him even in his dreams? He noticed their hair had grown longer than he remembered. After death, the hair follicles continued to function for a short time growing as the body decayed. Then the hair would stay with the corpse long after putrefaction. Was he talking to corpses? Something was wrong.

It's just a dream, Tyler. Control it. Tyler said, "I have missed you both for so long." He had crossed half the room but could not catch a glimpse of their faces. "I am sorry I wasn't there that night.........that night you died. I think about you both every day. I never was a man of words, but I hope you know just how much I miss you. I am drowning without you in my life. My life.......is nothing but ashes without having your laughter or your love. I understand if you hate me, but please....please at least say something to me."

He was behind them now, not quite daring to reach out and touch. The window cast no reflection of their faces. Tyler broke out into a sweat and licked his lips which were cracked with blood. A part of him wanted to wake up now, but deep down he never wanted to leave. Even condemnation from his family was better than no family at all. He needed to see their faces. See their eyes and tell them it was ok.

Tyler reached out for his wife's shoulder. His fingers brushed the dress's strap before lying flat near the curve of her neck. Her skin felt warm and soft like it always had. He smiled when he saw fingers rush up to cover his own. Emily and Grace Morgan turned towards him and their smiling faces made his heart surge in joy.

"Daddy!" Grace raced forward to wrap her arms around his waist as Tyler's whole life welcomed him with open arms. "Tyler...." The warmth, the hugs, and the kisses encircled him. He felt a weight lift from his shoulders. But the weight didn't go away. Not in the way that it should. It was a dream, and now he couldn't wake up.

"Never again. I will never leave you again. I promise."

"We know, Tyler. We know."

The words were from Emily, but the sounds came from a throat charred and blackened. He looked into his wife's face, and it was as beautiful as the day he had met her. Her skin was soft and pale and her lips full. Something about her was a little too soft, a little too beautiful, as if dying had only made her more glorious. More pure. A mortician could only dream of this kind of perfection.

"Emily. Grace. I hope you know....."

"Shhhhhhhh"

Emily placed a finger on his lips as he looked down into Grace's eyes. His daughter looked up at him with nothing as simple as love. She looked at him more in hunger. A hunger that could eat a world and still look for more. Grace smiled up at him, and he saw with horror that her teeth were black and jagged like razors. They glinted dully in the light of a grin his daughter had never used in life.

"Daddy," Grace said as she burrowed her face into his stomach. She bit into his flesh and burrowed deeper as her arms gripped him in an embrace impossible for a child. Tyler yelled in pain as he tried to push his daughter away without hurting her. She didn't budge as Tyler stepped backwards, trying to break the hold that held him fast.

"Don't worry; we've forgiven you, dear."

Tyler turned towards his wife's blackened smile. It was stretched into a predator's grimace, and her eyes had become a maroon color. Emily grabbed his throat in a grip of unearthly strength. "We're waiting for you, Tyler." Emily said. "We're waiting for you down in the fire, and we are so hungry. I am so hungry." Tyler screamed as she bit into his neck, ripping through skin and muscle as though it was living paper. His blood splashed into his wife's hair as she bit him over and over. His arms rose in a reaction of survival, but he willed them down to his side. He deserved this. He deserved to die like this. Tyler kept screaming long after he had run out of blood.

CHAPTER 22
Dangerous Arms

TYLER WOKE WITH his hands pressed to throat as though he were trying to choke himself. He had seen many victims with their throats cut who had died in similar poses, trying to keep life from spilling out. It was a horrible way to die. A gush of fatal violence. Tyler put his hands down and took a deep breath. He closed his eyes and willed away the images like a mirage dissipating as you drew closer. He was alive for another morning at least. That was something.

The dreams were becoming more vivid as though his subconscious was taking over, to become some kind of perceived reality. They were also becoming more violent as time went on. He tried to sleep as little as possible, but he needed rest to keep him sharp for the tasks at hand. Tyler's side of the family had suffered from insomnia for generations. Tyler's father used to roam the house at night and when he was a boy, he had thought it was a ghost. Later on, it used to make him feel safe knowing that his father watched over them while they slept. Only recently had Tyler grown to appreciate how much his father had probably suffered from his disorder with no complaints.

Tyler had never had problems falling asleep until the murder of

Emily and Grace. Now, whenever he closed his eyes, all he could see was his family dead or in agony. The recent surge of violence was probably due to his activities surrounding the investigation. Deep down a voice had begun to whisper in his mind. *"Hey, remember your wife and daughter? You know the ones you let die? What do they think of you now? Huh? Just wanted to bring that up to you in case you forgot. You know that your family is dead, and you have disgraced their names. Don't want to lose track of that one! Ha ha!"*

Tyler hated these self-doubts and had tried to bury that voice in the ultimate goal of justice, but it seemed to be getting stronger not weaker. It was feeding on him as surely as his dreams had. His hypocritical view of justice apparently did not fly with the thoughts and feelings that swirled around his mind.

Tyler got up feeling around the unfamiliar room for the bathroom. He had switched hotels last night and was not yet oriented to this one. An old habit of his, never staying in the same place for too long. The more grounded you were, the easier it was for you to be found. Even worse, you were predictable. Tyler wondered if the manufacturers of Abyss had made a point of staying mobile. It would be difficult to move a heroin lab but not impossible. Of course it was easier to just sever ties, aka shoot people in the back of the head, but the way the manufacturer had avoided detection so far was almost supernatural. No one could make that amount of product and get away with it forever. Tyler needed to find these people before the police did. It would be even worse if a strong competitor found them. Then there would be nothing left.

Why would that be a bad thing? He thought to himself. Does it matter how justice is served? Whether behind bars or decaying at the bottom of the Chicago River, they would be finished and that should be enough. Except that it wasn't. He wasn't sure if jail was justice enough, and if they were dead how would he know about it? No, the best way was still to take care of this himself and pay the consequences afterwards. Whatever they may be.

After a shower and shave, Tyler was across the street at a local diner illustriously called Di's Dinerama. The name seemed to ward off most of the customer base, but the coffee was strong enough to make up for it. His waitress was just old enough to be out of jailbait age, and she seemed to know it. Extra-long smiles and exaggerated bend overs for refills kept her busy until he made the ring on his left hand a little more obvious. She puffed away in a jitter of frustration that lasted until the next customer came in.

Tyler twisted the ring with his thumb. He had wanted to take it off, not as a sign of singularity, but rather of moving on. He stared down at the simple silver band. He had spent months learning and comparing the 'Cs' of the diamond business before finding a princess cut with a platinum band that Emily had loved. His ring had been given on their wedding day, and Tyler had never taken it off since. Emily used to clink their hands together like they were performing a wedding toast all over again. She would smile whenever they did that.

He had tried several times to not wear the ring in the last few months, but the best he had managed was to move it slightly off his finger like he was washing his hands. The ring had become loose as though his dreams were also eating away at his body. It felt like one day the simple band would slip off and disappear down a drain or gutter. Then Tyler was sure he would never find the symbol of his marriage again. He pushed the ring further up the flesh of his hand and finished the coffee.

After he left his tip, Tyler went outside and brushed off the light dusting of snow that had already accumulated on his car. He had mentally added an hour to his travel because of the weather, but the roads were clear due to rush hour traffic grinding the snow down under the tires of countless cars. Tyler tapped his ring on the steering wheel as he drove towards an all too familiar storefront.

Scott Eladio had been selling everyday convenience foods to everyday people for the last three years. The Chicago police department had become aware of the store owner because of his 'special' sales to MVP customers. These sales involved firearms that were either illegal or stolen. The unfortunate problem was that they had never been able to tie the guns back to Eladio. The store owner had maintained a calm disposition during several investigations, and no hard evidence had been found to tie him to the weapons. Several shootings were definitely linked to his products, but still Scott Eladio continued his business through selective sales and the luck God bestows upon drunks and illegal gun salesmen. Tyler was sure they would arrest him eventually, but eventually was not today.

The store was well-maintained and brightly lit. Tyler put the car into park and walked towards the front. The sliding glass doors opened to the usual assortment of convenience foods that were overpriced to ward off casual customers. An easy listening station emitted a saxophone solo at a volume low enough to be almost unnoticeable. The counter was close to the front doors. Eladio must have seen him coming before he had entered the store. The gun dealer wore his usual grimace and beckoned Tyler to come over to him. Tyler turned and locked the sliding doors behind him before turning off the nearby OPEN light.

Scott Eladio looked more like a dour uncle who hunted bear in east Maine than someone who would sell you a gun to rob your neighbor. A shaved head matched the short beard that he perpetually rubbed with the palm of his hand. Tyler doubted Eladio looked nervous often, but this was probably about as close as the man got. Not really the ideal situation. A man with a lot of guns could get itchy on the trigger if backed into a corner. Unfortunately, what Tyler planned was only going to make the situation worse.

"Hello, Detective Morgan. What can I do for you today? Is there a reason you are closing my store?"

Tyler continued walking and went past the counter ignoring the greeting. He moved towards the back of the store passing shelves of batteries and motor oil. He walked through an aisle of candy bars marked up four times any grocery store's price. It was a wonder Eladio made any profit at all off of his legitimate goods.

"Detective Morgan?!"

Footsteps behind him echoed on the polished tile floor, but they would catch him far too late. He had reached the back of the store and went to the door he was seeking. He placed his hand over the gold "Employees Only" sign and pushed. The door opened without a whisper as he shook his head at the brazen arrogance of Scott Eladio. A lock would have at least slowed him down. The man was confident in his form of incognito apparently. It would have worked legally with the police anyway.

"You can't go back there!"

The back area was dark but clean with a hallway at the end of the room. Tyler was surprised by the neat organization. He started looking in the opened boxes on the shelves and had reached his fourth one when Scott Eladio burst through the door like a tsunamic wave.

"What the hell do you think you are doing? Do you have a warrant to look back here?"

"Do I need one?"

The split second pause was all that Tyler needed. He turned around to look at Eladio's furious grimace. He continued, "If I look through this whole back area Scott, what am I going to find? Handguns? High-powered rifles? A rocket launcher?" Eladio stood with his hands curled into half fists as he visibly struggled not to attack Tyler. He waited several minutes for Eladio to calm down as the dour man took deep breaths.

"You are dead."

"People keep saying that, but I am still alive to hear it. How many guns have you sold to children in the last month? Any idea?"

"I guess you are a fucking saint then huh, Morgan?"

"There are no saints in this room, only monsters. I didn't come here to arrest you. I just wanted your undivided attention. I want to buy a gun." Tyler had seen many reactions out of Scott Eladio, but this was the first time he heard him laugh. It reeked of sarcasm and the genuine amusement of implied stupidity. He waited while Eladio took several breaths for a different reason now.

Eladio said, "Sure, I will sell you a gun! Then you can take me to jail and make your quota for the week. Everyone comes out ahead, right?" He laughed again but stopped as he looked back at the taller man. Tyler reached into his coat and pulled out a stack of bills, wrapped straight from Grace's college fund. He tossed it to Eladio who caught the money in his right hand by reflex. The gun dealer couldn't help but start thumbing through the cash before staring again at Tyler. He tossed the money back to Tyler.

"Bullshit. Get the hell out of my store."

Tyler said nothing and reached into the next box in line. He began pulling out bags of coffee filters and dropping them on the floor as he emptied the contents. Who would come here for coffee filters?

"Stop it! You don't have the right to do this!"

"Here is the deal. If you have anything illegal in this whole store I am going to find it and pretty quickly too, I might add. I am not concerned about what happens to your stock. So, either you can take a chance that I am legitimately interested in a gun and take a slight risk, or you can definitely go to jail once I find something here. I know I will so it is really just a matter of how you want to do this."

"Ok. Ok........" Eladio scooped up a handful of the coffee filter bags and threw them back into the box. He walked past Tyler, moving to the back of the room. It almost felt staged how quickly the gun dealer had given in. Maybe he had made up his mind before the protests had even begun. The thought that a search like this was actually inadmissible in court without a warrant did not seem to cross Eladio's mind. He was either stupid, or he could tell that Tyler was here on his own rather than as a representative of the CPD.

Tyler followed the store owner past boxes of high-fructose corn syrup and individually wrapped headache relief medicines awaiting the next recall. While the front of the store and beginning of the storage area embodied the essence of cleanliness and modern convenience, the very back area looked more like an alley than a supply space. It was like digging through the layers of time to find the beginning of corruption. Tyler half expected a rat to scurry in front of them or a large, black spider in a ceiling corner for a real-life cliché. The symbolism was not lost on him as they reached the very back of the hall.

Scott Eladio slowed his walk in reverence like a monk entering a temple for the first time. The boxes back here were stacked with marker code as a form of hieroglyphics no one but the convenience store high priest could decipher. Eladio walked over to the boxes and lifted several as though he were handling explosives. Maybe he is, Tyler thought, as the boxes were laid out in a widening circle. Eladio pulled out a box cutter and slashed the tape across the top of one with professional efficiency. He looked over at Tyler, perhaps thinking of using the box cutter on him, before reaching into the box and pulling out a handgun.

"This is a Heckler & Koch Mark 23 handgun. The magazine holds ten rounds and the stopping power is second to none. I recently acquired this item as they do tend to sell quickly and I….."

Tyler held up his hand and said, "Thank you, Eladio, but I have access to handguns." He gestured to the Glock holstered at his side before continuing. "What I was looking for was something a little more unique."

"Unique? What the hell do you mean? This is a quality gun!"

"I was thinking more along the lines of an assault rifle or machinegun. Something with *significant*…..stopping power."

"I don't sell that shit."

"I don't have time for this, Eladio. Yes, you do. Now either you can show me what you have or get on my bad side. It isn't a side you want to see. It is uglier than your face."

Eladio stared at him in silence. Tyler waited knowing the gears were turning, thinking about how he had already shown that he possessed weapons for sale illegally. There really was no other conclusion in the end. Eladio moved several boxes around before pulling out a longer box hidden behind several others. Here was the hidden treasure Tyler had been waiting for. Except this treasure didn't add wealth or longevity. It dealt death to others.

Eladio opened the box and pulled out an AK-47. The AK-47 had a 7.62x39mm cartridge and this one looked to hold the 75 round magazine. It could fire over 600 rounds a minute and was used by revolutionaries fighting for whatever cause was available to the many divisions of armed forces. It was a deadly assault rifle in the hands of a trained mercenary, or a cop who knew how to handle it. An impressive weapon, to say the least.

Tyler whistled and said, "Eladio, what kind of people are you talking with, and what kind of shit have you been selling them?"

Eladio grimaced. His tone was one of apology. "Come on, this is a rarity! I sell maybe one or two guns like this a year at best. Most people just come in looking for a handgun, not any type of real equipment. I am not putting anything out there that someone three blocks down wouldn't also sell."

Tyler nodded and once again tossed Eladio the wad of cash. "Great. I will take it and as many bullets as you have for it. I also want you to gather up every other gun you have here." Eladio's smile was directed down at the money rather than his customer. He said, "You want to peruse all the merchandise at once? That is something I can understand."

"No, you don't understand. You are going to gather up all the other guns so I can take them. The money in your hand is all you get. I am taking your stock and destroying it. You aren't giving anyone else a chance for murder. You are officially out of the arms business. Focus on selling your single serving shampoos and earn your money legitimately."

"Are you crazy? That is over half my profit and all of it is tax-free. No way, you evil bastard! Fuck that."

"Well, it is either that or I make a phone call, and you are busted before you can sell another battery pack. I will take the AK, and you can keep the rest at least until my backup arrives. I will look you up in ten years. Give or take a few months."

Tyler started turning towards the front of the store. Both of them knew how this was going to end again. Eladio sighed and murmured something that Tyler took to mean agreement. The man had slumped over in defeat as quickly as he had agreed to sell the gun. Tyler stepped back to where Eladio stood.

Tyler said, "Great, gather them up while I run a spec on this AK and gather up the ammo. Remember, I want all of them. Every last one."

Eladio slumped his shoulders again and walked over to the nearest pallet with the box cutter outstretched. He slashed the top of a box as though he was cutting Tyler's throat. It was probably what the gun dealer was envisioning at that very second. Tyler allowed himself a small smile as he ejected the magazine to confirm it was full. If he could shut down illegal arms and get one step closer to finding the manufacturers of the Abyss at the same time, there really wasn't anything else he would rather be doing. Looks like closing the store for the day had been the right move after all.

CHAPTER 23
Suspension of Disbelief

By the time Tyler arrived back at the hotel, it was late and the sun had disappeared. The cold continued to suck all the warmth from his bones. He had dumped all the guns from Eladio in a storage unit he had rented before his family's home had been destroyed. A lot of his old clothes, a microwave, a television, and other apartment items had been stored there when he had moved in with Emily. Now it was the home to over twenty handguns, a shotgun, and an Uzi. Eladio had winced at the look on Tyler's face when they had pulled it out of another box in the endless unveiling of weapons. He had wanted to punch the gun dealer in the face, but instead put it in one of the trash bags he had taken from the front of the store. All without the ridiculous prices of course.

Tyler shook his head at the thought of that storage unit. After he and Emily had gotten married, they had always joked that he was paying every month for a backup plan in case she kicked him out. She had even once threatened to ship him off to the storage unit after he had tickled her continuously during a movie. Now it was another contaminated memory filled with dozens of weapons that had probably killed dozens of people. If he had been working with the police department, he could have had them log it all into evidence until trial. Afterwards the Bureau of Alcohol, Tobacco, Firearms, and Explosives would have confiscated them and had the guns destroyed in a nearby scrap metal processing plant. Unfortunately, it looked like these particular weapons would be around for a little longer.

Tyler had brought in the AK-47 broken down into its components to his room. It was almost impossible to be inconspicuous with an assembled assault weapon of that size. The pieces were stuffed into a duffel bag with the stock wrapped up in his coat. He had also gotten several magazines, though who knew how much they would actually be put to use? Each part was now laid out on top of a plywood dresser. They were balanced on a clear finish that was so slick he was surprised the pieces didn't slide off. He would have to move them before the next cleaning took place by the housekeeping team of the hotel. Chancing do not disturb signs for too long was a really bad idea.

He laid down on top of the bed with his hands crossed behind his head. It felt good to be warm. He could hear the wind howling in frustration as it took its wrath out on civilians walking on the streets outside. Tyler wondered if anyone was braving the weather to visit Scott Eladio, looking for a gun. They were in for quite a shock. That at least brought a brief smile to his face.

The warmth was like a blanket wrapped around him. It was soothing but also made him tired and Tyler felt his eyes begin to close. He pushed them open and sat up shaking his head. It would be so easy to drift off into sleep, but he knew what awaited him were more bad dreams. No more nightmares he vowed to himself. At least not right now. Maybe if he held off until complete exhaustion, he could sleep through the night with no problems. He flicked on the television to distract himself with today's news.

The reporters didn't mention any stories about police detectives on the run though there was a brief piece on the escalation of Abyss usage. Tyler shook his head as a pretty blonde speculated that it would surpass cocaine demand by the end of the year for the entire city. Crime had risen significantly in all districts though there was no reply yet to any of this from the mayor's office. Apparently no one had a real solution or at least not one they wanted to share with the public. The channel had moved on to national news reporting on economic turmoil ravaging the country when his cellphone began to rumble on the dresser.

The phone was dancing frantically as Tyler got up and walked over to the frenzied device. He glanced down at the name on the screen and held his breath. It was Lieutenant Rooks.....again. Tyler had been ignoring and deleting messages for days now, but the phone continued to rumble with a high degree of urgency. He half expected it to fall off the dresser, as he waited through another ring, considering his response. If he didn't answer, he would probably have to get rid of the phone for tracking purposes. Plus, they would have complete access to his phone records anyway. Tyler owed Rooks this call. He owed him for being patient when so many others would have issued an APB on him already. Maybe there actually was one in the works, but Annabelle hadn't mentioned it.

Tyler reached out and picked up the phone. Rooks's voice spoke as soon as he hit the button to answer.

"Detective Morgan, you answer me and do not hang up this damn phone! Please confirm you are listening to me right now!"

"I am here, Lieutenant Rooks. I hear you."

"You are suspended, effective immediately."

The words were expected, but he still doubled over as though someone had punched his throat. It was a quick jab that started to throb as soon as he took his next breath. He felt another thread of his life break as quietly as all the others, revealing another small piece of the black hole growing inside his body. It was a hole so deep he couldn't see the bottom, but there was a cold hell in there waiting for Tyler. Guaranteed.

"Detective Morgan, I have Internal Affairs beginning to look into your recent actions with a charge of police negligence being the very least of their investigational stance. Do you understand what I am saying? The very least. Next will be a formal inquiry with an arrest issued if I don't get you in here soon. That would mean press coverage as well as interrogation. Not interviews, Detective Morgan. Interrogation. Implied guilt regardless of how it is portrayed outside our building."

"I understand everything that you have just conveyed, Lieutenant."

"Goddamnit, Tyler, that is not the answer I am waiting for! Do you understand the gravity of the situation you are in? I don't want a good detective getting pulled from our roster because he is becoming a vigilante!"

"I understand, Lieutenant Rooks. I don't want any of my actions to tarnish the department in any way." Tyler ran his hand back and forth over the top of his head. He said, "I can issue a formal statement absolving the department of any……"

"That isn't what I want, you son-of-a-bitch! I want you down here so we can get you cleared of all of this shit. Eventually anyway."

"What does the term 'eventually' mean, Lieutenant? A month? Two?"

The dead silence on the phone was more than answer enough. They both knew it would be longer than a few weeks before Tyler could resume active duty. The inquiry would take months at a minimum. He would not have access to his badge, gun, or any resources available to a detective. He would also be under surveillance or possibly jailed. The only thing that would continue in the intermediate would be his pay. That was the last thing Tyler was concerned with. Paychecks were for people with a future.

"You son-of-a-bitch, you have thought this through haven't you?"

"That is the second time you have called me that, Lieutenant. I appreciate the fact that you care. I am grateful for everything you have done, but the truth is I can't come in anytime soon. I'm sorry."

"Because of your family, right?" Tyler could hear a snarl in Rooks's voice. He imagined the phone in the Lieutenant's office being held in a death grip. It was his turn to be silent. There was nothing else to say. He stared at the ceiling in the hotel room, looking at the bumps in the stucco above that seemed to resemble a face mocking him. He waited for the Lieutenant to gather his thoughts before speaking again. Finally a long breath exhaled in his ear.

"The best I can do is forty-eight hours, Tyler. Then they will begin hunting you. You do understand that, right? Once IAD is involved, there is no turning back. Even Detective Herrera will have no choice but to disclose any information she has on you. I will have to do the same. We will not rest until you are brought before a formal inquiry, and you WILL be brought in. Am I making myself clear?"

"Yes, Lieutenant....... Alan, thanks for everything I appreciate it. I know Emily thought you were always looking out for me, and now I can see she was right. She is always my better half, even now."

"Tyler......Goddamnit......."

"Goodbye Lieutenant Rooks."

Tyler pressed the disconnect button. The call ended his career in law enforcement. He almost expected the phone to ring again, but it was silent. He got down on hands and knees next to the hotel bed and put the phone under the framework. It would be missed by the cleaning crew, but not damaged, so it could still be traced through GPS. Tyler wanted to pack up and leave that very minute, but instead he lay on the bed staring into the ceiling.

No one took even a hint of police corruption more seriously than the Chicago Police Department. His other "family" would turn against him in a matter of days. They would come for him relentlessly. He had been alone for a while now, but this was the first time he had lost even the safety net of his profession. He would have given his life to feel Emily's breath on his shoulder right now. Just a single heartbeat's worth.

CHAPTER 24
Dog Days

THE HARD FLOOR underneath Will's feet echoed as he walked through the warehouse. It felt like he had walked its length a thousand times. In reality, it had probably been a dozen at most. For the first time, he looked down at the ground wondering why anyone would paint their floors the color of rust. It was an ugly and drab shade that resembled dried blood mixed with countless other hues. Maybe the initial logic was sound, but why make it look like you had just slit the throats of your employees in hundreds of places? He wanted to laugh about these crazy thoughts, but a sense of humor could be dangerous in his line of work. Usually it was associated with weakness and that was something he could not afford. The only man he had ever seen pull it off successfully was also the same man he was walking toward at this very moment. Will made his way through the back section towards his boss.

Usually their Abyss chemists would be here working frantically, but Will didn't see anyone else around. Maybe right now they were on break hiding among the 55 gallon drums that lined the eastern wall of the building. If they were, Will didn't blame them. They were much smarter than he was for that reason alone. It didn't pay to be near Robert Baxter unless he was in a good mood. Even Will couldn't always tell when that was. He felt the beginnings of a smirk develop on his face and strangled it before Baxter did it for him.

Baxter acknowledged him with a brief nod of his head before turning his gaze back to the various beakers, incisionary tools, and boiling vessels. Will knew almost nothing about the production process other than they imported the residue of poppies from a supplier which was then somehow converted into opium by boiling. Baxter had once explained that they extracted the morphine from the opium which was then converted into bricks. These bricks were combined with acetic anhydride along with several other chemicals Will couldn't even spell. Eventually it was catalyzed into the unique red and black color of their custom product that was spreading rapidly on the streets of the city and beyond.

Baxter had several people working on the production however the man himself could probably replicate the process on demand. The ability to create Abyss was not in Will's skillset, but it was obvious they had to produce and sell as much of it as they could while it was a trade secret. Eventually someone would replicate the process, and then the product would be beyond control. It was best to hold onto the lever of the machine as long as you could. It was important to remember though that the lever could get hot. Very hot. Eventually you had to let go.

Baxter gestured to the warehouse around them before issuing his greeting. "Do you know what separates us from the zombies working in their tombs of steel and concrete?"

Will was always thrown off by the questions Baxter asked him. He knew they would come eventually, but sometimes he could be working with Baxter for hours and not hear a sound. Other times they would talk about everything from philosophy to theology, though most of the talking was by Baxter. Will enjoyed listening to him even though it was like listening to the sound of a rattlesnake. It could be interesting as long as you didn't forget what the sound really meant.

"I don't know."

"We are taking what we really want. Where do you think you will be by the time you are forty?"

"Retired. Well, either retired or dead, but I would prefer retired."

Baxter smiled in genuine humor. "That is what I like about you, Will. You are a cut above most of the people in this profession because you are simple. So, you want to retire before most people do and live a life of luxury few can afford, correct?"

"Sure, Baxter. That would be great."

"See, you are doing it for money. Within two years, you will be on a beach fucking a gold-digging whore and planning how to spend the next forty years in luxury. It's blunt, honest, and, more importantly, logical. Outside of getting a fix of heroin or cocaine, most people commit crimes for money or some sort of material wealth. All you have to do is ride the wave, don't stab your partners in the back, and try not to get burned. You then retire for life. You have a simplistic goal, and you stick to the formula to reach that goal because you know it works."

"I guess."

"Why do so many lose sight of their goals?" Baxter asked the question before Will could say another word. "Usually, it is because of drugs or loyalty only to themselves. Some people are simply batshit insane. Sometimes the only way to keep things on track is a harsh lesson. Sometimes you have to kick even your most loyal dog to keep him in line. Why? Because if you don't, the dog starts to think he is the pack leader and not you. Then it is only a matter of time before he goes for your throat. I want you to pull together all of our main contacts. Everyone that directly interacts with you or me."

"All of them?"

"All of them, Will."

"Why?" Will dared to question the order. Baxter arched his eyebrows slightly but more in amusement than any real sense of confusion.

"We need our dogs loyal. We need to ensure that none of them steal our product or sell anything on the side. Individually none of them could stand up to us, but as a pack? We would be torn to shreds in a matter of seconds. They would rip out our throats and then fight each other for scraps."

"But none of them are stealing from us are they? I haven't seen or heard anything."

"No, because right now we all need each other. Besides we are making a lot of money which keeps the pack well-fed. A well-fed pack is a complacent one. Even a mean dog won't bite you if there is a steak sitting in front of him. No, this is more to keep everyone's focus on the consequences of biting the hand that feeds you."

"Is this about that junkie? Big Time or whatever the guy is called?"

"Alvin Keth. Yes, that would have something to do with it."

"But he's just small time. He will probably be dead in six months. Why do we care about him?"

Robert Baxter gave that unique smile of his that could be mistaken for kindness. Will knew better. He scratched the side of his face and looked away for a moment while the taller man stared. It felt like a long pause, but then he heard Baxter take a breath and continue.

"The fact is that he stole from us and now wants to renegotiate terms to sell back product that is ours in the first place. Surely you see the problem with that? I would kill him just on principal alone, not just because he is costing us money. It takes a special kind of junkie to try to rip off the people who are supplying him and succeed at it. Mr. Lynd may have kept a clean profile, but he certainly failed at protecting our investment. Now some single celled organism has our product and has the audacity of trying to evolve. You don't evolve without casualties, Will. Natural selection can be a real bitch."

"Then let me go kill him now, or I can arrange for someone else to do it. I doubt he will be too hard to find. We can kill him today."

"Will, you haven't been listening. We kill them if they are a potential threat, but what do you do to someone who has already stolen your property? This act of greed tells our competitors and our allies that it is possible to hurt us. No. It is better to make an example of Keth and show our friends in low places that it would be unthinkable to attempt anything like this again. To show them that we will not only kill the man, but make him suffer. Rape his wife and children. Burn down the neighborhood that housed him. Tear apart everything that made him what he was and erase any trace of his memory. Do you understand?"

"I guess." Will said. The words were more of an appeasement than an agreement. The conversation only reinforced that he would follow Robert Baxter more out of fear than anything else. Will didn't believe in Satan or any malignant force bent on destroying the human race, but if there were such a thing, he would bet Baxter was the prince of darkness himself. The man did not miss anything, and even scarier was that he was usually right.

"I will set it up, Baxter."

"Good. That is all I ask."

Will turned and began to walk out of the warehouse. A glance over his shoulder showed that Baxter had not moved. The man looked more like a fucking statue than a human being. He forced himself to try to slow down but before he knew it, he was outside and walking towards the car. His feet sprinted their way to the driver's side of the vehicle. It was only when he sat down in the seat of the car that Will realized he was out of breath.

CHAPTER 25
Nothing to Lose

TYLER WOKE UP more refreshed than he had been in over a month. There were blessedly no dreams that he could remember, and it was the first time that he could recall having slept through the night. He stretched his arms out on the unfamiliar bed. He was in a different hotel than the night before. He hadn't even glanced at the name or the rates, but it was definitely cheap based on the peeling wallpaper and bolted television with four channels. He mentally reviewed his routine from last night, hoping to identify some pattern that had allowed him to sleep. No change in food or the type of beer he had drank. He had stared at the walls until oblivion had come. Nothing stood out in his mind, except maybe his body had finally recognized his sleep deprived state and had bolstered him as best as it could.

Tyler got up and stretched, feeling an ache in his back from the lack of support in the mattress. The pain rode up into his shoulders, and he thought of Emily's backrubs after a particularly grueling day. There was something very intimate about a backrub. Feeling a woman's hands soothing the muscles and making your skin warm. Emily would always lean close when it was over and kiss his ear softly. Not in a sexual way, but more in a gentle, sweet caress, letting him know she was there for him. She had always been there for him, and he had failed to be there for her. Tyler felt a pang in his heart at the thought of being able to sleep through the night without even a thought for his family. What right did he have to rest when his family could not? The thought spiraled rapidly into a loop that continued on and on in the back of his thoughts. *You are sleeping while your family is dead. You are sleeping while your family is dead. You are sleeping while your family is DEAD.*

Tyler said, "Jesus Christ, Tyler, now you are berating yourself for getting a good night's sleep."

The words echoed off the wall, making them sound like they were from a stranger. The repeating inner voice had shut up for the moment, but Tyler was sure it would return. Even speaking out loud to himself was outside his normal patterns. Didn't that used to be considered a sign of insanity? Tyler shook his head and grinned at that one. There must be a lot of crazy people then, from the number of times he had witnessed others talking to themselves. Chris Wessler would mutter under his breath constantly when he was writing reports. Usually most of the team would stay away from his dour sounds, but Tyler had always loved sparring with him. Chris had never seemed to mind. The muttered curses would at least then have a smile behind them.

Tyler's grin faded with the thoughts of his former partner. He had done Chris a disservice by not letting him know what was going on. If anyone had earned that right, it was the one friend who had been there throughout this nightmare. Tyler remembered the constant phone calls and offers of support from his former partner. At the funeral, Chris had been one of the first to show up and the last to leave, outside of himself. Now Chris had moved on to Vice and Tyler had moved on to......... whatever path he was on.

Tyler picked up the plastic receiver of the phone and dialed Chris's cell from memory. Luckily it was a local call, or he would probably have had to deal with the hotel staff in some way. It was a miracle the phone even worked. The line rang until the gruff voice answered in the annoyed tone Chris had for phone numbers he didn't recognize.

"Yeah?"

"Chris, it's Tyler."

"Tyler! What the fuck have you been up to? Last I heard you've become some sort of rogue vigilante gunning down the homeless and drinking the blood of virgins in the dead of night."

"Funny."

"Yeah, you never were one for jokes. Seriously though what is going on? From what I hear, Rooks is in an uproar and whenever I see that new partner of yours, she looks like she is in mourning for someone near and dear who just died from self-immolation."

The tone of Chris's voice was jovial, but the question behind the words was real. Tyler was reminded of one of their cases where they had captured a man named Wayne Teller who had just murdered his wife and son. Tyler had spent hours browbeating him in interrogation. Usually his scare tactics worked wonders, but Teller was an inhuman machine. He had repeated the same answers verbatim time after time with no emotion. That had been the most damning evidence. His complete lack of regard for his wife, who looked like she had been run through a blender, and a son whose head had been lopped off. Just a blank stare that would have been at home on a dead fish in the Chicago River.

Teller's solid alibi was his sister who had confirmed his whereabouts during the time of the murders. DNA evidence was almost useless as it was the suspect's house. Of course, there would be his DNA everywhere. No murder weapon and a cold automaton that was immune to Tyler's anger. Tyler had left the room feeling that the murderer was silently laughing when Chris went in. He watched from the next room as Teller confessed his crimes to Chris within the span of a thirty minute conversation. Tyler couldn't believe it.

As Chris was leaving the interrogation room, Tyler grabbed his arm and asked the typical questions of How, What, and Why. "Simple, Tyler. Empathy. He thought I identified with what he had done." Chris had replied, "A kindred spirit, or at least he believed that in his fucked up head. When you speak the same language as the psychos, they begin to view it as 'us' versus them, not just 'me' versus them. Make sense?

You are a lot better than me at assessing crime scenes, putting together scenarios, and figuring out why the criminal mind thinks the way it does. I can even admit that you are smarter than me. But the fact is, you can't relate to the people we put away. Until you learn to understand why they do the things they do, you will never catch them all."

Tyler had begun his criminal psychology coursework and had discovered a lot of truth in what Chris had taught him. Now the same man who had once helped him become a better detective was subtly asking what was happening with Tyler. He had no time for self-doubts, but he did have time to talk to Chris one last time. He took a breath and began his last conversation with his former partner.

"I was just suspended, Chris."

The dead silence on the phone was potent and heavy. Tyler was silent too in astonishment that he had actually made Chris speechless. Son of a bitch there really was a first time for everything.

"Jesus Christ. That is fucking low. Rooks is out of his head if he thinks he can get away with it. I am logging a complaint as soon as I get off the phone, and then I am going down to that self-righteous prick's office to strangle him with his goddamn tie! They can't do that to us!"

"Me. Chris. They can't do that to me, and yeah, they can. Rooks made a tough decision, but he made the right one."

Tyler could hear the gears of rage grinding in Chris's head and shook his head in wonder. Still loyal after all this time.

"Bullshit. I realize you have gotten a little rougher around the edges lately, but you were worse before you met Em. You were always a mean bastard but a good cop. You were better than I was at that part. Now Rooks is hanging you on a meat hook for the butchers. I know I don't know all the details, but I know you."

"I'm not the cop I once was Chris. That part is gone now. It's in the past." Memories flashed through Tyler's head as he spoke. Picnics. Parks. Saturday morning breakfast. The past was a demon torturing him with visions of his previous happiness. Talking to Chris brought some of that past bubbling to the surface. "It has been decaying since Emily and Grace died and now it's gone. I'm different now."

"Well, I bet you aren't so different that you are going to sit back and do nothing. If you have gone off on your own, tell me what I can do to help. How can I help make any of this right for you?"

"You can't, Chris. I just called to say goodbye. I don't know what is going to happen in the next couple of days and I wanted to say thanks for being a good friend. I know Grace loved you like an uncle, and that always meant something. Emily and I appreciated all the support. You were a good detective to work with. Take care of yourself."

"Tyler? You can't just hang up like that! Tyler.........."

The call ended with the click of the receiver. Tyler left the phone off the hook. After a few moments, the phone started to beep. He was sure Chris was trying to dial, but this was really the best way. Now he had nothing to lose. He packed up his things quickly and prepared to change hotels for the last time. The weight of the assault rifle was comforting in his hands as he gathered up everything left of his life. It was reassuring in a way that did not bear close examination. Now all he had to do was find a new place, reach out to Alvin, and then wait. The trap was set.

CHAPTER 26
Lincoln Park

THE BENCH SLABS felt cold even after the snow was brushed off onto the ice-crusted ground. The rough wood whimpered as Tyler sat down. He had arrived in Lincoln Park expecting to be amazed by its beauty in the dead of winter, but today was not one of introspective admiration for the surroundings. The park was the largest in Chicago, at over 1,200 acres of land. It was visited by millions of people every year and boasted a large variety of facilities ranging from harbors and tennis courts to the conservatory. He was currently right outside the gates of the Lincoln Park Zoo. The last several days had been a blur of nightmares and terrible hotel food, so at least the outside air cleared his lungs. Tyler caught himself thinking about Tolstoy's *Master and Man* as the snow flurries increased in intensity. The temperature was dropping already, and the crowd out today lowered their heads as the wind bit into faces. Everyone trudged on like monks following their own pilgrim paths.

He had suggested the spot to meet with Annabelle more out of a subconscious need to see the place his family had spent so many afternoons than any strategic reason. Grace had loved coming here to draw sketches of the animals. She would eat hot dogs and spicy Korean street fare that was a trademark, as much as the park's beauty. Emily would also come here to work on a story typing on a laptop, while Tyler would throw Frisbees with his daughter. It was a pleasant memory made bitter, and the taste of it made Tyler smile with a complete absence of warmth. Emily and Grace were not buried here, but so many of their memories were and they gave off an ethereal aura that was hard to ignore. If he wanted to, Tyler could spend all day walking through the park, standing on many of the places they had picnicked. The thought was not at all comforting.

Tyler had called Alvin two days ago and had found out their meeting was scheduled in just four days. The junkie had sounded high on something stronger than marijuana. Tyler could almost see the watery red eyes darting about nervously above the whispering voice. They were supposed to meet at an abandoned building off of South Springfield. There never seemed to be a shortage of those types of meeting places, Tyler thought. Once Alvin had outlined the details, Tyler told him he would be there a few hours early to go through their strategy. Alvin had agreed and hung up with a speed that made him think they had been disconnected.

He had spent the next two days in an exhausted coma, living out of his hotel room. There was no contact with the outside world unless you counted television. Tyler found himself missing his books but could not find the energy to go buy new ones.

He had grown accustomed to being alone for extended periods of time after the funeral. It had seemed like living in a Cold War fallout shelter right after the first bomb had dropped. His entire world had been wiped out in a radioactive haze of murder. He could picture the three yellow inward triangles emblazed on a black background warning him not to leave his sanctuary. Through the use of creative takeout food options, he had spent weeks alone pacing the small rooms of his apartment with only ghosts to keep him company. He realized now what he really had been doing was waiting to die. Waiting for that last day when he would either see his family again or the void of non-existence.

But now this was different, wasn't it? Yes. Tyler felt a need to keep on living and to finish his purpose. What was that purpose exactly? He wasn't sure if he could answer the question unless he voiced dark thoughts. Was he going to arrest these people or kill them? Murder and Justice could sometimes be the same word, just taken in different context. It was semantics plain and simple. Just a problem in the connotation of the words, nothing more. No, what he wanted was revenge. Revenge for the mindfuck this last year had become. The year that had seemed to go on for a lifetime. How he had reached this idea of revenge was irrelevant. He would know when it was time and would carry his guns wherever he went.

He had called Annabelle around 6:00 a.m., who had answered right away in that breathless voice more at home in a choir than a police station. He had wanted to see if she had heard anything more or if any further leads had surfaced. The surprise was that she had heard more, a lot more. Annabelle had refused to give him the information unless they met face to face. Tyler understood why, but a small part of him still wondered if she was setting him up. He realized she could have turned him in when they had met at the bar. It would have made more sense to do so then too. Still this meeting seemed a little too coincidental. His paranoia whispered in his ear, speaking in a hiss. Wouldn't it be funny if he was arrested when he finally cared?

Annabelle appeared in the corner of his sight, walking down the snow-tracked sidewalk like a bullet flying towards his head. He could tell as she drew closer that she had already spotted him, and her pace had increased almost to a run. She was dressed in a gray chevron tweed coat which would have looked plain, but on Annabelle, it looked perfect. Her hair glistened with pearls of white and her breath came out in wisps from the exertion.

Tyler had to look away for a moment while she settled onto the bench next to him, laying a laptop case at her feet. They were both silent staring at the people passing them by. Staring into their own thoughts before they needed to speak. It was unusually quiet due to the wind cutting off the normal banter of the crowds. Annabelle broke the silence first, speaking as though trying to pull off a Band-Aid.

"You are to be apprehended for questioning on sight, Tyler. The announcement was issued during the morning gathering, and it is in effect as of 8:00 a.m. today. Any officer that spots you is to take you back to the station for interrogation at once. We are also to issue a prompt call to Lieutenant Rooks upon apprehension or location sighting."

Tyler nodded in a motion of understanding that seemed to frustrate Annabelle to nervous agitation. She bit her lip in a subconscious movement as she stared at a tree naked of leaves. They both shuffled their feet. Tyler could tell she was waiting for him to say anything so he prodded her with the question she wanted to hear.

"What does that mean to you, Detective Herrera?"

"It means I am off-duty today, so I am meeting a friend in the damn park to discuss unverified rumors and speculation. Right? That is what we are doing right? Because otherwise I need to try to arrest you right now. I am saying try because I don't know what you would do if I made the attempt. So we are just friends meeting today, ok?"

Tyler could see the tears gathering as a sheer film over perfect eyes. She turned her head away to mask the emotions, letting the wind wipe them away. A part of him wanted to put an arm around her and comfort her, but it was far too late for that. There were too many ghosts who needed his attention every second.

He waited for Annabelle to compose herself. The snow drifted down between them in a veil of cold and purity. It was ephemeral and filled with naïve carelessness. It felt like a lie. Tyler wanted to leave. He wanted to get up and walk away, and it was probably the most selfish thing he had ever felt. It felt like drowning.

Tyler said, "Ok, we are just friends talking for a little while. Whatever you want, but as your friend I don't want you to risk meeting me here to tell me that. We both knew the arrest issuance was coming sooner or later. This meeting isn't worth the risk. If you got caught, you could lose your badge and your future."

"That's not all, Tyler." Annabelle interrupted while reaching into her laptop case to pull out a manila file. She turned slightly towards him to shield the papers and opened the folder to show Tyler the contents. "There is more. Within the last couple of days, we have heard about several accounts of new sale activity for Abyss. It stands out from the rest of the business structure because it isn't flowing through the usual channels. In fact it is pretty easy to trace and not at all discreet." Tyler knew even before Annabelle moved the report aside and held up the picture that it would be Alvin Keth. His junkie key to unlocking the Abyss manufacturing market kingdom had just graduated to the highest levels of stupidity. Alvin Keth could fuck up the whole deal without even meaning to. What a cruel joke.

"This is Alvin Keth or 'Big Al' but I think you already know who he is. Apparently, Mr. Keth has moved up about two dozen rungs on the drug ladder in one day. Used to be a small time hustler of marijuana, maybe a little coke on the side for some extra weekend cash. Now this burnt out junkie apparently has an elusive, high-demand product that he is pushing with a vengeance. Also, interestingly enough, he has another tie that goes above and beyond the usual lowlife scumbag. He is a CI for Vice and assisted a homicide case for a former Detective Tyler Morgan. Isn't that just a strange coincidence?"

"How did you hear about this?"

"Got a phone call from a Vice detective you also know by the name of Chris Wessler. See, Chris apparently can't reach out to his former partner anymore, and when he spotted this, he called me hoping I could help him get in touch with you. I told him I would see what I could do, but not having a phone number makes it kind of hard to reach out."

"Jesus Christ! How long ago was this?"

"Yesterday."

Tyler's head spun realizing the tightrope he was walking now had a pit of razors waiting to greet him at the first misstep. Alvin had probably started selling almost immediately after Tyler had left the apartment. He had made the fatal error of trusting a junkie with the supply of a valuable drug in the hopes of getting an audience with the supplier. Now that audience had been granted, but if Alvin were arrested or exposed in any way it would mean prison for Alvin and a loss of the only connection Tyler had. He had to get to Alvin now and ensure no further damage was done. Otherwise he might need to put a bullet in both their heads right there in the tiny apartment. It would be a mercy they didn't deserve.

"Annabelle, thank you for the information. I really appreciate it and I know this isn't what you want to hear, but I have to get going." Tyler stood up and she matched his movement. He realized for the first time that her head barely reached his shoulders. "I know you are taking a risk telling me this. I don't want to run but there is a lot hanging in the balance. You have been a good friend to me. Thanks again for coming, but I need to go if I am going to have any chance at all of solving this."

Annabelle nodded her head in defeat and sat back down on the bench without a whisper. She sat staring at the concrete beneath her feet, ignoring the cold as it pulled strands of hair away from her face. She murmured something he could not hear over the wind. Tyler could feel time ticking away, but he couldn't just leave like this. It reminded him too much of all the people that he should have been there for.

"What did you say, Annabelle?"

"Go ahead, Tyler." She said more clearly as she smoothed the coat fabric on her lap. "None of this matters except getting one step closer to dragging down the people responsible for your family's death anyway, right? I didn't see much of a reaction out of you until I mentioned Alvin. Then you were ready to bolt out of here without a goodbye." She turned to look up at him, and her eyes blazed with a fury he had not seen before. Her voice still sounded calm as she continued. "Last time we talked, I asked you about what type of man your family would want you to be. Obviously that talk hasn't changed your thinking, so I want to ask you one more question. Have you thought about the fact that you actually could still have a life? You still have your job, although maybe by a thread, and you still have a future. When did you decide that you didn't have the right to be happy anymore?"

Annabelle paused and looked down at the sidewalk for several seconds. She said, "You know the path in front of you is suicide. Either you wind up dead, or you will find yourself surrounded by dead bodies. Then what? You still have that gaping hole inside you. Killing everyone that ever wronged you won't make the emptiness go away. The only thing that will help is time and healing. I'm not saying it will take the ache away completely, but it will be enough so that you can live. Isn't that supposed to be the best revenge, Tyler? Living well?"

Tyler remained quiet through Annabelle's words, and now that she was silent he turned them over, shifting through her plea. He appreciated everything she had done and owed her the small courtesy of taking her words seriously. What she was talking about was trying to find a kind of happiness as best he could. Tyler was surprised to realize he had also been thinking of the concept in the back of his mind. It would be easy to just let go, walk away, and mourn his family. Maybe one day he start another life in a new place? Forgive himself for the crime of being more dedicated to his work than spending time with his family. Forgive fate for taking what he cared about most into its steel grip and crushing it until there was nothing left but bits of bone. Forgive and forget, wasn't that the way of good men and women?

Tyler shook his head and Annabelle's shoulders slumped. He said, "You know my answer already. I wish I could justify what I am going to do with some noble cause or ideal." He laughed for a second, but the sound died as soon as it had begun. It sounded fake so he pressed on. "I wish I had some grand philosophical statement that we could debate until a satisfying conclusion was reached, but I don't have one. The fact is there is no divine goal or retribution for the weak. I was a selfish man before I met Emily or held my daughter in my hands. I am once again a selfish man who wants to ruin the lives of the people who took away my happiness. I want them to suffer until I can't make them suffer anymore."

His face visibly hardened and Annabelle involuntarily raised a hand as if to ward off his anger. "I want those murderers to feel more pain than I have, and then I want them to die screaming in agony. I have the skills and the will to do so, Annabelle. Don't stand in my way or try to make me doubt what I am doing. I will not stop until I find these men, so step aside, and let me do what needs to be done!"

Tyler turned and walked away as Annabelle sank to her knees in spite of herself. She clasped her hands together as if in prayer. He could almost hear their bond of partnership snap as he moved with a purpose that made several tourists step out of his way. His boots crunched into the wet concrete beneath him. The sound was loud to his ears but strengthened his resolve with each step. It was the type of walk Robert Baxter would have recognized.

CHAPTER 27
Splinters in the Mind's Eye

THE DOOR OPENED with one solid kick, sending shards of wood flying as Tyler moved in with his gun drawn. The air reeked of marijuana and some type of cheese he couldn't place, creating a sickly sweet smell that clung to his clothes. Alvin Keth's apartment was littered with beer cans and food wrappers, making his walk into the living room all but announced. He was not going for subtle at this point, but the detective in him warned against any potential threats lurking in the darkness. The living room was deserted though the television was on, blaring about the record snow levels. Tyler pointed the Glock out in front of him keeping an open line of sight as he walked towards the bedroom area.

Alvin Keth lay sprawled out on a mattress, covered in a dirty sheet and a thin sheen of sweat. He looked like he was dead. Tyler felt a twinge of guilt as he wondered if they would miss the meeting because of an overdose. He drew closer and saw the rise and fall of lungs. Tyler shook his head in disgust. The junkie turned kingpin was still sleeping and apparently hadn't heard his door being kicked in. The fact that

Alvin was sweating in one of the worst snowstorms was an irony for them both.

Tyler walked over to the headboard where he saw a 1964 quarter, the last year of silver circulation, lying as the only object on the nightstand. Must be his lucky quarter he thought, and then pushed the barrel of his weapon against Alvin's temple. He pulled back the Glock's hammer and leaned down, keeping the weapon buried into the flesh covering the man's skull. Even then, Alvin continued his blissful slumber, unaware of the loaded weapon less than an inch from being in his brain.

"Alvin!"

The junkie's eyes flew open, and he jerked to get up, but Tyler pushed the gun's barrel hard. Alvin relaxed recognizing the metal for what it was, though his breathing sounded erratic like his heart was dying. This probably wasn't the first time this had happened to Alvin, Tyler thought, though it may be the last. The trigger felt like smooth glass. It would be so easy to push down.

"Waaahzzz. Morgan? Holy shit, you gave me a heart attack!"

"Don't even try to lie to me, Alvin. Why try to sell the drugs?"

"I didn't…" Tyler pushed down on the barrel again until there was silence.

"Look, I did what you asked, man. The meeting is set for two days from now!" Alvin started coughing as he took ragged gasps. "We are good, right? We are good to go!"

"That is not what I asked. What I asked was why are you trying to sell the drugs we are using as leverage for our meeting? Let me put it in simpler terms. Why are you fucking up our meeting by giving the supplier a reason NOT to meet with us?"

"I did what you asked! You got the meeting!"

"You are starting to sound like a broken record. Have you even considered that setting up a meeting with these people and then selling the product might give them an alternative?"

"Like what?"

"Like killing you and taking whatever you have left in this shithole?"

The silence was deafening. He watched as the problem worked its way across Alvin's face. Tyler's lip curled in disgust despite the fact he didn't want it to. "Big Al" clearly hadn't thought this through and was just trying to make some cash on the side while helping a police detective. Or at least someone he thought was a police detective. The problem was not thinking things through could make them dead, or worse, missing the meeting. There was nothing he could do to alter what had happened. Tyler shook his head. This was beyond idiocy.

"I just......I just........"

"Never mind, Alvin, what's done is done." Tyler yanked the gun away from Alvin's temple. He stood up trying to control his rage. Alvin seemed to sink further into the mattress and his breathing started to slow down. Tyler eased the hammer of the Glock down. The gun vanished into his holster like a puff of smoke. Threatening Alvin would not help anything right now, no matter how good it felt.

"The important thing is we need to stay focused and sit tight for the next two days. Now when I get back, I want you to be sure we don't get any visitors. Also, we need to get this garbage cleared out and fix the door so we don't have any more intruders."

"Sure, ok. Wait. What do you mean when you get back?"

"Apparently, you need some supervision until we go through with the meeting. I am going to be your tenant, so you may want to remove any syringes sticking out of the couch. That is where I am going to sleep."

"Wait, what? You can't stay here! You will frighten my friends away!"

"That's the idea." Tyler started walking back towards the front door. He was not looking forward to the driving conditions of the streets outside. The sky was a gray womb and only Chicago's natives would dare to trudge through the hazardous conditions. The drive was short, but he planned on the snow costing him several hours. Not that he wouldn't have the time to spare. Tyler had two days he wished he could just throw away like trash lodged in the cracks of his life. What was that saying about being 'sick and tired of being sick and tired'? It was apt in this case, but it didn't make him smile.

He heard Alvin call out for him to wait as he put his hand on the doorframe. His former CI took staggering steps towards him as Tyler turned back. Alvin said, "Why don't you just have some other cops watch the house? I'll be good, scout's honor."

Tyler shrugged and said, "Because they have other cases to look into and criminals to apprehend. You are my CI through assignment and protocol. We will see this through regardless of what you want. Now we can either do this the easy way or the hard way, and that really isn't a choice when you think about it." He opened what was left of the front door. Tyler could already feel the cold outside begin to seep into his bones. He closed the cheap wood on Alvin's protests and went to get the rest of his guns.

CHAPTER 28
Intermission

THE ENTRANCE TO Rosehill resembled a castle's barbican and parapet walk more than a home for the dead. It was the largest cemetery in Chicago and was named erroneously from the area's previous title Roe's Hill. The entryway had always interested Emily when they were visiting the gravesites of Tyler's parents. Every member of his family had been buried here since his grandparents had chosen the site. It would be where Tyler would be buried as well. He passed through the entrance and felt calm wrap around him as he remembered past visits with Emily and Grace when they were alive. There had always been an annual visit on his parents' wedding anniversary to lay lilacs or roses on the graves in remembrance.

Grace had been scared the first time they had brought her here, but Emily had only smiled and told her that they were visiting family. "Cemeteries are a place to visit those who aren't with us anymore," she had said in her gentle voice. "We get to keep them alive in our hearts and memories." Grace had looked up with her old soul eyes. "Keep them alive forever?" Emily had smiled her special mother smile and said, "Yes, sweetheart. We keep them alive forever."

At the time Tyler had found the moment endearing, but now it hurt. God, it hurt to think about it. The second of tranquility dissipated as quickly as it had come and in its place was a sense of unease.

The cemetery had always been beautifully kept. During the summer, the grass was green and evenly trimmed. The meticulous lawn work made the gravesite flowers burn like beacons of color. He had chosen the plot when his father had died of lung cancer. The location hadn't been just because of family tradition. It was obvious the caretakers here took pride in watching over the dead. Tyler had not hesitated when choosing for Emily and Grace. It had been the one easy decision while choosing coffin wood types and headstone markings. Discussing epitaphs made it impossible to live in true denial.

The trees overhead were stripped of their leaves, arching over him as he made his way toward the graves of his family. Tyler thought he could have found the way with his eyes shut. There were many famous businessmen, mayors, athletes, and actors buried within the cemetery but Tyler had always been more fascinated by the monuments. Several had been brought here from City Cemetery and were protected from the snow by glass casings. It was a beautiful place tinged with sorrow for those that had been lost. Right now, it was the only place where he felt like he completely belonged.

The graves of his wife and daughter were facing east as most graves did throughout the world. This custom could be traced back through many belief systems including the Egyptians who worshipped Ra the sun god who supposedly rose each morning. The practice continued all the way to a Christian belief that the deceased would rise to face the new day when Jesus returned to pass judgment. The only judgment that Tyler saw right now was cruel and bleak. He brushed the snow off the plaques that topped each headstone for his wife and daughter, wishing he had worn gloves. It had been such a short time and already they seemed forgotten in the cold ground. Meanwhile the people who had done this were probably inside staying warm and enjoying all the benefits of being alive. Tyler put his fists into his pockets to keep from pounding them into the ground.

He watched as the snow began to work on covering the headstones again while a burst of wind cut into his face. Tyler found himself waiting several minutes as the noise and the cold drowned out his breathing.

"Hello, Em. Hello, Grace." His voice came out as a whispered croak, but now that he had started he didn't want to stop. "I came here because I guess I wanted to say goodbye before anything else happens. If you are looking down on me, I wanted to ask if you could forgive me for what I am going to do. I know that's an impossible request, but I miss you both so much. God knows I miss you.............."

Tyler waited, wanting to cry. He willed his eyes to tear up, but they wouldn't. It seemed his body was incapable of a simple function that many people experienced regularly whether they wanted to or not.

Tyler said, "I was talking with Annabelle, and I think she was right about a lot of things. She mentioned you would want me to be happy. You would want me to go on living and rebuild my life. The funny part is I know she is right. I know that is what you want for me, and that's another reason why I'm here. I want to apologize because I....can't. I just can't. Maybe that's not even true. Maybe it's that I won't. I won't go on and pretend I am a whole person. Sometimes, I feel like I am a phantom or a ghost just waiting to disappear. It sounds so cliché. I don't know. All I want now is to know the people who did this to you are dead, and I hope you can forgive me for it. I need you to forgive me for it."

The headstones were silent as he stared, listening to the wind howl in frustration. It was a caged beast whipping around his face and hair. Tyler reached into his pocket and pulled out a neatly folded piece of paper. It was the origami hummingbird he had made for Grace the day she had died. The paper still looked fresh with the folds crisp and neat after being kept safe all this time.

He held it up for his daughter to see and said, "I made this on that day. I never got a chance to give it to you. It never seemed like the right time afterwards. It doesn't now either, but this may be the only chance I will get. I had hoped to teach you how to make it. You were always so quick with your hands, Grace." Tyler smiled. "A future artist if I ever saw one." He placed the hummingbird against the front of Grace's headstone. It lay flat and unmoving. Tyler knew the wind would carry it away in minutes. For one moment it was his daughter's. That was all he could ask for.

"I like to think both of you are in a better place now. I don't think it will be a place for me, but I hope you can read my heart and see why I am doing this. I love you both more than anything. When they killed you, they killed everything that was good in me too. I hope you can look down on me and smile, but if you can't, I understand. Please know that my heart is always with you no matter what happens."

The graves were still silent and the wind continued to roar across the cemetery. Tyler turned before he could see the hummingbird disappear. The lines of grief eased away from his face as he trudged through the snow, leaving only a grimace of hate in his footprints. He resisted the urge to draw his weapon at his side. He wanted to feel the weight of the Glock in his hand but there was no culprit here to point it at. It made no sense, and it felt insane.

Former detective Tyler Morgan got into his car and pulled away from the cemetery, weaving through the other cars and the snow as though Hell was behind him. The tops of the headstones of the Morgan family had already accumulated enough snow to blur the engraved letters. The hummingbird left behind was gone, perhaps carried off by the wind or buried, to be unearthed next spring. Either way he would never see it again. The cemetery lay silent keeping any secrets it had heard to itself. The dead had nothing to say.

CHAPTER 29
Wake Up Call

By the time Tyler got back to Alvin Keth's apartment, he saw the junkie had made the most of the time, by cleaning up the living room. The smell of marijuana had dissipated somewhat, and Tyler was sure there were several trash bags that had been dropped off to the incinerator. Still, drops of water from his shoes made little pools of grime on an even dirtier floor as Tyler shut the door as best he could. The bag slung over his shoulder carried the remainder of his meager armory including the AK-47 disassembled to a more compact level. The suitcase he brought had his clothes and enough Abyss to overdose every person on the block. The thought of a mass of people all screaming in ecstasy and horror until they collapsed into a coma of death was a frightening prospect. Tyler was more worried that it wouldn't buy him the meeting he needed.

He found Alvin collapsed on the couch using a frayed cushion for a pillow, covered in an overly large white, hooded sweatshirt. The fact that this was the second time he had been here and found Alvin napping was a little disconcerting but nothing that he had time to examine. The light snores and drool accumulating on Alvin's chin told him that there was a little bit of time to get settled. For the first time, Tyler noticed an odd Cheshire cat clock on the wall whose smile widened with each swish of the tail as time slowly died. The cheap novelty looked like it would be more at home in a demon child's room rather than a drooling junkie's den. He walked past it into the smaller bedroom which was more akin to a closet than a place for sleeping. There was a sleeping bag on the floor that smelled of sweat and possibly worse excrements.

It was fine for Tyler's purposes. He sat down and began to assess what he had brought with him. The AK-47 was easier to assemble than take apart, and he checked each of his four magazines which put him at three hundred bullets. He examined every component including the spring and the barrel itself. All looked in order, and when he was done there was no doubt the weapon would work effectively. Tyler then began to dissect each of his Glocks. He was busy looking at the magazines when Alvin walked in holding a .357 Colt Python in his hand as if he were carrying a briefcase, or in Alvin's case, a bong.

Tyler smiled and said, "What's going on, Alvin? I hope that gun isn't loaded."

"Yeah, it is. You know it is. I will use it too."

"You don't want to do that. Is the Abyss really worth it?"

Alvin stammered and tapped the gun on his hip in an irregular pattern. "I've been thinking while you were gone. You know about how I'm only talking with you anymore? How I haven't seen any formal paperwork or real paychecks made out to me. So I started making some phone calls while you were gone. Even tried getting hold of you directly at the police station. Got your voicemail several times, and the last time I tried, I got transferred to someone higher up. That type of stuff never happens, man. So that gets me thinking some more."

"Be careful, don't want to hurt yourself." Tyler inwardly winced. He had a guy threatening him with a gun and now he decided to start cracking jokes? Maybe he really did have a death wish after all.

"I'm fucking serious as hell, man. I don't think you are a cop no more, let alone some high level detective. Something just doesn't add up. If that's true, then I ask myself what's going on? Why are you doing this? The only answer I can come up with is you are looking to make some sort of move in the drug world. Maybe you lost your job on the side of the law, so you are looking to make it on the other side. I know you went through some heinous shit a while ago. It was all over the news. Maybe you lost your mind, man. You could be mad as a hatter and are looking to get rich or get killed trying."

"Ok. You got me." Tyler said and held up his hands in mock surrender. "I'm actually suspended. I'm not acting as a representative of the police right now."

"Jesus Christ." Alvin said the words as a prayer. "Jesus Christ." He slumped down onto the sleeping bag on the floor, the gun forgotten. Tyler reached over and took the Colt out of his hand. Alvin didn't even seem to notice. He was bent over with the sweatshirt's hood covering his face like a monk in prayer. A monk with the face of Jesus, drugs pumping through his veins, and stained lips. Tyler waited for the anticipated questions.

Alvin said, "So, what now? I can't call shit like this off! I thought I had the CPD backing me up, but it is just you. Don't get me wrong, you are one scary motherfucker, but even you can't score a good deal off these guys. So are you just trying to get rich? Shit, man, why didn't you say that from the beginning! That's something I can understand. Maybe we could be partners. Get some more guys and….."

Tyler interrupted, "Alvin, that isn't what I'm trying to do. Abyss is evil shit that is starting to corrupt our whole city." He sighed at Alvin's confused expression. "Quite honestly, it has probably spread to the point that it will be produced by others soon. I have no illusions, but I want the people who started this to suffer. They need to go down for what they have done."

Alvin stared at Tyler for so long he began to wonder if the junkie's brain hadn't overloaded. Tyler was trying to figure out what to say next when Alvin said, "Shit. Your family……Shit. That's what this is about! Your family got killed and you want revenge. Shit!"

Tyler couldn't keep the surprise from showing on his face. Any average person would have probably deduced the scenario, but this was usually beyond someone who had been strung out on almost every illegal substance known to man. Apparently there was still enough circuitry in Alvin's brain to make some basic connections.

"Yes, that's right."

Another long pause as Tyler watched greed war with self-preservation. They crawled across Alvin's face in a tide of emotion. He would have killed to play poker against people like this. Maybe he could have retired a long time ago and never exposed his family to all the filth and violence that crawled on his skin even now.

"So what's in it for me? Don't tell me about some informant's paycheck or the goodwill of the law. We both know that ain't fuckin' comin'."

Tyler nodded his head over to one of his bags. He said, "In that is all the remaining money I have. My family's life savings. It's yours. Plus any money that we get out of this deal is all yours as well. I have no interest in money at this point."

"How much is in there?" Alvin seemed to be asking the question more to the bag than to Tyler. His eyes seemed stapled to it. This was something Tyler understood.

"From my guess, I would say there is enough for you to be comfortable for a long time. Just my rough estimate, of course. If you decide to take up a new coke habit, maybe it will only last you a few months. Just depends where you are putting your money."

Tyler saw the cogs turning in Alvin's head, grinding away until the inevitable conclusion when human greed and a large sum of money intertwine. He saw the idea of betrayal gradually register in Alvin's eyes, even if the junkie thought he was hiding the concept behind a glance away. Tyler had hoped that he could count on his newfound cohort so that somehow, someway, Alvin could maybe walk away to the seventh level of druggie paradise. That was unfortunately probably not going to happen now. It seemed even a man who resembled Jesus could betray and kill people when there was enough personal gain on the line. It was a long train of thought for reading body language. Maybe he was misreading the whole situation, but at this point it didn't matter. What mattered was getting close enough to the people he wanted to hurt and damn any other costs involved.

"Ok, I'll do it." Alvin said the words, but his eyes never left walls that looked like they hadn't been painted in over twenty years. The snap decision and the obvious gesture told him everything that needed to be said. Tyler knew he was walking into a trap. The signs were all there, and if he died he would have no one to blame but himself. Still it was the only opportunity he was going to get. There was no other option. If he did have to die, he could think of no better way than crushing the men who had killed his soul.

"That's great, Alvin. I appreciate it." He said the words with great effort. They sounded awkward to his ears. He had never been good at being insincere, and the false sense of camaraderie felt like a coat of ichor on his tongue. Tyler would need to keep a constant eye on Alvin. It was important not to tempt fate.

"We should go over how we want to plan this." Tyler said, "If we stick together, everything is going to turn out just fine. First, I am going to need your cell phone."

Alvin handed it over without a second thought and then said, "Who are you calling?"

"No one. It's so that you aren't making any calls. They are supposed to call your cell, right?"

"Uh. Yeah."

He walked out into the living room with Alvin in tow. Tyler strode over to where he had seen the landline phone on a psychedelic TV tray. He picked up the phone and ripped the cord out of the wall without too much trouble. The sound of the phone jack dying was a short groan in the confined space. Alvin jumped back and shook his head in shock. Tyler threw the phone against the wall just to be safe.

"Any other phones in the house?"

"What the hell?!?!"

"Sorry, but I can't trust you that much. Any phone calls have to be through me, and you can't leave this apartment from now on. I just can't chance anything else going wrong before the meeting."

"Motherfucking cop. Why don't you trust me?"

Tyler had to smile at that one. It was time to look through the rest of the apartment.

WHEN THE CALL came, Tyler had been staring at the phone wishing for it to ring. Of course, he had been doing that for hours, so there was no telepathy or arcane sorcery involved. The phone vibrated loudly for several rings. He reached over and picked up the small device.

"Alvin." Tyler whispered but the junkie had already moved over to him, brushing long hair behind his ears. When you were around one person for any extended period you got to know their tics and body language, even if you didn't want to. He could tell the junkie was far beyond nervous.

"Is that them?" Tyler asked.

"I think so." Alvin said.

"Ok, then please answer it."

The conversation was brief and to the point. Tyler knew the information before Alvin disconnected the call. He closed his eyes seeing images of his wife buried in the ground. Was she at peace? Was she smiling down on him from Heaven or screaming his name in Hell right now?

"It was them. They want to meet in two hours."

CHAPTER 30
Rendezvous

ALVIN DROVE A newer Volkswagen Beetle which didn't surprise Tyler in the slightest. It was the type of car that would appeal to the wannabe hippie spirit of Alvin, though it was a terrible choice for any drug dealer. The Beetle was a small compact car that was reliable, but hardly known for speed or power. In a police chase Alvin would have been caught quickly, but Tyler didn't want or need to bring up that topic. He was surprised the car was a gun metal grey rather than a bright blonde or neon green. Tyler's height caused him problems getting into the car, and when he was finally seated, it felt like a metal coffin wrapped around him.

When he had first spotted Alvin's car, he had considered protesting, but only Alvin knew where the meeting was going to take place. It wouldn't benefit Tyler to push on little things as long as they got there. After that, very little mattered and he doubted they would be using the car to drive away. Another problem became apparent as they pulled out onto the street in a sluicing motion. The roads had gotten worse as the snow began to fall in what Tyler could only think of as "blizzard building proportions".

Alvin hunched over the wheel, squinting into the traffic as the wind battered away at the small vehicle. The car shook against the onslaught. Alvin muttered under his breath, driving well below the speed limit. He had told Tyler that they were leaving with several hours to spare and apparently they were going to need every minute of the extra time. It didn't matter. All of the snow in the world was not going to keep him from the meeting.

Tyler touched the window, feeling the cold as he thought about the first time he had taken Grace outside in the snow. Emily had bundled her up so tightly in a coat and snowsuit Tyler knew he would have to pick his daughter up if she fell. Grace's eyes were twice their normal size as she waddled forward reaching down to scoop up snow as best she could with her mittens. She had smiled holding it up to Tyler like a great discovery or treasure. He had laughed so hard that he was in danger of toppling over himself. They had made snow angels and a snowman, playing all day until they could stand the cold no more. They had gone back to the apartment with teeth chattering and smiles on their faces, hoping to find some hot chocolate.

Tyler's memory dissipated like his breath on the glass, leaving him inside a different kind of climate. This snow reeked of malevolence and danger. It was bad weather to be out, especially in the streets of a large city. Even the Chicago natives, used to the ice and snowfall, were extra cautious. There was an unwritten guarantee that at least a few people would get hurt or killed in these kind of conditions. Still there was a silver lining. The less people out, the less chance of running into any problems before they reached their destination.

Alvin handled the car as best as he could though it was obvious the Beetle was becoming more difficult to drive every minute. He didn't talk or turn on the radio, being solely focused on not getting into an accident. Tyler appreciated the time to gather his thoughts even when it looked like they would slam into another car or the curb. They had taken so many twists and turns Tyler almost entertained the thought Alvin was trying to lose a tail or perhaps get him to lose his sense of direction before they reached the location.

The Beetle pulled into a warehouse district he didn't recognize, though that could be because of the weather more than anything else. Warehouses, docks, and abandoned business buildings were all popular places for criminals to meet as they were secluded, and granted a modicum of privacy if business went bad. Usually, it was the criminals who came with murder on their minds, and the police who tried to stop them, but this case was different. The irony was not lost on him. Tyler wanted to check the AK-47 and his Glocks one last time, but he had stripped, cleaned, assembled, and loaded them hours ago. The feeling of not being prepared still circled his mind.

Tyler noticed there were not a lot of tire tracks through the snow on the street. It became rougher on the Beetle as they pulled up to the side of a large warehouse. The building had seen better days several decades ago. If it were summer, Tyler wouldn't be surprised to see a wrecking ball nearby. Chicago had made a lot of progress from a business development perspective, but the poor economy had taken a toll on a lot of places, with this location being a prime example. As Alvin parked the car, you could almost smell the desperation in the air even with the windows rolled all the way up.

"You know," Alvin said looking out, his eyes still squinting from driving in the blinding white. Tyler waited for several seconds to hear more, but Alvin said nothing else, just continued staring outside.

"Do I know what?"

"You could just walk away." Alvin said still not looking at him. "Just get out of the car and walk away. I could keep the money and go through with the deal. It wouldn't be a big thing, man. Just consider the money and the drugs my reward for helping you. I'm not saying forget any shit or anything, but just walk away. You don't even need the money anyway, right?"

"Are you done?" Alvin looked at him with arched eyebrows and then looked away. Tyler dropped his gaze to look at the AK-47 and feel the comforting weight of the handguns at his side. "Let's go," he said grabbing the case between them and opening the car door into the cold outside.

Tyler found himself wanting to smile as they exited the car. Even if his family hadn't been murdered. Even if he didn't feel like an empty husk. Even if he was willing to give the money to Alvin and had no problem with letting the junkie become a drug lord selling heroin to burnouts and children there was no way this would end well. As soon as he was able, Alvin would sell him out. Quite frankly Tyler wouldn't blame him. Too many 'even ifs' for everyone.

The snow crunched under their feet as it bit into their pants and coats. Tyler found himself hunched over, but that had more to do with the assault rifle he was carrying in one hand and a large amount of designer heroin in the other. There didn't seem to be anyone around, but that was deceptive in a large city. Real privacy was an illusion and as rare as true wisdom. The air was crisp and clean in his lungs to the point of pain. He let Alvin lead him into the warehouse which loomed like a mausoleum in front of them.

They were still about half an hour early, which meant they were probably the last ones to arrive. This was the type of deal that favored those who were ready for anything. The only advantages Tyler had were that he was trained, and he didn't care if he got out of here alive. The second advantage didn't sound like a strength, but in reality it was his only true wild card.

They trudged into the building leaving tracks as they moved forward. Tyler noticed a separate slush trail leading across the warehouse to the other side that anyone could follow. He kept Alvin in front of him as they walked in silence. There really wasn't anything more to say. They had discussed how the deal was supposed to go down, but Tyler doubted it would work out how they had planned anyway.

Alvin was clearly on edge. His hair was wet from snow and now sweat that had begun to stream down his face. His head seemed to be mounted on a swivel, looking at every inch of the place and cringing at imagined noises. Tyler felt the same way but allowed his peripheral vision to stay open. The key was not to focus on any one object or area for too long, or you could lose awareness. This was not a situation where you could afford to be distracted.

They continued to follow the trail of breadcrumbs in the form of snowprints past several steel racks that must have held countless pallets of some sort of product. They were stark and empty now. It was warmer inside the building, but not warm enough to indicate the heat was still working. Tyler was glad they had chosen the daylight hours for this, otherwise it would have been much worse. He doubted any electricity ran through the arching ceiling lights. The bulbs themselves undoubtedly dead. There were several empty wooden pallets on the floor that promised to hold only rot and perhaps a few starving rats.

Their boots echoed on the concrete. There was no hope for the element of surprise here. The open space promised a clear scope of vision, and Tyler could see a group of people coming into focus. They had been inside the warehouse for a couple of minutes, but it already felt like an hour. Cold feet bringing them closer to their goal.

Tyler could now spot a group of five men spread out in a half crescent around a table. A few steps further and it was obvious there was another man sitting at the table with his feet propped up, lounging and at ease. Tyler's grip on the AK-47 tightened involuntarily. He tried to control his breathing as they passed more of the pallets and discarded refuse of a dead business. The men that were standing wore gloves, all carrying handguns or assault rifles in their hands. Tyler would bet that if he ran their fingerprints, every single one would come back as clean. He would also bet that none of them were Chicago natives.

One of the men stood closer to the chair than the others and looked uncomfortable in his suit. He was of average height but seemed muscular and competent. The man bent down and whispered something to their relaxed leader, but the words were silenced with an upheld hand. Tyler and Alvin approached the table, stopping far enough away to not take a bullet in the face. That was the idea anyway.

Tyler could now get a look at the leader sitting at the table who still had not moved from his position. He tried to think of a word that could describe how he felt around the man and the closest thing would be unease. He looked tall like Tyler but more lean. His clothes were dark and nondescript, but his face was feral and unique. The man wore a smile that was as uncomfortable as the fact that he appeared good-natured. Beneath the dark brown hair, Tyler saw a pair of eyes that were cold chips of steel. They were dead eyes in a way Tyler didn't like to think about. The eyes glared at Tyler, inspecting him like he was a favorite insect of a seasoned lepidopterist. They glanced unconcernedly at the guns and the case before settling on Alvin. They dismissed the junkie in less than a second. The man's voice was quiet, but Tyler heard the words as clearly as a razor cutting through the cold air.

"Gentlemen, I believe we have some business to discuss."

CHAPTER 31
Bullets

TYLER MORGAN, FORMER detective of the Chicago Police, held an AK-47 in one hand and a case of heroin in the other. The men in front of him were in an obvious state of alert with their weapons half raised. These were the types of professionals who had smelled nitroglycerin many times or handled large quantities of thermite without breaking a sweat. The whispering man had taken a step back and had his right hand resting at his side, presumably to pull some sort of handgun at any hint of treachery. Tyler thought he could probably kill one of them before dying in a hail of bullets. Which one deserved it most was debatable. It was too early to tell.

He had reached the epicenter of the task he had been given the moment that Emily and Grace had died. Now it was all about timing. Tyler watched every movement he could, every twitch of the finger or spasm of the eye. He had to be ready when they relaxed and realized that Alvin had brought the Abyss. A simple blink could cause this whole scenario to end with both of their deaths.

"If we are going to be business partners, then we need to sit across from each other like business partners." The seated man spoke in a dead voice, the smile dropping from his face as though it had never existed. He took his feet off of the table and sat up. The chair barely made a sound. "My name is Robert Baxter and yours is Alvin Keth, so now we have been formally introduced. Your associate holds what we are interested in so there is no harm in you behaving properly. Now. Sit." Baxter gestured to the chair across from him in a short palm chopping gesture. The men around Baxter tensed, and Alvin moved forward a step as though he were a marionette being jerked on lines of steel. Tyler could feel his control of the situation slipping already. There was no SWAT team or backup for him here.

Alvin moved forward and sank into the folding chair like it was a vat of oil. He was encased in sweat while Baxter seemed completely at ease. An awkward silence settled into the area as Baxter stared up at Tyler, not even looking at Alvin. Finally, he lowered his gaze to Alvin and said, "Thank you. Now let's not waste any more time on pleasant conversation. You have several kilos of my drug, and now you want to make a deal with it. Does that about sum it up?"

Alvin seemed to be struggling to swallow like he had just traversed the Mojave. Finally he was able to croak out his words in a whisper.

"Not. Not exactly like that, Mr. Baxter. We brought you this Abyss as a bargaining chip for bigger things. We are looking to become partners in the business and would like your experience in…uh assisting us with this….. hmmmm endeavor."

"My experience, Alvin, lies mostly in killing things, unfortunately. You called for this meeting, but the main reason why I am here is because I have this question that I just can't get out of my skull." Baxter shook his head in mock confusion. "You see, since I started this 'endeavor' I have witnessed all the forms that people take. From beggars who would stab you in the throat for a bag of weed to the stockbrokers who smile large shark grins during the day and then rape prepubescent girls in alleys at night. All forms. Most people are stupid or ignorant, but I think that is common knowledge. Yes, the majority of human beings are idiots, but I would venture to say almost no one would be stupid enough to steal from an illegal drug manufacturer and then try to sell the product back to them. Well, no one who wanted to live would be that stupid anyway."

Alvin had to wipe the sweat from his eyes. He rubbed them like a scared boy. "Mr. Baxter, I....This wasn't...." Robert Baxter's mouth tightened into a grimace and the room was silent. The warehouse felt like a cave that was collapsing around the group. The walls seemed to shrink until they were all trapped in a clandestine closet. A claustrophobic's nightmare. The air was pregnant with tension. Tyler knew the chances of anyone in this room relaxing their guard now was nothing. The plan had failed before it had even began.

Baxter said, "I was saying no one is that stupid, so I have to ask myself what other options are there? I believe there is a certain logic to this world. I'm not talking about karma or the wings of destiny. I am just talking about pragmatism, plain and simple, and this situation just doesn't make sense. But," Baxter held up a long finger to punctuate his point. "But, this whole scenario would make sense if it was needed for an ulterior motive." Robert Baxter reached into his coat and pulled out a Glock 30 with a speed that surprised Tyler.

Tyler raised the AK-47, facing a wall of guns all pointed right at him. He cursed himself for not just starting to shoot as soon as they entered the warehouse. Maybe he would have died right away, but it still would have been better than this.

Baxter leaned over the table and pushed the barrel of the Glock into Alvin Keth's forehead. The junkie hadn't moved and was starting to pant in ragged breaths. Alvin said, "Baxter, it isn't what you think! I wanted to warn you, but I didn't get a chance! I want this bastard dead as much as anyone. He was with me the whole time! Listen..."

"Shhhhhh, quiet little man." Baxter said, nudging the barrel deeper into Alvin's skin. He looked up at Tyler and for the first time their gazes locked. Baxter's eyes were an almost metallic blue and Tyler saw intelligence, but it was calculating like a machine more than a man. The eyes said they had no mercy for anyone under any circumstances. The eyes said don't fuck with me. He knew if he lowered the AK-47, Robert Baxter would have him dead before he could blink.

"Detective Tyler Morgan of the Chicago Police. Age thirty-four. Graduated with top marks from Academy. Highly intelligent, according to aptitude tests. I would go into the scores, but it would be lost on our current circle." Baxter gestured around the warehouse with a hand wave. "Unfortunately your file doesn't go into hobbies, or I would cite that as well. Widowed. Recently widowed, I might add. Also lost a daughter in a travesty that Chicago still talks about. You look a little more desperate in person than your picture, but that's understandable considering the circumstances. You are also currently under investigation by IA and potentially facing criminal charges. Did I leave anything out that you want to add?"

Tyler's mind reeled at the information. They had known all along. They had known who he was before he had walked into the building. Baxter must have a world class hacker helping him if he was able to gain access to the CPD server. He had walked into a setup, but it was not the type of trap he had been expecting. If they had known then, why was he even still alive? The question whirled around his head like a biblical plague.

"So where do we go from here?" Tyler asked. "It is obvious you know all about me, Baxter, and I know almost nothing about you. Well, other than you are an evil motherfucker who sells designer heroin."

"Ah, but that's enough, Detective Morgan." Baxter said. "If there is one thing I have learned, it is that even a pinprick of information can be dangerous." He pushed the gun further into the forehead of his hostage. Alvin whimpered and muttered something about shooting Tyler rather than him, before falling silent. Tyler took a half step back. Baxter continued as though he hadn't noticed. "Now, what I want to know is who else knows about this meeting, about the Abyss, and most importantly, about me?"

Tyler replied, "No one. I didn't even have a name before this meeting. I know very little, which is why I was using Alvin in the first place. Desperate times. Like you said, I am under investigation. The 'rogue asshole cop', right? Who is going to listen to me anyway? Why don't you let Alvin go, and we fight it out ourselves? You can keep the

Abyss, but at least let him walk out of here. I'm telling you the truth, no one else knows about this."

Baxter stared at him for several moments. The air was dense, and it felt hard to breathe. Alvin Keth continued to mumble promises and pleas like an ancient litany for protecting the soul. Baxter smiled at Tyler and said, "I believe you, Detective." He looked at Alvin once again and shook his head. The bullet tore through Alvin Keth's skull and exited with such force that a spray of crimson splashed Tyler's arm. He lunged backwards towards a pallet lying on the ground as the whole warehouse erupted in a crescendo of noise. Bullets clanged off girders above his head like a swarm of angry, metallic locusts.

Tyler popped up over the top of the pallet and fired several short bursts from the AK-47. The thunderous sound of the assault rifle boomed in his ears as he shot at the men scrambling to find their own cover. A cry of pain rode along the sound of gunfire, as he ducked back down again. It was impossible to tell who he had hit, but, with Alvin dead, Tyler didn't really care. They were all armed, and every one of them wanted him dead. Bullets thudded into the wood that was his only shield. He could sense the boxes begin to give way already, as he shifted to an adjoining pallet, hoping to gain a little bit of distance.

Tyler surveyed his surroundings for any possible advantage, trying to ignore the constant gunfire. The warehouse was vast, but there was little cover outside of the two pallets he was crouched behind. The supports in most warehouses might have offered better protection, but this location was definitely not one of them. If Tyler attempted to make a run for it, he would be shot a dozen times before he made it five steps. His options for guerilla movement were nonexistent. He was trapped until either they ran out of bullets or the pallets had enough holes to stop protecting him. Judging from the sounds the pallets were making, it looked to be the latter. Tyler prepared to pop up again when the shooting stopped.

No words had been said, but Tyler could almost hear the body language communication that was going on right now. Maybe they were circling around him and wanted to be in a good position to avoid a crossfire? Tyler had no doubt Baxter would risk his men if it meant taking out his target. He strained to listen for any sound. Any slight movement or hint of a direction the men were moving in.

"Detective Morgan?"

Tyler heard Baxter's calm voice echo. It was difficult to tell where the sound was coming from. He was outgunned, outmanned, and outmaneuvered. They knew exactly where he was. He spent a second checking the magazine of the AK and thumbed the holster for one of his Glocks. It was better to die shooting than as a rookie fumbling for his weapon.

Tyler said, "Is this the part where you tell me to come out, and everything will be fine?"

"Not at all, you son of a bitch." Tyler could hear the shark smile in the words. "I want you to give up your weapon and surrender, so I can torture the information I need out of you."

"Not much of an incentive for surrender." The AK-47 was set and his Glock was ready. Tyler moved a little closer to the pallet and readied the rifle in his hands. It felt warm like a heart or the blood pumping in his veins. He could detect movement thanks to the open environment. The scuffle of boots on the concrete floor was unmistakable. It was hard to be silent when you were ducking from a man with an assault rifle.

"The only alternative for you, Detective Morgan, is to turn the gun on yourself right now. Take that AK, put the barrel in your mouth, and bite the bullet. I personally don't want you to do that because I need to know what you have locked in your head, but that is because I am always cautious about information. However, if you did kill yourself right now it would solve my immediate problems. Just a thought."

The voice was slightly closer, at least it sounded like it was. He struggled to hear everything over his pounding heart. His pulse throbbed to a beat that only psychotics and dead men hear. It was clear they were closing the gap which meant he had minutes if they were taking their time. That was what they called in training a "best case scenario".

"Did you kill my wife and daughter?" Tyler said the words that he had waited to ask during this entire dark journey. It seemed like a lifetime ago that he had begun to ask the question.

"Me, directly? No. But you might as well consider me guilty because I am the one who gave the order. Heavy is the head that wears the crown right? Sword of Damocles. Now that we have met, I would change things a little bit. Yeah, I would definitely change things now, Tyler, I promise you. I would have been there personally, and then I would have personally fucked your whole family while you watched. Then I would have gutted you like a squealing pig because obviously you are not a man to be left alive when bloodwork begins. A man like you, we should have just scattered your ashes to the four winds."

"Yeah, that was a mistake."

"Fair enough. Listen, Tyler, this is all......." Tyler made his move and jumped up firing the AK-47 in clipped bursts, the gun sounding like thunder. He felt no fear and a sense of calm enveloped him as he aimed first towards where Baxter's voice had been coming from. Several of his shots shredded the table which had been turned over on its side, either intentionally or during the uproar. Tyler saw movement on his right and began firing. He thought he heard a cry of pain, but it was hard to listen to anything over the assault rifle which had begun to get hot in his hands again.

The responding fire was immediate, and Tyler felt something brush against the sleeve of his jacket. He fired towards where he thought the shots were coming from, but it was impossible to tell. Bullets ricocheted off the walls and his pallet was being destroyed as though it were being attacked by a whirlwind of nails. Pieces of wood flew around him, throwing splinters that were more than likely burrowing into his skin, if only he could feel it.

The assault rifle clicked, and Tyler ducked down as he realized it had jammed. He found himself absurdly considering how this would never happen to the hero of a movie. Unless he was the villain, then it all made perfect sense. He dropped the AK-47, thumbed his other holster, and pulled out both Glocks, taking his time while the gunfire chipped away at his cover. Tyler had no illusions about taking them all down. He just prayed he would take some of them.

In any sustained firefight the side with the most guns and the most people to pull the trigger usually won despite what movies might say. That plus the fact that he had no intention of trying to escape left little option. His best hope was that he had killed Baxter and hopefully the triggerman of his family's deaths, but he doubted that was the case.

The gunfire rose and fell as men reloaded, and he waited for a lull, pausing for the tide to go out. Tyler leapt up again and began firing before he even had a target. The sound of the handguns roared in his ears as he scanned for potential threats. He was still firing when he felt a sledgehammer crash into him. He spun around like a mad dervish, but instead of whirling gracefully back up, Tyler slammed into the ground.

There was no pain. Had he been shot? His body betrayed him as he tried to rise back up. The ceiling blurred above him as he struggled not to black out. The guns of his family's killers would be focused on him soon, and he needed to take them down into the depths of death with him. His arms felt like lead as the light above blurred into a new sun that burned into his soul. Finding him unworthy of any afterlife paradise. Tyler's eyes closed despite his silent scream.

CHAPTER 32
Immobile

THE HUMAN BODY has an enormous amount of sensory reception with pain receptors being the most numerous. One square centimeter of skin contains hundreds of receptors with all of them communicating to both the spinal cord and the brain. This is why a prick of a needle can be felt, all the way up to a loss of a limb. Some areas of the body have more of these pain receptors which explains why burning your finger feels differently than burning your tongue. Tyler found himself wondering where shoulder wounds would lie in the receptor spectrum.

His eyes opened, and he knew he wasn't in Hell yet because only his arm was dipped in fire. It throbbed to a beat of unbearable pain that made him wish he wasn't conscious. At least while he had been knocked out, there had been no dreams and no pain.

It took several seconds for Tyler to realize that it was completely dark around him. It was as though he were inside a coffin buried six feet down in the earth. There was a feeling of being hooded, but no cloth brushed his face. It was the type of darkness that could make someone go mad after an extended period of time. The sensory deprivation drove his mind to the pain, which made him grit his teeth in anger. He needed to stay focused.

The air reeked of dust and mold. Perhaps he was still in the warehouse? It felt too warm to be the same place. He was seated in some sort of chair and Tyler believed he could feel wood underneath his legs.

The act of moving brought a fresh wave of pain that almost made him cry out loud. Only ghosts in the darkness could hear him now. The pain told him that he was bound somehow which explained why he was still upright. His arms were tied behind the stiles of what felt like a chair. He was possibly tied to the webbing or splat. There was very little give when he strained as his body fought back a wave of dizziness. Whoever had tied the rope or wire had done an expert job. It was almost guaranteed that ligature marks adorned his wrists. It was a depressing thought. There was no easy way out of his immobility. He mentally filed this away as he focused on his other senses.

The lack of sound was deafening. Tyler listened for any subtle noises and heard nothing but his own breathing which came out in ragged gasps like they were last breaths. The breathing became so loud to his ears that he needed some sort of sound. Any sort of sound.

"Hello?"

The words croaked out of his lips, disappearing into memory. He didn't really expect an answer but the sound confirmed what his pain had first told him. He wasn't dead, and that was something. There was no use wondering how long he had been here. It could be days or potentially weeks, dependent on whether there was drugging involved as well as the accumulated dosage of said drugs. He didn't feel muddled or disoriented, but it was hard to tell in this black room with no light to guide him.

Tyler's thoughts drifted to the past, no matter how much he wished otherwise. He began to think of late nights reading to Grace before she drifted off, still wanting to put her thumb in her mouth. Then creeping out of the bedroom as only a parent could, to go join his wife in their bed. It was a comforting kind of darkness that wrapped you in a warm blanket of security, completely unlike what he was in now. Tyler smiled. Intentionally or not his captors were torturing him right now, forcing him to relive memories he didn't want to think about. They hurt too damn much.

He heard something from behind him in the dark. Tyler couldn't make out what it was, but the noise sounded like it was far off in the room. Was it the broken dragging of feet? Some sort of odd movement. The shuffling seemed to be getting closer.

"Is someone there?"

The sound stopped immediately at his words. Tyler held his breath as he strained to listen. Nothing. His heart pounded in his chest as he imagined his family standing behind him. Standing behind him dead. Standing behind him, waiting to drag him into flames for the ultimate sin of being lax. The silence seemed to mock him for a second, and then the sound started again. This time coming closer. The noise unnerved him because he could hear no breathing. Nothing but that soft slide of broken bones and dead flesh.

Tyler's breath quickened, and he felt sweat sting his eyes. He couldn't see anything, but he strained to look behind his back. The shuffling sound had come closer and was right behind him when it stopped. He still couldn't hear breathing. Tyler tried to move regardless of the pain, but the chair held him fast. His neck could almost feel dead fingertips and he wanted to scream out loud. He gasped for breath as sweat fell down to soak his clothes. It was hot and cold at the same time. This was another form of torture as he sat bound. Just waiting for something to happen. His ears hurt as they strained to hear anything outside his own ragged sounds.

"If you're going to do something, do it. I deserve it."

His words bounced off the walls coming back to him without any new information. Finally true darkness stole over him as he fell asleep, exhausted and alone. No other sound emanated from the prison of darkness but his own shallow breathing.

CHAPTER 33
Oubliette

A SLIVER OF LIGHT snaked across the floor almost blinding Tyler. How long had he slept? Was he even awake now? He realized he could see the faint outline of a door and the room surrounding him. It was like staring directly at the sun compared to what he was used to, and he half expected spots or jagged lines to dance in his vision. The room had finally come into focus at least a little. It was a storage area with no furniture or boxes just a lot of empty space. There were a few indentations on the floor which told him that whatever had been in here was now long gone. Maybe it was an area for processed Abyss or a location to hold people that would soon be buried outside the city limits of Chicago.

Tyler heard footsteps, but this time coming from outside the room. They too moved closer, though these were more substantial. More human sounding. Perhaps he had imagined the footsteps he had heard before? It was hard to tell what was real when half of your body thrummed with pain. Bullets could be a bitch that way.

He glanced down and saw an unusual outline attached to his shoulder. Bandages perhaps. If they had some further use for him, then of course they would fix him up. Nothing could be finer than pre-torture medicinal administration. Tyler chuckled in spite of himself. It was all he could do, given the circumstances.

The footsteps stopped outside the sliver of light, making several dark shadows under the doorframe. They stood there, not moving to open the door. Tyler could hear the muted voices of his captors speaking. The tones were low and calm as though they were discussing last night's television or the insane amount of snow Chicago was receiving. "Come on you lazy bastards, let's get to it." he muttered and almost as if they could hear him, the door opened, blinding his eyes in a flash of white.

His head turned away involuntarily, sending a fresh wave of pain up his side. His eyelids tried to staple themselves together to stop the strain. He let them relax as he adjusted again. The light still felt brighter than it should be. Gradually slits of vision were allowed in as he squinted at two large shadows that stood in the doorway. At first, they looked the same, but as his vision increased, he could tell one was probably half a foot taller than the other.

"Can you see yet? We are going to have to turn on a light in here, but it's a lot to get oriented to. Let's wait another minute." The words oozed with pseudo-sympathy in a voice he wished he wasn't hearing. There were no regrets about any people he may have hurt or killed in the gunfight, but Tyler did regret that the one person he wanted dead was still alive and well.

Another minute ticked by, and then the room flooded with light. Tyler lowered his head in spite of himself. The adjustment this time was faster, but it still took several minutes to open his eyes to slits once more. A wave of nausea rode along with the constant pain as he experienced what he could only assume was extreme vertigo. The room swam into focus coming to a clear concise point with Robert Baxter smiling down on him. The man looked more akin to a demon with the large smile and dead eyes than anything human. In Baxter's shadow, stood the man he had seen whispering earlier. The whispering man wouldn't look at him, but instead seemed to find interest in every area of the room except where Tyler was.

He was tied to a chair as he had suspected. It was old and made of poplar. If Tyler had a decent amount of time, he might be able to break free, but that didn't seem likely. The room was large and empty, maybe 30 X 32 feet. It was hard to estimate. Many dark maroon drops stained the floor, mixing with a faint detectable trace of ammonia, telling him that he wasn't the first person that had been in here tied to an old chair. There was nothing to do but stare into the eyes of a man he wanted to kill.

"I really hope you are enjoying the hospitality, Detective Morgan." Baxter said as he stared at his captive. "We had to fix you up as best we could. My medical knowledge is limited, and we didn't have access to Rush University Medical Center or Northwestern Memorial Hospital. We did what my father would have called a 'patch up'. It kept you alive, but I can't guarantee you will live long-term. Not that it seems to be that big of an issue for you anyway."

"How do you know who I am?"

Baxter looked annoyed at the interruption and chopped it away with a motion of his hand. "I'll get to that in my own time, but right now I am the one doing the talking. Not wise to interrupt while shot and strapped to a chair. There is someone I want you to meet."

"Who? Your whispering friend here?"

Baxter moved with a speed that Tyler wouldn't have thought possible for any man his size. His fist struck Tyler in the jaw, causing a dull cracking sound. His face burst into pain. He wanted to howl in agony but ground his teeth shut. He couldn't keep his eyes from watering. He glared up through the pain as he spit blood onto the spotted floor. It seemed to match well with the previous decor. Baxter resumed his position in front of Tyler and looked down at the floor as well. He seemed satisfied with what he saw.

"My 'whispering friend' here has a name, Detective Morgan. This is Will. Will is somewhat of a special case. He is the last surviving member of a group of dangerous men. This group was given the job of slitting the throats of some people you knew. I guess it is kind of funny that this is how you get to meet the last person who saw your family alive. Say 'hi', Will."

Will stared down at the floor, not even trying to hide the fact he was ignoring Tyler as best he could. Tyler felt his rage eat away at his organs, gnawing on his stomach and spleen before moving on to tear at his lungs. The old saying about how looks could kill echoed in his thoughts. If only it were true. Here was one of the men who had murdered his life and burned the corpse. Here was the man who had ordered his little girl to die and his wife to suffer. Here was the source of his alcoholism, his emptiness, his nightmares, and his lack of any real joy. They were right in front of him, and he didn't even have a gun in his hand. If he could trade his life for five minutes of mobility and a gun with two bullets, there would be no hesitation. A Faustian deal with a satisfying conclusion.

Baxter nodded as if he were reading all of Tyler's thoughts and could relate to the intentions. He said, "You are probably wondering why you aren't dead, so let me set you on the right path. We need some information out of you. That's it. No hidden agenda here, right, Will? You are more than likely going to get tortured because it is something I'm good at. I am sure even God in Heaven delights in those who know their strengths. The real question for you is how long is it going to last? That's entirely up to you, Detective Morgan. Before we begin though, I mentioned that there was someone I wanted you to meet. Maybe you thought it was Will here, but guess you are in for several surprises today. Just a minute, I'll be right back. Don't go anywhere." Baxter said and winked. Just a couple of friends sharing a joke.

Tyler's mind raced as Baxter walked out of the room. All the questions he could ask himself right now would be pointless. He was stuck in a goddamn chair and not going anywhere, so he turned his attention to Will who was dripping sweat and had found a very interesting ceiling tile to observe.

"Is it true you killed my wife?" Tyler said. The words hung in the air like an invisible hammer beating down the wall of lies for a glimmer of truth. The sweat on Will's forehead rolled down the sides of his face as he continued to be silent.

"Is it true you killed my wife and daughter?"

Tyler continued to wait.

"Is it true you killed…....?"

"Yes, it's true." Will spoke, but true to form it was barely a whisper. The voice was devoid of emotion, completely contrasting with the body language. It was the sort of voice used to discuss driving conditions on the way to work or some other task that had been done countless times.

Tyler sagged back in the chair feeling his bonds tighten, but even that was a relief in a way. His anger was focused onto that single admission of guilt and allowed the rest of him to be at peace. The rage that coursed through his body had become red and vivid. In a way it felt good. In a lot of ways it felt good.

Now that he had found the people responsible, it was no longer a question of whom. What needed to be done to the people who had taken everything about you that was human and ripped it out of your chest? He had known the answer all along. There wasn't even an illusion of choice in this. He had debated lies with Herrera.

Will looked at Tyler, expecting some words in return for his admission of guilt, but Tyler continued to stare at him memorizing his features. He would know every inch of skin and every hair follicle. This man would never escape from him. Never. He hoped this would intimidate Will, which it seemed to be doing. It was better to be around people who were uneasy with you than those who felt they had complete control. Arrogance could lead to sloppiness, but fear always made people lose sight of their purpose.

The next few minutes were purgatorial in nature until Baxter walked back into the room, along with Tyler's surprise. Tyler struggled to keep his jaw from dropping as Chris Wessler stepped in, as big as life with a mauve tie and a heavy step. A familiar juggernaut with a Beretta strapped to his side. Tyler's former partner was once again a part of his life.

CHAPTER 34
Reunion

"Well, are you going to say anything?" Chris asked, meeting Tyler's gaze with a smile. "At least cite the Chicago oath of office or something. Gotta admit I am glad to see a shocked look on your face for once."

Tyler's mind raced back looking for warning signs. A police detective has many opportunities to commit illegal acts, more than most professions. The discovery of a cache of drug money tempts even the most disciplined police officer clearing a pathetic salary. Why work your whole life to retire on a small 401K when a simple grab of some cash before logging the rest into evidence assures an easier life? The crimes of the CRASH anti-gang unit of the Rampart Division had shown how easy it was to turn a blind eye to corruption until you were a part of it.

He had worked with Chris for years, but Tyler couldn't recall a time Chris had shown any inclination to turn his back on their oath of service. Had he missed a sign that might have saved his family's life? This question was more disturbing than any that Chris and Robert Baxter might have for him. He wished he had the time to review his glaring mistake, but he doubted he would get the chance.

"I'll be honest with you, Tyler; I never thought I would see you here." Chris said, "I thought maybe you would keep living like a zombie until you died of a blackened heart. Maybe I would open the paper one day and see a headline about you hanging from a rope. Maybe one too many pills. Anything but seeing you strapped to that chair. I am truly sorry about this fucked up situation." A look of sympathy crossed the large detective's features. Tyler thought it looked genuine.

Chris said, "Believe it or not, you are the closest thing I had to a real friend, which is why this is so terrible. We were good partners you know? You were always one cold son of a bitch, but you were good at the job. I respected you, which is more than I can say for most of the stiff fucks we dealt with. We would have some fun, you know? But things just got fucked up. Killing your family was bad karma. I actually was against it. Completely against it. But I am not the head honcho. Once you trade in the badge, you lose a lot of your power. There are gains, of course. There have to be for this kind of shit."

Tyler hoped he had managed to pull the stunned look off his face. Thoughts of Chris at the funeral, sticking up for him during the performance review that he hadn't even bothered to attend, the phone calls always offering support. Chris Wessler was the type of partner who would give you the shirt off his back, wasn't he? If Tyler had to make a list of his friends (it would have been a short list) there would be no doubt Chris Wessler would have been number one, followed up by Annabelle. Hell, he couldn't think of a friend that wasn't also a co-worker now that Emily was dead.

Now his former partner was looking down on him as he lay strapped to a chair. His former partner who was a cog in the death machine that had destroyed his family. It was funny not in a 'ha ha' way but in a 'laugh as the world burns down while it sets your skin ablaze' kind of way. Sometimes laughing was the only thing you could do to cover up the screams.

"Why?" Tyler said.

"Why?" This time Chris did laugh out loud. "Money, of course. More money than I would ever see taking in ten detective salaries! What other answer did you expect? I wish I had some noble cause like you. Deluding yourself into thinking you aren't a bad person, but I don't. You have done horrible things. Lots of horrible things, but in the end you justify it to yourself. I don't. I doubt you are even really a police detective at this point, but I can still say I am that, at least. Funny huh? Believe me, Tyler, I feel bad for you, I really do, but I wouldn't change anything if it meant losing what I have gained. I wouldn't change any of it, even looking at you helpless right now. That's the honest fucking truth which is more than most people usually get."

Tyler had no words. He lowered his eyes to keep his disgust from showing to his former partner. He wanted to kill Chris now as much as Robert Baxter or Will. In a way it was worse because this man had been to his home as a friend. Had eaten dinner with his family and bought presents for his daughter. Had his family died because of who he was partnered with, or was it all just a pathetic coincidence? This sick feeling extended far beyond gut wrenching disgust. It was the stench of a vile disease bloated into a mass of cancerous cells.

"Now Tyler, I wish I could say I am here to say hi, but Baxter and I are business associates. I'm somewhat of an Intel type of guy. I would say the offer was on the table for you too, but we both know you wouldn't take it. You would just try to kill us as soon as you got free." Chris shrugged his shoulder in a motion that said *What can you do friend?*

"Baxter just needs to know how much you know and if you told anyone else. Between you and me, I think he enjoys torturing people and is using the situation as an excuse, but the end result is the same. They thought I might be able to get you to see reason, so here I am. I also have a different deal on the table, if you would just hear me out."

Tyler said nothing and after several minutes Chris cleared his throat in a friendly awkward pause before continuing. "We both know you aren't leaving here, but I can make it quick for you. It's the best I can do under the circumstances. Those circumstances being that you are fucked. The question being how much. Am I right? I know you, Tyler, probably better than you know yourself right now. How many times have you thought about turning those Glocks on yourself? How easy it would be. Well, I am offering you the chance. The chance to see your family without a guilty conscience that you didn't try your best. I'm sure you did, really. Look how far you got, but this is the end of the line. You can either go through torture and God knows what else Baxter has planned, or you can just tell me and the pain is over. Done is done as my mother used to say. So what do you think?"

"No." Tyler's word came out in a croak, but he stared into Chris's eyes until the larger man looked away. Chris seemed almost surprised, which he shouldn't have been. Nothing was logical anymore.

Chris said, "No? That's it? You know I am offering you what you really want. Peace. Just a few answers and then you get to see them again. Isn't that what you want? Like I said, the end result is the same, but you are heading for a world of hurt. Baxter is one crazy son of a bitch, and you know how much I am against criminal labeling." Chris smiled his "friends sharing another joke" smirk. "Do you have a good reason why? Outside of goddamn stubbornness?"

"I have a good reason, Chris. Probably the best reason you will ever hear for not cooperating. I hate. That is my reason. I hate." Tyler strained at his bonds but got nowhere. He said, "You will get nothing from me. It isn't for some grand goal or noble ticket to Heaven. I'm not going there. I just hate. Those are my only words for you, and my suggestion is that you put a bullet in my head right now without the information. Not for my sake, but for yours."

Chris shook his head in sadness. "Well, my friend, you can't say I didn't try. I thought you had more common sense to go along with all that intellect. You could have at least died in peace. For what it's worth, I am sorry. You got the raw end of a shitty deal, and if there was anything I could do to……"

"Enough. Get the fuck on with it." Tyler's words were monotone in nature but his fists ached and he could swear there was blood flowing down his fingers. Chris nodded and said, "No aces over kings this time, Tyler."

He walked out without another word, leaving Tyler to his thoughts. He had no time to focus on an escape plan. Not that there were many options. He wished he could blow up the whole building right now, taking down his family's murderers in an explosion of fire and debris. No prayer for such carnage would be answered except from an insane god. Tyler would pray to anything if it brought him what he wanted. Knowing his partner had been indirectly involved made it worse. Who else on the police force might be expediting the custom heroin distribution? Herrera? Rooks? No, not them. Then again Tyler would have said the same thing about Chris a few minutes ago.

The door had been left open making Baxter's appearance almost silent. Tyler was alone for the first time with the tall man who had issued the death sentence of his family and countless others. His step echoed with bestial grace as he shut the door behind him without seeming to move. Baxter's hands were in the pockets of an ash gray coat that swept down behind him almost like a cloak. His eyes were cold and the smile on his face was one of mockery.

"You didn't disappoint me, Detective Morgan. I knew you wouldn't."

CHAPTER 35
Another Type of Pain

RED WAS THE only color Tyler could see. It throbbed and pulsed with a life of its own as he tried to understand it. It blurred and melded with different hues becoming a shade of scarlet before gradually darkening to a maroon quality. He tried to stay focused on the red as it engulfed him. There was either the color or the pain. Tyler didn't want to focus on the pain. It was all around him and wanted to be let in like an angry stranger. The color was preferable. It moved in front of him and covered all fallacies. Like everything else in his life, it faded away, leaving only the alternative in its wake.

Tyler's vision gradually returned as he realized he had screamed himself hoarse. His voice let out a dull croak, sounding more like a jar being opened than a living person. The pain surrounded his body, gnawing at his mind. It rose like a tide in the ocean, engulfing him in waves like large monoliths. He tried to make it stop; compressing it into a small corner in his body, but it grew until it felt like he had been set on fire. His blurred vision became more focused. He realized he was soaked in either sweat or blood, he couldn't tell which one it was.

In front of him was Baxter stepping back in half-steps, as if to admire his handiwork. The tall man held a chisel in one hand and a claw hammer in the other. Tyler shifted to look up into the murderer's eyes and lowered his head, as he stifled a scream from escaping his chapped lips. The bastard broke one of my ribs! He thought. The pain was almost all consuming to the point that he didn't want to open his eyes and see the damage. How did his ribcage look underneath his shirt? He could feel the broken bits of bone inching their way towards his lungs to puncture the breath out of his body.

Baxter stood like a leviathan over him with a smile that was a mask of pseudo emotion. A true demonic automaton risen up from hellish depths to become a plague on humanity. It was easier to identify him that way rather than what he really was. Just another human being. "I would ask if it hurts, but that's a rhetorical question isn't it?" Baxter said as he dropped the hammer and chisel. They clattered onto the concrete. "Any chance you are willing to talk yet? Give up the ghost?" Tyler stared at Baxter as he nodded. "Yeah, I thought not. Matter of fact, I was hoping not. In the end, it wouldn't have mattered anyway. At least not yet. You're going to suffer. Hopefully worse than your little angels did, but we'll see. It's still early. If you cooperate, things will get a lot easier for you, but I hope you don't for a while. Hang in there, Detective, I am going to go prop my feet up for a moment and ponder man's existence. It sure beats watching television, right? Don't go anywhere, all right?" Baxter waved as he walked out of the room, shutting the door behind him.

Tyler tried testing his bonds, but the rope was still tight and professionally tied. His side throbbed in protest, but he was beyond the point of feeling it right now. His consciousness flickered like a firefly in the middle of a summer night. Tyler fought the waves of pain to stay conscious. It would be so easy to black out right now. He could do it; he knew he could. The problem was unconscious men didn't get justice. All they got to do was wake up in Hell.

Since the rope was not a solution, Tyler focused on the only other piece of his confinement he could. The chair felt old. If he shifted his weight, it creaked and swayed somewhat like a willow tree. The maker clearly had not envisioned a man of Tyler's size and height when it was built. Time had caressed the piece of wood like it did everything else, making it weaker with each year. He believed it could be broken if he used his body correctly. Tyler was grateful for not giving up on his exercise even in the depths of despair. He hadn't done it for any aesthetic purpose, but rather as one of the few activities he could do to help forget about the pain. He had read about people in depression literally killing themselves from excessive exercise. It was just as easy to make your heart give out from running that one more mile as it was from eating that extra slab of steak.

Tyler leaned forward as much as the bonds would allow, gathering strength. He imagined muscles bunching into a coil as his chest cried out in agony. He rode the pain as he gritted his teeth, seeing himself shooting Baxter in the head then turning the gun on Will and Chris. Maybe then himself? It didn't matter. He focused on the anger of Grace never going to prom or dancing with her father as she got married. He focused on the anger that he would never see his daughter grow up to be the beautiful woman she should have been. His mind screamed in silent anger as his body lunged backwards in a movement that propelled him at frightening speed. He slammed into the ground like a semi hitting a brick wall. A new wave of pain rose up and crashed down onto him, taking him into a state of unconsciousness. He might have smiled if he had been given the chance.

CHAPTER 36
Splinters

Tyler woke in a sweat staring at the ceiling. He tried to get up but fought a haze of nausea that argued with the pain for his attention. The room was silent and unforgiving, waiting for him to gather his strength. He sat up after several long minutes and examined his shoulder. The gauze wrap was still holding. It felt secure and tight. Whoever had done the job was certainly more than competent. They didn't want Tyler to get off too easy. Maybe he could return the favor. He didn't even try to examine his ribcage.

He struggled to stand and almost fell. His legs wobbled and shook. The weakness was sickening. He rose, groaning at the pain that had subsided to a dull ache. Tyler finally was able to look around the room. Outside of the chair, there was nothing else except walls and dust. The faint hope for some kind of weapon dimmed. His vision had been limited by the chair, but now he could see the rest of the area. No hope for a phone or, even better, a gun. Outside of the one door that Baxter and Wessler had walked through, there were no other exits or even a window to break. Tyler wondered about all the sounds he had heard behind him when the lights had been off. Where had they come from? Again in the grand scheme of things, it didn't matter.

Tyler reached down to pick up one of the legs of the chair that had broken off. He did this with a hiss escaping between tired teeth. It seemed to take forever. When his fingertips brushed against the leg, he had to stop himself from falling over again. He inched downward and was rewarded with a large wooden weapon. It felt heavy in his hands and came to a jagged point. A club was no good against a gun, but made a great bludgeoning weapon if he could get behind someone. The chance of ambush in the condition he was in was almost laughable.

He shuffled towards the door frame and waited several minutes, listening to the ragged sound of his own breathing. He could hear the building settling around him, but no other sounds reached his ears. Tyler was short on time before someone checked on him, so he had to take a chance. The door was a sliding latch lever with no lock. It was fortuitous in a way, but also depressing to think they had considered him finished so completely. Either that or they were distracted by something else.

He leaned out the doorway and looked into a narrow hallway that broke off to both right and left, curving around the building. He chose to walk towards the right by random choice. One way was as good as the other with what little information there was at this point. His window of time died every moment he wasted.

Tyler stopped at the corner and couldn't help from leaning on the wall. He wondered what kind of stain he was leaving and what the next person who walked by would think. Standing up and moving made him feel a little better as his circulation improved, and the pain abated to a tolerable level. He tried not to look at the wounds and focused on his senses. This time he was rewarded with some faint sounds around the corner. The sounds of friendly voices that were certainly not friendly to him. A brief laugh, that grated on the nerves, echoed as he waited.

What should he do next? The odds were that the voices belonged to people working with Robert Baxter. Calling out would surely kill him faster than he could bleed out. The voices continued to rise in volume until Tyler could start to make out words. Casual conversation about people he didn't know. Just another day at work while a police detective was being tortured in the next room. He didn't recognize the voices.

One of them could be Will. One certainty was, but neither of the voices had that metallic quality that Robert Baxter used so effortlessly.

The talking had stopped completely. He strained to hear anything else. The silence roared in his mind as he waited, trying to control his breathing. A sound of movement came in the distance, growing closer. The sound turned into footsteps as they came down the hallway he couldn't see. Tyler tightened the grip on the chair leg as breathing turned to silent gasps. His hands clutched the weapon in the semblance of a batter's pose. The sound grew closer as shoes struck the concrete floor beneath. He found himself holding his breath. His heart threatened to betray him for taking this course of action, demanding his attention. His focus was sharp as time crawled forward.

A flash of blond hair and moving feet was all he saw before he swung as hard as he could. A soft grunt came out of the man's mouth as wood connected with skin and bone. Tyler caught himself on the wall to keep from stumbling, and his weapon fell to the floor in several large shards. He wasn't dead yet which told him everything he needed to know about the attack. No one sounded the alarm or ran towards him with gunfire. After several long seconds, he looked down at the man on the ground.

The man did have blond hair and was wearing nondescript clothes. Tyler guessed he was around five foot eight and couldn't tell if the man was still breathing. The body lay sprawled out in the narrow hallway as though he had decided to take a nap right there. Tyler had thrown his strength into the swing, but there wasn't a lot left to give. The blond man probably had a concussion rather than more permanent damage.

Tyler's body protested as he lowered himself down to the concrete. He noticed every movement his muscles made and each one had a flare of pain to go along as a price. His fingers found a pulse in the blond haired man's vein though it was faint. Tyler started searching through the man's pockets. He tossed aside the wallet without a second thought. Finding out who or what this man was had become irrelevant. A cell phone was in his front left jean pocket. More importantly, the man had a gun in a holster looped into his pants. Tyler flicked open the black leather and pulled out a Springfield XDM 9mm. A compact and well-made gun known more for accuracy than true firepower, but it was still suitable. He checked and made sure he had the 19 round magazine. There were no extra magazines or bullets. The chamber was loaded, so he had a grand total of twenty bullets for a scenario that might have twenty men. It was better than nothing.

Tyler laid the gun on the concrete floor right next to his foot. He wanted to keep the gun close just in case. In front of him lay a weightier problem which was, of course, the phone. Tyler picked it up and touched the home button. The energy bar read at full, and he had an excellent signal. It was an older model of phone that used fingerprint rather than face unlock so Tyler could open the phone by using the blond man lying in front of him. The phone glowed with a hellish blue light as Tyler used the unconscious man's hand. He knew he did not have time for this. Any second someone else could come down the hallway. The fact that the body was too heavy to drag away was obvious as well.

He needed to decide whether to use the phone or not. One would think the decision would be easy so why was he hesitating? The tiny voice of reason that Tyler had left spoke out from whatever closet he had stuck it in. *Call the police and hide. You can still live through this. You wanted justice? You got it. They will surround this place before Baxter, Chris, and the quiet Mr. Will can leave. The scum will all go to jail for life. Hell, the heroin alone makes them guilty even before your testimony of gunshots and torture. You already have enough blood on your hands, my friend. Find a corner to hide in. Make the call. Wait and live to see another day. It's a win for everybody, right?*

"Wait and live to see another day. It's a win for everybody. A win for everybody." Tyler realized he had uttered the words out loud due to the echo of the hallway. Phone in one hand and gun in the other made it hard to stand, but he clutched them like talismans as he grunted his way to his feet. He waited for his vision to focus as he tried to slow his breathing down again.

The gun was pointed towards the end of the hall as he stared at the phone for one more second before making his fingers dial the tiny buttons. A brief moment later, he was listening to the phone ring. It was time for someone to get a win even though it wouldn't be him.

CHAPTER 37
Trace Evidence

"HELLO?"

The second Tyler heard Annabelle's voice he was grateful for the fact that she always carried her phone, and she always answered it, even for unknown numbers. The slight edge of drowsiness in her voice told him the clock on the phone wasn't lying, no matter how hard it was to believe.

"Uhhhh……HELLO?"

"Annabelle, it's Tyler."

"Tyler, oh my God, where the hell have you been? I've been trying…"

"Annabelle, please just listen right now. There is no time for talking or questions, do you understand? I have literally a minute, and then I won't be speaking anymore. Do you understand?"

"Ok, Tyler." Her voice had changed from concern to professionalism in less than a second. The drowsiness was gone, and she was completely focused. It made what little time he had left all the more impactful. He had made the right choice for his phone call.

"I need you to trace this call. I am going to leave the phone line open as long as I can, but you need to send every available cop here immediately. I don't know where I am. The weather made it hard to figure out my exact location, but the last known address was in a warehouse district, so that should help. I may have been moved since then, and I am inside a building, so the best call is just to use the signal."

"Ok, Tyler I am on it. Just keep talking to me." The noise of scrambling in the background was reassuring, and Tyler smiled in spite of himself. Even in his situation, there was still some humor to be found from Herrera.

"I would run the names Robert Baxter and Will though they are probably aliases. The name Will doesn't help much I know, but run it anyway. I want you to also put out an APB for Chris Wessler too."

"Chris Wessler?! Tyler, are you serious? What kind........."

Tyler interrupted, "There's also......nevermind there's no time. Sorry, Annabelle, I am going to put the phone down now somewhere to keep the line on. Trace the call using the phone number that just called you."

"Tyler, it would have been faster if you had called the station directly. They could almost be done tracing this call already. Why........ Wait, you already know that. Of course, you already know that. What are you doing?"

"Thank you, Annabelle. Thanks for being there for me. It made a huge difference when I tried to go to sleep, knowing I had at least one friend on the force. I don't have the words for the debt I owe you, but if you can do this last favor, you have my gratitude. Please just trace the call and get here as soon as you can."

"Christ, you know what you're doing, don't you? Tyler, Goddamnit! You are buying yourself time, aren't you? Is the CPD your backup plan in case you don't kill them all yourself? Tyler, listen don't do it! You are still a good man. A man with a lot of demons, but a good man. Don't throw it away! You are putting yourself in danger purely for revenge. Don't go after them. Are you hearing me, you bastard?!"

"Take care of yourself. Try not to talk anymore. It will bring attention to the phone." Tyler heard some yelled words for a few seconds as he dropped the phone to his side but then dead silence after that. Yep, a true professional, he thought with another smile. There was no real hiding place for the phone except on Mr. Blond Hair who was the first thing anyone would search if they came by. Being unconscious got people's attention unfortunately. He kept the phone in his hand for now, but focused his line of sight down the hall with the gun outstretched in front of him.

He shuffled forward feeling stronger in spite of himself. Maybe it was the sense of euphoria that people sometimes got before death? Tyler wasn't going to complain if it allowed the pain to recede enough so that he could accurately pull the trigger on his newly acquired weapon. The hallway curved around leading to a metal door with a small glass window. Tyler leaned down to look through. Even though the glass was old and dirty, it was clear that where he had just come from was the office area of a large warehouse. It was probably the same one he had been in before, but he wasn't sure yet. A rust encrusted pole partially obscured the room overriding any aesthetic choice the architect might have envisioned. The large area had several racks that looked empty and stretched onward with no end in sight.

Tyler leaned his shoulder into the door pushing open the handle with a creak that sounded like a gunshot. He crept forward holding the gun out in front of him, so that it poked through the doorframe, giving him a shield for his body in case he had to pull the trigger. Nothing moved or made any noise outside of himself. It was eerily quiet for such a large room. The door eased to a click behind him, and he went to the left keeping the back wall behind him for cover.

There were a multitude of crates lying on the floor in unorganized piles. It was as though when they had closed the warehouse down, the workers had thrown everything down in disgust. He took several more steps away from the door before selecting one of the crates as the hiding place for the phone. He checked the small screen one last time. The energy bars on the phone were still on full and the signal was good. The ticking minute counter told him the call was still live. Keeping the phone active should help with GPS and wireless detection.

The crouch down hurt like hell, but it was worth it. Tyler put the phone under the right side of the crate until it was invisible. No one would be able to see it unless they were lying on the floor. At this point, he probably needed only ten minutes for Herrera to get the phone's signal location once she had communicated with CPD. It didn't really matter for him personally, but it was the only backup plan he had. Twenty bullets and the CPD on their way was more than he could have dreamed of thirty minutes ago.

After taking a long minute to stand up again, Tyler walked forward, reaching the edge of the wall. He moved sideways keeping the buffer next to him, again trying to block as much space as possible. He took occasional glances behind as he moved. That was when he noticed the drops of blood on the floor. It was not a consistent trail, but even the most inexperienced of trackers would have no trouble finding which way he had gone. His body was just too fucking tired to care.

He could feel the wall shift and tremor as a gust of wind pushed with all its might outside, currying for favor of entrance. The winter storm seemed to have grown, but inside he felt a little calmer. A little more at peace when he held a gun in his hand and knew what had to be done. There was no more doubt as to the who or why. No celestial wonder of predetermined fate or the odd way death spared him, but had punished those he cherished most. There was nothing right now but the act of breath and the inner desire of pressing forward.

Tyler had reached the point where he could see the far wall of the warehouse room and the outline of a human shape. He trained the barrel of the 9mm on the figure that grew clearer by the second. It was a man with his back turned toward Tyler. The wind masked Tyler's shuffle forward as the building shook under its frantic assault. He had not yet been heard, so his body closed the distance as quickly as it could. The guard could have been the one he had heard earlier talking with Mr. Blond or someone else entirely. The rifle slung over one shoulder made the man's alignment clear as Tyler drew closer.

The wind died without a hint of protest, and Tyler stopped. His gun was trained on his captor's back, but it felt heavy now after holding the weapon outstretched for an extended period of time. The weight still felt good and he was surprised how steady the barrel was. He had been trained to only keep his finger inside the guard when ready to shoot and right now the trigger was half depressed. The man would have no chance if he tried to raise his rifle or turn suddenly. Tyler waited with his breath held. It seemed he was doing a lot of that even though he needed oxygen now more than ever.

The wind picked up again, and he dared a little closer. He could now see the rifle was an M27 automatic rifle which was favored by the Marine Corps. It was a deadly weapon to have in the hands of someone Baxter employed. The man himself was nondescript except for a scar on his ear. Brown hair and average height and weight from what he could tell. He was smoking a cigarette of some kind, and Tyler was close enough to see the thin wisps of smoke dissipate into the air above. The distance closed to twenty feet and he had pushed his luck about as far as he could. The guard still had not yet turned around, as though determined to ignore any other presence.

The sights of the gun aligned with the man's back, making it a life or death situation with just the pull of a trigger. Did this man have anything to do with his family's death? Obviously he was involved in the heroin business somehow, but was that enough of a reason? Tyler felt a flush in his face that had nothing to do with his blood loss. He lowered the gun a fraction of an inch and spoke.

"Hey motherfucker. Turn around slowly."

CHAPTER 38
Seth Miller

THE MAN'S BACK stiffened in recognition that he had been caught with his attention lax. His ass hanging in the wind, figuratively speaking. The inevitable turn was accompanied by slumped shoulders, dejected in every way. His hands were raised high in the air as the automatic rifle dropped to his side by some sort of custom strap attachment. It made Tyler want to punch the guard in the face. The constant wave of anger and pain made his teeth grind together until he thought he could taste blood.

"You're not supposed to be...."

"What I am supposed to be doesn't really matter. Not at this point." Tyler said, "What matters is who are you supposed to be?"

"Seth Miller." The two word answer was accompanied by a look implying that the name should answer everything. Tyler wondered if Seth was high on something. Most illegal drug organizations were notoriously strict on such matters, but when you dealt with junkies on a regular basis, certain expectations couldn't always be met.

"Well, Seth Miller, I want you to unclip the strap that is holding that rifle to your shoulder and let it fall to the floor. Then I want you to kick said rifle over to the crate on your left. I am also going to need your phone. Once you've done that, walk five steps toward me slowly. Does that all make sense?" Seth nodded and reached to unclip the automatic rifle. It fell to the floor with a clatter that made the man cringe, but he managed to move it under the crate within three kicks. The cell phone came next which the smaller man bent over and slid it across the floor. Tyler bent over slowly before putting it in his pocket. Seth then stepped forward as though he were performing a minuet.

"How many more of you are there?"

"You're dead, you know that, you stupid asshole. You are fucked."

"I'm also the man with the gun aimed at your face." Tyler motioned with his hand indicating the barrel. "How many more?"

Tyler continued to stare at him until the man dropped his eyes. Seth seemed to count in his head before saying "At least five, though it is probably more. I don't fucking know. I don't keep count. I got put here just to look out for the building. That is what I do. I'm here to keep people safe, that's all."

"Sure, with an M27 and crates of heroin. You are a fucking traffic guard alright. Makes sense to me. Next question. Where's Baxter?"

"Who?"

"Baxter. Your boss. The man who tortured me and put me in a mood for shooting people. Especially shooting people who forget the fucking answers to simple questions."

Seth's eyes widened to the size of soup bowls. "I don't know, I have no fucking idea! I saw him maybe two hours ago, but I haven't seen him since! You gotta believe me." The voice had taken on a whine that made Tyler cringe in spite of himself. "He doesn't talk to me much. I don't really deal with the drugs at all, really."

"What do you deal with?"

"Security. Safety. Anything other than the drugs, pretty much."

"Yeah, you said that already. Ok, let's go." Tyler made a move along motion with his gun that allowed him to drop it slightly. Holding up the weight of a 32oz gun continually had become a labor of will.

"Go? Go where?" Seth's voice became higher pitched, and he seemed to be hyperventilating at this point. "You going to take me somewhere and shoot me? You can't do that. You're not going to do that, right?"

"Not right now I'm not." Tyler's eyes glared into Seth's. "I'm not going to shoot you as long as you do what I tell you. I need to put you somewhere you can't do any harm or alarm anyone until this is all over. Look, I believe you. You don't know where your boss is, but I can't just leave you here. Unless you want me to put a bullet in you, it's in your best interest to tell me where we should go."

"How about the weapons area? That room is a fucking vault. It's really close to here too. I could take out all the ammo and shit."

Tyler smiled in spite of himself. Yes, Seth Miller was definitely on something in order to suggest having himself locked in an armory, as though that would be an ideal place to store a prisoner. The irony of the request might not have been humorous a few painful, shuffling steps back, but right now it was downright hilarious. It took all of Tyler's control to smother the hysterical laughter bubbling inside. Once he started down that path, he might as well give his gun to Seth Miller and let his fate be finished.

Seth noticed Tyler's look and held up his hands. He said, "No, seriously. The guns would be worthless without the bullets right? I could move that and all the other stuff and then you have a prison room. It wouldn't take long. What am I going to do with an AK without any ammo for it? Crowbar my way out of there?"

Tyler realized he must have grimaced because Seth added. "Or we can do whatever. You are the man with the gun and not one to be fucked with. I get it. I would just give up now, but it's your call."

"No, I like your suggestion Seth." Tyler said his mind racing. "Let's go to the weapons area. You walk in front of me." Tyler held up the Springfield XDM 9mm again. "Stay ahead of me by two steps. If you move any faster than a slow crawl, or if you make any sudden movements I am going to assume you have turned hostile. Do you understand the term hostile, Seth?"

"Yeah, yeah, sure." Seth nodded with his whole body, eager to please. It made Tyler's stomach turn.

"Good. I don't want to shoot you, but I won't hesitate if anything goes wrong. If it goes wrong for me, it goes wrong for you." Tyler made another waving motion with the gun. "Now I am going to search you and then we get moving. All right?"

Seth sidestepped around the crates until he was in front of Tyler, holding his arms out in a compliant manner. He turned so his back was facing the former detective. Tyler reached around and checked his captive's pockets. He found keys which went in his pocket and a wallet that went back in Seth's. The gun had begun to get slippery in Tyler's hand. He couldn't help but lower it since no one was watching him.

The M27 was still there on the ground, but he wasn't familiar with it and the Springfield XDM 9mm was far lighter. He found himself breathing hard, as though he had just run the twenty-sixth mile of the Chicago marathon. His heart was screaming to him for help. It was too bad he didn't have a good answer.

They made their way weaving through the warehouse like drunkards as Tyler thought about what Seth had said. The man had wanted to move out all of the ammunition as well as "the other stuff". Three simple words that had changed his mind about everything in his immediate future. The other stuff. What type of stuff exactly could that be? It was certainly food for thought.

CHAPTER 39
Armory

THE WEAPONS AREA would never really be classified as a vault, but it stood out as a large steel cage about twelve feet tall by thirty feet wide. A testament of lithe strength and economical construction within the decay of the forgotten warehouse. Tyler guessed that in the glory days of business it was possibly used as a controlled substance storage area or a separated space for transport materials. He could see why Seth had thought of it immediately, it resembled an independent prison cell more than anything else.

They were facing the side of the cage and had to walk around to the front where the door was slightly ajar. A large Krieg lock hung on one of the bars. It was open with the key still inserted. It was obvious Baxter didn't need the cage to be locked when he was around. Seth continued forward until he was standing a few feet in front of the door as though waiting for permission to enter. Actually he probably is, Tyler thought, as he stopped seven feet back and began to study the inner space of the cage.

The far wall had racks set up with steel clamps hooked into the bars. Each space held some sort of assault or automatic rifle with the barrel pointing up towards the ceiling. He saw AK-47s, AR-15s, M27s, among others. There was a table in the center of the area with what looked like several Uzis and an assortment of handguns. Tyler nudged Seth closer, and they took a few steps before standing outside the door.

Tyler said, "Any sudden movements, and I will pull the trigger. You won't have a chance, and that is a bad situation for both of us. Put your hands behind your back and walk through the door. Walk over to the left, and then turn so your back faces the cage bars. Do it slowly." Seth reached behind his back and clamped his hands together. They walked forward almost in unison as though their time together had made them conspirators. Tyler blinked away a bead of sweat as he watched Seth's arms. Walking a criminal into a room with a large arsenal was intuitively a terrible idea in every way. There just wasn't any other option at the moment.

Seth did exactly as he was asked and walked toward the left side of the cage which was bare compared to the rest of the area. He reached the bars and turned toward Tyler, the scuffle of boots making it seem like they were walking on gravel rather than cold concrete. The rotation finished with Seth staring death at Tyler. He found himself wanting to laugh in spite of it all. All of it was goddamn absurd.

"Not too late to reconsider, asshole." Seth said, "We can forget this whole fucking thing. Your time's about up. Give me the gun, and let's go back to your room. I promise I will put in a good word for you. Who knows, maybe Baxter will let you go. I can't promise anything, but stranger shit has happened, right?"

"You don't know your boss very well. Be quiet and reach behind you with both hands." Tyler said, "Grab the bars and slowly slide down towards the floor. When you reach the floor, cross your legs and don't make another sound." Seth shrugged in a gesture of a man holding the winning hand. Tyler waited until Seth was positioned so he couldn't make any detrimental movements and then looked around the cage again.

The central table held a variety of handguns though, regrettably, no knives. There were several crates in the cage secured with rope. That definitely helped. Tyler had hoped for an easy way of securing his prisoner. He did see a pair of trimming shears lying on a crate that might work. There was also a piece of knotting that looked like something from a hangman's collection. They were probably leftovers from the binding. Tyler saw some schematics of what he assumed were the warehouse. They had been thrown down on the table as though the owner wanted to forget about them. Satisfied he wasn't missing anything of importance, Tyler looked around the rest of the cage and had to stifle a whistle from coming out.

The crates were stacked almost five feet high and each one had been labeled according to the contents. "Uzi ammo" one of the lower crates read, and he could see enough in between the boards to verify it was true. Apparently, once the cargo had reached the warehouse Baxter had no real fear of it being confiscated. Other labels read like a gun collector's Christmas list. "AK ammo" "Colt Python rounds" and Tyler's favorite "Misc. Ammo". Normally he would have pried open every one of these for documenting evidence, but now all that he was doing was trying to keep his jaw from dropping.

Tyler's ragged breath began to quicken as he began to panic. He could barely hold the Springfield XDM 9mm he had, let alone arm himself with the variety of weapons lying around him like discarded toys. The crate names swirled by faster as his mind raced, searching for the one thing he had come for. Tyler had hoped to see the disassembled components of a rocket launcher or grenades. The type of item that only ex-military, terrorist, or in this case, well-funded criminal groups carried. The AKs were nice, but they were more run of the mill than what he had been hoping for.

The most insane part of this whole situation was how badly Tyler wanted a drink right now. Scotch, vodka, or rum, it didn't matter. His lips felt like sandpaper. He would be tempted to drop his gun if there were a glass and some hard alcohol in front of him. The torture had kept his mind off of it, but Tyler realized he hadn't had a drink in potentially days. Certainly the longest span of time since his family had died. One shot would have made a world of difference right now. His hand involuntarily spasmed.

Tyler knew time was about up when his vision began to blur at the edges. Any peripheral sight he used to possess was gone, giving him a tunnel that mirrored his mindset. He opened his mouth to utter the final phrase of departure to Seth when he found the crate he had been looking for. It was on top of one of the stacks arching a little lower than most of the others. Tyler walked over to the crate in a movement born more of will than actual energy.

"Hey, jackass, what are you doing?" Seth said the words with a hint of cockiness as Tyler's vision faded. He ignored the captive as his hand touched the top of the crate. It had been sealed shut. He rested his hand on the corner of the wooden planks and said, "Change of plans. Seth, get up and help me get this crate open. Be careful with the rope, we are going to need that too."

"Crazy asshole." The words meant nothing to Tyler as he felt a smile begin to appear on his lips. His fingers traced the three letters marked on the side of the crate that he needed. Tyler had traced the letters three times before Seth stood up. Each letter meant nothing, but combined their meaning was powerful and talismanic like an arcane rune. Seth continued his muttering as Tyler's hand traced the letters again and again. P. B. X.

CHAPTER 40
P. B. X.

The acronym P.B.X. stood for plastic bonded explosive more commonly known as C-4. The chemical composition consisted of everything from Polyisobutylene to everyday common motor oil. C-4 has been in regular use for decades due to its malleable form and the explosive power it contains for a relatively small quantity. A little over a pound of C-4 could destroy a car or truck with little problem. You could mold the C-4 into almost any shape desired, allowing control over the direction of the explosion. C-4 was also known to be especially stable for an explosive.

Usually military divisions kept a tight rein over explosives like this, but if you had enough money and connections there were ways of getting such materials. There was little doubt that Baxter had enough of both to make acquiring something like this a simple task. He shook his head in wonderment of having drug dealers with funding and weaponry to rival guerilla warfare tactical units.

Seth did most of the prying of the crate using a board of another box while Tyler kept an eye on him. The lid came off with a snap of splinters. Before Seth could do anything further, Tyler motioned with his gun for him to step back. He looked into the crate to find what made this entire trip worthwhile. He guessed there was over ten pounds lying in a cushion of straw. It was more than enough for his purposes. Tyler reached out and touched the C-4 with his hand to make sure it was real. The explosive was surprisingly cool to the touch and felt more like putty than any kind of dangerous weapon. He was sure that if he looked closely where his finger had touched, he would see a passable print. His fingers involuntarily rubbed together trying to get the feel off. A fresh crime scene complete with his own signature.

Tyler looked at several of the boxes near the C-4 and found one labeled DET which he knew was the other component he needed. He motioned for Seth to open this crate as well. The lid came off much faster than the first. Tyler wasn't sure if it was rage or frustration that fueled Seth's movements, but he didn't care. When it was done, Seth moved back without even being told to. "Ok, Seth." Tyler said, "Walk over to the crates on your left, and remove the rope from two of the stacks."

"Yeah, how am I supposed to get the rope off? With my teeth?"

"If I let you keep them, I might suggest it." Tyler said, "But it would probably be easier to use the shears on the crate over there." Seth snarled as he moved towards the box but said nothing further. Tyler made sure he kept his distance with the gun leveled as Seth picked up the shears, looking at him out of the corner of his eye. It looked as though Seth was trying to gauge if he could reach Tyler and stab him before the gun would fire. Tyler again wanted to smile but motioned for Seth to begin. Seth tried once and the shears seemed to bounce away from the tough cord. Seth looked at Tyler, but he again motioned the captive to continue, well aware that every second they were undiscovered was more valuable than blood.

After what seemed like hours, Seth had cut off two long sections of rope that would more than serve his purposes. "Great. Now I need you to lay down face first on the floor right where you are. Press your heels against the bars of the cage and put your hands over your head. I am going to tie a knot in this rope which is going to require both hands. Just keep in mind the gun is going to be right next to my hand. Before you could even get up, I would have two bullets tearing through your skull, so no movement on your part would be a good idea."

"Fuck you. You think you can even stand again?"

"Let's find out. Even if you are right, that just makes me all the more desperate, right?" Tyler said, "Lay. Down."

Seth stared at him for several more seconds before lying down on the floor. Tyler walked around the entrance frame keeping the gun trained on the prone man. He shuffled around Seth and lowered his body to the ground. Tyler tried not to gasp in pain as he sat down, but it came out involuntarily. Seth's head whipped around like a snake sensing prey. Showing weakness was not something he could afford. A gun nudge to the back reminded them both of the situation.

The strand of rope was knotted into what was affectionately known as the hangman's noose. Once he had finished the knot, Tyler began to stand up, feeling needles in every part of his body. A wave of nausea hit him as he finished the movement and shut his eyes. He willed himself not to vomit. It was much worse than the pain. Would any blood come up or just the meager contents of his stomach? He didn't want to find out and crushed his eyelids shut. The darkness was somewhat soothing as he took deep breaths. The nausea disappeared as quickly as it had arrived, and his eyes opened once again.

"Seth, I am going to drop a rope over your head now." Tyler said, "It is a noose that is going to tighten if you fight in any way. I don't think you want rope burns and a crushed windpipe, so I suggest you don't struggle ok?"

It was disconcerting that Seth didn't say anything, not even a casual 'Fuck you', but stayed on the ground with his shoulders slumped. Tyler dropped the noose over his neck and tightened it without any resistance. The rope looked beige on the very pale skin of his captor. He again felt a twinge of….something as he asked Seth to stand up. Were these the actions of a police detective? A human being who took prisoners and planned on using C-4 sounded more like the type of person he would have taken down. It sounded more like the actions of a criminal or a terrorist than an advocate of the law.

Tyler opened the box labeled DET and saw a feast of destruction. Multiple blasting caps, two rings of det cord, and several detonators. He had never been part of a bomb squad, but these were simple enough to hook up. They were probably intended for demolition usage rather than military operations. There was no real formal casing on the C-4, just the brilliant white color in the shape of several bricks. The det cord also did not appear to have the same labeling that would be used for military purposes though he was unsure about that component. It didn't matter as long as they worked.

Tyler grabbed both the blasting caps and detonators. He slung the det cord around his shoulder. The equipment was surprisingly light, but even so it was still a burden. There was no way that he could hang onto the rope and his gun while carrying a crate of C-4, even uninjured. "Seth, get up." Tyler said, "I need you to pick up this crate over by me and carry it out of the cage."

Seth stood up, taking several seconds before turning around to face Tyler. He walked over without a word of protest. His eyes widened when he saw which crate Tyler wanted him to carry. "The C-4? You want me to take the C-4? Fuck no. I am done playing this game, asshole. You are going to kill us both. You are a crazy motherfucker I will give you that, but I'm not doing it. Fuck you and hell no."

Tyler had been through numerous police interrogations and you could always tell what was referred to as the point of no return. In this context, the criminal, victim, or informant was shut down emotionally on a specific line of questioning. Usually you could tell by repetition of phrases, vocal tone, or body language which all would synthesize to indicate a dead end. The detective would then have to alter his or her approach to try to reach the information through another line of inquiry, but Tyler just didn't have the time. Also this was a little more extreme than trying to identify a thief or murder suspect. Unfortunately with the state he was in, there wasn't any other option to get the C-4 out without Seth's help. He was going to have to take a risk to make this work. Improvisation had always been a strong suit of Tyler's.

"Step back, Seth." Tyler said and when Seth stared at him, he yanked on the rope making the man backpedal away from the C-4.

Seth smiled showing he knew he had some leverage in the situation. The smug look had the shine of freshly laid tar. Tyler walked over to the crate and looped the rope around his wrist freeing up his hand. The lid to the C-4 crate weighed less than a pillow as he pulled it off of the crate, placing it on top of another. The look on Seth's face drooped as Tyler pointed his gun at the exposed white bricks.

"I really like the saying 'you always have a choice'. It has a nice ring to it doesn't it?" Tyler said, "It lets us pretend that we are in control of our lives. Lets us pretend that we aren't the puppets but the puppet masters. Are you a puppet master, Seth? I bet you think you are. Well, I guess we are going to find out. This is your chance to make a decision for both of us. You can either agree to pick up that top crate of C-4 and carry it out of here, or I will pull the trigger, potentially blowing us both up."

"Bullshit. What have you got to gain from dying right now?" Seth snarled, "You got some kind of plan. I don't buy you will kill yourself for nothing."

"If you don't help me, what have I got to lose? You see what kind of condition I am in." Tyler said gesturing to his body with the gun. Even that movement had a momentary pain associated with it. He was in bad shape. "I need you to carry the C-4 or I might as well blow us both up right now. Nothing lost and nothing gained. Unless of course, you want to live longer. Me? I can go right now if need be."

Seth shook his head. "Sorry, I still call bullshit. You can try to convince me you came in here with your vigilante attitude all you want. Deep down I still don't think you are one of the bad guys, and good guys don't blow themselves up for no reason. Maybe now is the time we sit down and figure out how to get you back to being a prisoner without getting killed, eh?"

Seth's eyes reflected the grin on his face as he stared at Tyler, silently daring him to do something. Tyler took the Springfield XDM 9mm and again pointed it at the C-4 crate, his eyes never leaving Seth's. Seth's grin wavered but he shook his head. He said, "No way mother-fucker. You ain't got the bal...."

The rest of his words were drowned out as Tyler pulled the trigger. The roar of several bullets tearing into the explosive crate echoed in the confined space. Seth screamed as he held tied hands in front of his body to ward off the incoming explosion. Tyler watched as the other man fell into a heap on the floor. The fetal position wasn't flattering for anyone. Seth lay there for several seconds shaking until he opened his eyes in small slits.

"Maybe the C-4s faulty? Or maybe we should try again?" Tyler said and again aimed the gun at the explosives. "Want to try your luck a second time, or are you going to pick up the goddamned crate?" He continued to stare at Seth who looked away, nodding his head more times than was necessary. The urge to sigh in relief weighed on Tyler, but he suppressed the breath as Seth put his arms underneath the crate and picked it up.

"Leave the lid on the floor. We don't need it." Tyler said and the cheap wood clattered to the ground. Seth carried the small crate out of the cage with Tyler right behind him. There was no place for displays of weakness in front of anyone in this building.

One of the rules Tyler had learned about C-4 early on was just how stable of an explosive it really was. You could drop it off of a building and nothing would happen other than having a blob of flattened putty on the sidewalk. Even a gunshot or setting the explosive on fire would have little effect without the proper combination of heat and some sort of shockwave. There were supposedly cases of people using it to cook. A detonation tool or some kind of blasting cap was required to initiate the explosion within the composition.

This knowledge had probably just saved him from being in a dangerous situation, though the cost was high. The gunshots he had just created were loud, and if there was anyone else nearby, they would have heard the noise. The narrow timeframe of avoiding detection had just sharpened to a razorblade right on his carotid artery. Each footstep was a life wager, though right now he just felt disgusted with it all.

They walked out of the cage and into the warehouse where Seth paused with indecision. "Just keep walking straight unless I say otherwise." Tyler said. "We will get to where we need to be soon enough." He looked upward as they walked, looking for the exact place that he wanted. Their movements were silent except for the exhalation of breath from both terrified men.

A few minutes later, he spotted the structure he was looking for. Tyler whispered a prayer of thanks. The steel girder beam was one of the central supports within this section of the warehouse. It stretched all the way to the domed ceiling as though it wanted to crash through to the cold sky above. Tyler could wrap his arm around most of the beam, but the durability of the metal was unquestionable. There were many of these beams stationed throughout the area. This one had the advantage of being the closest. Tyler yanked back on the rope which caused Seth to lurch backwards. He turned and looked back with a glare.

"Put the crate down next to the girder and step back. Lay down ten feet over to your left like you were before." Tyler said, "Don't move and don't say anything." It would have been ideal to have Seth complete this part of his pseudo-plan, but the arguing would cost more time. Tyler could handle the setup more efficiently anyway. He stepped over to the lidless crate while still facing his silent captive. Seth's new tactic of complacence was more unnerving than the previous threats of torture and death.

Tyler jammed the Springfield XDM 9mm into the side of his pants, making the gun accessible if needed. He reached down into the crate and pulled out two handfuls of the cool plastic, feeling like a potter. The C-4's putty-like consistency made applying it to the support beam simple as he molded the substance to the middle portion of the beam. Soon there was a ring around most of the beam. It grew thick as he reached for more until all of the C-4 had been used and the crate was empty.

Tyler stepped five feet back and looked at his work. The explosive was slightly uneven, but it covered the segment in a ring that touched all sides of the beam. It would be more than sufficient. The blasting caps slid into the C-4 like butter. Tyler put all of them into his circle. It was overkill, but this was an overkill type of situation that brooked no room for malfunction or error.

Tyler rubbed his hands on his legs as he turned to Seth and said, "Ok, let's go back to the cage. Stand up. We have to move." Seth's shoulders began to shake and for several seconds Tyler thought he was crying, but a bark erupted from Seth as he raised his head back laughing. "Ssss….Stupid." He said, "Ssssssoooo fucking stupid." Seth continued to laugh until Tyler had heard enough and jerked on the rope, which cut off the sound for a second.

"On your feet! Let's go."

Seth struggled to stand, still chuckling as tears streamed down his face. *I am not the only crazy one here*, Tyler thought. He would have smiled but even that was becoming more difficult. His face felt like a frozen rictus of pain, and he wondered if there was blood on it.

The walk back to the cage was faster since he knew the way and had Seth leading, still trying to control his laughter. They did not encounter anyone, and Tyler could feel his luck stretched to the point of ripping to tatters. It felt like he had escaped hours ago, but in reality it had probably been forty-five minutes. A military installation would have noticed the loss, but taking out Mr. Blonde and capturing Tyler's hysterical assistant meant that there was probably limited coverage. Still there was no way this could go on for much longer.

Seth walked into the cage and without a word sat back down on the floor, a mass of muscle, rope, and laughter. "Move over here by the door." Tyler said pointing right next to the metal hinge. "Turn around, sit with your back to the cage, and grab the bars." Tyler took two steps back so that he was out of Seth's sight and outside the cage itself.

A surge of pain rose through him again as he took off the noose from around Seth's neck. Tyler took one strand of rope and began to tie a knot around Seth's hands in a pattern that looked like a suture. The knot was well out of reach with the cinch between the wrists. He felt Seth go rigid, but there was no resistance or any other movements. He could tell Seth was wincing as the knot went tight. It would cut off circulation which might buy Tyler a few seconds should there be any Houdini acts.

Seth's mocking laughter had died down enough for him to speak.

"Piece of advice, motherfucker. When you want to blow something up, make sure you have enough explosive to blow something up." He said, "You can't destroy one support beam and bring down an entire warehouse."

"Who said anything about bringing down the entire warehouse?" Tyler smiled back at his captive's back and the smirking prisoner stiffened. "No, I was looking for something else entirely. Something a lot more simplistic." He reached into his pocket and pulled out the forgotten cell phone as he walked back into the cage to face Seth. He gestured to his captive to tell him the unlock code. Tyler had been very lucky on the other phone he had acquired. The battery showed a full bar as he opened the phone and started looking for an address book. There was none, but the dialed calls section showed him several different numbers to choose from.

"Which of these numbers calls Baxter?" Tyler said holding the phone for Seth to look at the list.

"None of them." Seth said, "I have never called the guy. Hell, I have only seen him a few times."

"Which of these numbers calls Will?" Tyler said.

"None of them again, fucker." Seth said but there was hesitation for a fraction of a second. Tyler knew he had a winner. He smiled. "Sure. Makes sense to me. We should play cards sometime. I think I could make some money. Let's just take a look."

Glancing at the list, there were only a handful of numbers to choose from. The phone looked like a pay per minute cell that had become popular for being a disposable source of communication. A lot of drug deals occurred through this type of device because it could be discarded when no longer needed. Nothing to easily trace and no evidence to carry around with you. One number had been dialed frequently and had been used this morning.

Tyler selected the number from the dial log and hit call. Seth's head slumped down towards the floor while Tyler waited for the other line to ring. It felt good to call someone with his captors' phone in one hand and a remote detonator in the other. It felt more than good. For the first time in over half a year, Tyler felt completely alive again. He wanted to laugh right then, but the other party answered the phone. Tyler began to speak. There was a lot to discuss.

CHAPTER 41
Baxter's Call

WILL THOMPSON HAD been around Baxter longer than anyone else to his knowledge, and yet he still didn't understand the man in the slightest. Baxter was ruthless in his efficiency and colder than the winter storm that seemed to be screaming right outside their walls, but lately it seemed even more so. Baxter's mood had gotten to a point where Will didn't want to say a word or make any sounds that would bring that icy glare to stab his eyes. The entire chain of their supply wove up to Will before reaching Baxter, and everyone seemed perfectly fine with that. Baxter had become a bogeyman that was used to frighten the little pimps and users more than just a man who sold heroin. He had grown stronger as they had lengthened their supply chain throughout the city. It was ridiculous when you thought about it by yourself, but when you were with the man, it made complete sense. What a fucked up world.

Will watched as Baxter sat upright in an oak chair, staring off into whatever hell he thought about. He looked like a machine waiting to be turned on. Will wished he had something in front of him to occupy his mind, as he inspected his gun for the tenth time this hour. He checked the sight and magazine before letting it rest at his side. He had no idea how long they had been sitting there, but they were waiting to get a phone call. He found himself mentally screaming at the phone to end the silence. Something needed to happen. Anything was better than sitting here with his boss.

Will wondered for about the hundredth time what drove a man like Baxter to do the things he did. The man was highly intelligent and money was probably no longer a concern for him. Why not retire to an island somewhere in the Pacific and live out your days drinking margaritas and getting blowjobs from expensive whores? Will wished he had enough money for things like that.

Deep down Will knew it wasn't money that kept Baxter going. Not in the slightest. Men like Baxter were a rare breed. They were the type that lived off of fear, power, pain, and anger. They would burn their mothers alive in a boarded up building just to listen to the screams. They were the ones who wore smiles and dead eyes on their faces while carrying an ax in their hands, ready to chop off heads just to see the blood soar. The type you didn't want to ever fuck with. Not if you wanted to live longer than five minutes anyway.

Will noticed Baxter was looking at him as though he was reading his thoughts. The former blank look had become a furnace. Will wished the phone would ring this very second. Ring, damnit ring.

"What's on your mind, Will?" Baxter said, "You look like you're deep in thought."

"Nothing, just wishing we could get this over with." Will replied, "The bastard should have called by now."

"Patience," Baxter said, "We have the product that they want and enough supply to keep everyone happy. It is a win-win situation. We just have to wait a little while, that is all. They will come around."

"I know, Baxter, but we are asking for a lot of fucking money here. The street value isn't going to……"

Baxter held up one hand, not saying a word. Will found himself silently cursing for the instant obedience. Baxter lowered his hand back into his lap and seemed to shut down as they continued to wait. The machine had come alive for a moment but now was back in suspended animation. The only sounds were from the building in the constant struggle to get settled on its foundation. Will would swear it was haunted, if he didn't have worse things to worry about than ghosts and dark specters. He would kill to hear even the monotonous click of a clock as it tracked the hours until mankind died. It was an apocalyptic and depressing thought but far better than boredom. Boredom had its own set of madness where the mind wandered into all kinds of insane ponderings.

Will jumped as the phone erupted in a jittery movement. It danced the frantic jig of most annoying, vibrating phones as Will scrambled to answer it. "Yeah," Will said into the phone, amazed at how calm his voice could sound when he needed it. Baxter's eyes were resting on him as he listened to the phone. The jabbering voice on the other end of the city told him the information he had waited to hear. "Ok," he said and Baxter nodded his head as though his point had been made. In a way it had, though Will didn't want to admit it. That was as much defiance as he could muster. He hit end on the phone without saying anything further and turned to Baxter.

"They agreed to your terms and the price. We can meet them first thing tomorrow and make the transfer."

"Of course they did." Baxter said, "It is a large amount of a product in high demand right now. Why wouldn't they? The next thing we need to figure out is where to next."

"Where to next?" Will knew his face was balled into that blank look he hated when he didn't understand Baxter.

"We need to think about expansion. This deal gives us enough money to leave and move on to a new area. New York. LA. Hell, Detroit could work too. Chicago was a good starting point, but there gets to be a time when there are too many ghosts. Too many loose ends to simply tie up with a bullet or a knife. Eventually you either have to become a nomad or die. Get what I am saying?"

"But I grew up in Chicago," Will said as his mind whirled. He realized this was the first time he had vocalized any rebellion against Baxter. It would have scared him at any other moment, but right now he didn't even have time to give it a second thought. He found himself staring at the concrete beneath his feet. He could almost hear the smile in Baxter's voice.

"You grew up in Chicago, and then you became one of the heads of a supply chain for a new type of heroin." The words were with as much sympathy as Will supposed Baxter could give. It still seemed insincere as hell. "What did you think was going to happen? We would continue doing this here until we die? Those who live by the sword, Will. Those who live by the fucking sword. Right now, we need to sell the rest of our product and move on to greener pastures. I had hoped to make things last a little longer, but between our fire sale and having ex-police vigilantes tracking us down, I can see we are too exposed here. Best to burn our bridges and make way towards a new Gomorrah. I've already got Wessler looking for some new contacts that might be sympathetic to our cause or at least our money. It won't be too hard to add on to our network until we can live in a new world. Now what do you say?"

Will slumped forward. Just another puppet with his strings slashed through. He knew Baxter was right on some base level. The cop they had tied up scared him almost as much as Baxter. Those angry eyes that glared at him through the pain, not even flinching. It was enough to make a man shit himself. The torture hadn't gotten them anywhere either, though Will doubted Baxter cared. Whether or not someone else knew where they were was inconsequential. It was more the fact that someone "would" eventually know where they were. In the end Baxter was right, but had Will also become a liability?

"What about me?" Will asked looking Baxter in the eyes. He was proud and stunned by his bold move. "What about my future? Am I just here for the final move out to wherever, and then you dump my body in a trash compactor? Maybe a goddamn incinerator?"

Baxter arched his head back and laughed. It echoed uncomfortably through the open space as Will waited for the sound to stop. Boredom looked kind of good right now actually. Baxter raised his arms as though he were a theologian greeting his favorite student to discuss a new revelation. "Will, if I wanted you dead, you would be halfway to Hell right now. No, I am taking two things from this city with me, and those are the money and you. No romantic implications behind that statement, I hope."

"Why?" Will asked.

"Because you understand exactly who I am. Do you know how rare that is? Most of the people we deal with will stab their own mother in the tits to make a dollar, but you won't betray me, and you know why?"

"You would come back and kill me" Will said without a breath of hesitation.

Baxter nodded and waved his hand in a "there you go partner" gesture. "Exactly," he said, "you understand the breadth of our relationship, and you don't cross it. That and the money are the two things I can trust. Now that I have your assurance for our future business proposal, let's move on to the rest of our current project. Everything needs to go. Any evidence or extraneous matters need to be dealt with. We have to be prepared to finish the job." Baxter reached onto the table and picked up the Beretta that always seemed close by. The efficient movement of checking the chamber and magazine told Will all he needed to know. The conversation was over. Will's future had been decided in the span of thirty seconds.

Will's mind whirled at the possibility of leaving. It wasn't even a choice really. Baxter seemed to assume it was done. Even if he wanted to go, there was something almost primal and wrong about leaving one's home because of a phone call. He supposed a lot of military personnel felt the same way, but his motives were far less noble than theirs. He had gotten into this business for money, but Will wondered for the first time if he could have made it in a more legitimate job. If he had more money, maybe he could slip away and start anew? Somewhere else far away from the eyes and knife of Robert Baxter?

While he followed Baxter, these thoughts circled around his head as well as other questions that were not going to be answered anytime soon. They moved silently except for the betrayal of their footsteps. Baxter moved with a purpose that was inhuman. As they walked, Will found himself looking up at the ceiling as though contemplating divine intervention. That was when his phone began to ring again.

He stared down at his pocket in disgust. The phone was out and to his ear before he even looked at the number.

"Yeah?"

"Hello, Will, you evil son of a bitch. This is Detective Morgan."

The voice rammed nails into his feet as Will stopped, out of breath. The movement caused Baxter to stop as well and turn to him. He felt a cold sweat trickle into his armpits or maybe he was just imagining it. The police officer? The detective they had captured was calling them on the phone? "Detective Morgan?" Will said and Baxter stared a hole through his skull. Will nodded his head at Baxter's unspoken question. The voice on the other end sounded like hot gravel grinding into tires, eating away at the rubber.

"That's right, Will. Apparently your loose end is now just loose. I wanted to give you and your boss a friendly call and let you know I was coming for you. Speaking of which, can I speak to him? I know talking to you really isn't going to accomplish much, so can you put him on the phone?"

Baxter seemed to possess telepathy and gestured with his hand for the phone as soon as Morgan was done talking. Baxter took the phone and spoke, "You are turning out to be more of a problem than I had originally thought, Detective Morgan. My congratulations." Will strained to hear the words that were being spoken but couldn't make them out. The detective spoke in a grim but even tone. Maybe it was better that he couldn't hear the words. Maybe it was better for the both of them.

Baxter smiled and said, "You do that, Detective Morgan, you do that. We'll be coming for you too. Just out of curiosity, why haven't you called the police? You forget your place of employment's phone number?" His grin widened, and Will was glad he was not on the receiving end of it. After Detective Morgan spoke again, Baxter said, "All right that's fine. That's goddamn fine, Morgan. Be warned though, you just went up on my scale of things to fuck with and that, my friend, is somewhere you don't want to be. I'll be seeing you soon."

Baxter hung up the phone without waiting for a reply. It fell to his side, a dead piece of plastic and circuitry.

"Will, our time schedule just got moved up. I want you to have someone load all of the product into the truck," Baxter said with a voice that was a razor's whisper. "Put everyone else on alert. We have to find Morgan fast and put him in the ground. Then we are out of here until tomorrow when we finish the deal. Within forty-eight hours we are out of Chicago and on to a different climate. Also, see if you can get a hold of Wessler too. We are going to need him sooner than I thought." He tossed the phone back to Will who almost dropped it, feeling like a drunken juggler. What had Detective Morgan said?

Will had already begun frantically dialing numbers on his phone when Baxter grabbed his arm in a grip that made him wince. Sharp pain rose into his shoulder as he stared at the floor, not daring to meet the eyes or plastered smile of the man who was furious in a way he didn't even begin to understand. Suddenly the urge to shit was upon him, and he wished he could just stop staring at the goddamned floor.

"Will.........." Baxter said in a tone that demanded an answer. "Whose phone was he calling from? Even more importantly, where would that person be right now?"

CHAPTER 42
Turmoil

TYLER MORGAN HUNG up the phone. Baxter's voice cut off with a click of finality. He had gotten what he wanted, and now all there was left to do was to get ready. The phone dropped out of his hand and cracked on the hard floor before skittering away. Even the lightweight handheld device was becoming tiresome to use, and his eyelids felt like someone had punctured them with tacks. It wasn't even that he felt tired but just used up. Like all that he had left to keep him standing was his anger. Anger could keep you sharp and push you further than you thought possible, but the long-term price was exhaustion. No one was an endless font of rage regardless of how they wished it. He checked his captive's knots to distract his thoughts.

Seth Miller was squirming, turning both directions with his head and body, trying to push away from the bars as though the cage was a Goodman furnace.

"You can't do this!" Seth said. Tyler could see the man was drenched in sweat. "You're going to get me killed! I am a dead man. They are going to kill you and then me just for being mixed up in this. I didn't ask for this bullshit! Motherfucker! Let me go now!"

"You need to stop repeating yourself, Seth." The words were supposed to have bravado, but they came out as a wheeze. "You're actually pretty safe right now anyway. There are worse places to be than a giant metal cage. Don't worry; no one is even going to reach you. Worst case, the police will be here soon to clean-up. Just live long enough for that to happen, and then you can live long enough to regret being born. Sometimes life can be a real bitch."

"Bastard! Asshole! Motherfucker! Crazy son of a bitch! I will kill you!"

Seth continued to yell, but Tyler turned his back to the struggling guard. He was relieved to discover he could tune out the words for the most part, as he made his way back towards the warehouse area. Stealth was no longer a part of his gameplan but speed still was. His feet moved forward, a slumbering lurch of exhaustion. Tyler had always been agile for his height and build. Now his limbs rebelled against him, fighting for every movement as it tried to conserve the leaking supply of blood. It was time to end this before his body ended it for him. He would need the M27 automatic rifle's power. He wondered if he would even be able to lift the weapon.

Tyler wasn't thinking clearly. He should have gotten the gun first before making the phone call, the trip back cost him another couple of minutes. He groaned like an old man rising from bed as he picked the weapon up by the strap. It felt lined with lead. He was glad he hadn't been carrying the gun the entire time. The Springfield XDM 9mm fit nicely at his side. He could feel the metal with every exhalation. The gun was his sole comfort right now.

The walk to the main warehouse area where Baxter would have to come from was five to ten minutes max, but Tyler knew it was taking too long to get back to the C-4. He felt a breath of air on his neck and turned around. There was no one there. At least not yet. Tyler stopped and stood trying to hold his breath as his heart beat to the thrumming of constant pain.

"There's nothing there," he whispered and regretted the noise. He could almost see time slipping away, ashes in the wind. God, it felt so odd. The room around him was silent except for his own shuffling. Tyler waited a few more seconds before continuing his shamble.

The support beam where he had planted the C-4 loomed ahead like a mystical tower in the distance. The blast radius would be small compared to the size of the building, so he stopped at what was probably a safe distance behind some crates that were stacked sixteen to seventeen feet high. His body leaned more heavily than he would have liked, but it felt so good to rest.

If the crates collapsed he would fall forward, but they seemed to be holding for the moment. It reminded him of when his daughter used to sing Ring around the Rosie. Emily had always rolled her eyes at the song and spoke of the disputed origin of the rhyme coming from the Black Death during the 17th century. Tyler had pointed out that prior to World War II no scholar had ever written any analysis or thesis of the song showing its origin tied to the gruesome disease. It was one of their countless debates that always ended in laughter. Regardless, they would both smile as Grace danced around the apartment singing the song to an orchestra only she could hear. Tyler shook his head at how erratic his thoughts were becoming. He just couldn't help it anymore.

"Ashes, ashes, we all fall down." Tyler mouthed the words as he waited. He licked dry lips and tasted salt. How long had it been since he had drank some water? More importantly how long had it been since he had drank some water and not lost any blood? His throat seemed to close as though a vise were clamped around his neck. The urge to swallow became a need he couldn't avoid. A man or woman could supposedly go up to fourteen days without water, but that was also assuming they hadn't been shot or tortured. What was the expected life duration for someone with those particular conditions?

Out of the corner of his eye, he caught a flash of long brown hair. Tyler whipped his head around to look at the crates and saw nothing. Emily?

In his head, he knew his dead wife was not there. Not behind the crates right next to him. It couldn't be his daughter either. Will's fire had seen to that, but still he couldn't help wanting to look. He shouldn't be moving from his spot at all, but Tyler knew he wouldn't stop wondering unless he tried to see.

He moved as quickly as he could to the crates. Tyler wanted to lay down the detonator and automatic rifle, but was unsure if he would be able to pick them back up again. He let the gun drop down to his side on the shoulder strap and lowered the detonator until it lay flush at calf level.

His hand grazed the edge of the crate, feeling rough splinters. They were probably digging into his flesh, but he couldn't tell anymore since everything hurt. Tyler leaned forward around the edge to see what was on the other side of the crates. Nothing. There was nothing there. His teeth ground together as he cursed himself for even looking.

Goddamned fool. I am just a goddamned fool! he thought. You have an evil psychopath bearing down on you and you are looking for your dead wife and daughter in the middle of a decaying warehouse. He shook his head, but it only served to make him dizzy.

The steps back to the original spot were a little harder to make as though he were mired in tar. No one had shown up, which was a miracle in and of itself. He was about to lean on the crate again when he heard a faint sound. The detonator was stuffed into his pants as he used both hands to lift up the assault rifle into a firing position. Tyler stared down the sight of the M27 as he tried to quiet his breathing. The sounds grew louder until they became the familiar scrape of boots on concrete. It sounded like a squad of marines rather than what was probably a few hired guards and maybe Baxter with Will.

Crashes of noise roared in his ears as he waited at the filter point. Soon he was rewarded when a leg stuck out followed by the rest of a man Tyler didn't recognize. The AK-47 that the man carried however was something he was familiar with. The man seemed to sense his thoughts as he turned and looked right at Tyler. Time turned to ice as the other man hesitated. The assault rifle was all but useless in the hands of his surprised attacker. Tyler held up a finger to his lips in a shushing gesture. He then motioned for the man to walk forward, and for one second it looked like it would work. The man moved like an automaton brought back to life, before catching himself.

"Shit." Tyler said as the man shook his head awakening from a dream. He stared at Tyler and yelled, "He's over here!" raising his weapon to fire. Tyler pressed down on the trigger of his weapon as hard as he possibly could.

CHAPTER 43
No Choice

THE FIRST BULLET missed his target, but whether that was due to poor aiming or exhaustion was debatable. Tyler didn't see where it hit because he was already firing the second, which tore through the man's leg as he tried to raise his assault rifle. The man screamed in agony, dropping his weapon and fell to the floor. He curled up into a fetal position wailing louder than any siren. Tyler raised his line of sight since his attacker was clearly out of the fight. He began to look for his next target when the roar of automatic gunfire precipitated a hail of bullets crashing around him. He fell backwards as splinters of wood and dust became a storm clouding his vision.

Tyler felt small fragments of pain, but it was from debris rather than bullets. He had just used up the last of his luck. He wished he could hear the sound of footsteps. Tyler fired off several shots just to make the shooters take cover and glanced out to see the C-4. The wrapped girder was intact, and there was no one nearby his trap yet.

Tyler felt for the detonator in his pocket, fumbling with one hand, trying not to push too hard. It was insane to even have such a device in a casual location, but it was an insane situation. No one could claim any of this was logical. The storm of miniature explosions stopped as quickly as they had started. Tyler allowed a smirk to crease his face at the thought of an autonomous reload by his attackers. Of course, that wasn't it. The shooting had stopped because someone had ordered it.

"Detective Morgan? Tyler Morgan? Are you still among the living? If so, let's talk. If you're dying just scream out so I can hear it."

Robert Baxter's voice echoed through the warehouse bouncing off the thin walls. Tyler hated the man's control even in a situation like this. Will may have been one of the men who had killed his family, but none of this would have happened without Robert Baxter.

"I'm here, you evil fuck. Tell your men not to move."

Baxter laughed and the sound engulfed Tyler in a wall of irony.

"Nobody's going to move because I say so, not because you have a hundred bullets to back up your demands. I really don't have a lot of time for this, Detective Morgan. I am impressed that you are still alive, believe me. It is a monument to your obsession over your dead and rotting family. But the fact of the matter is that you aren't leaving here. Let's get this over with like men. Drop the gun. Step out. I promise you one bullet to the head, and it is done. That is a much better deal than the anguish I guarantee you are suffering through right now. I should know. I gave you that pain."

Tyler could hear the smile in the voice of the man he wanted to kill. Baxter was buying time for his men to find him. It wouldn't be hard. They could just follow the moans of the man he had shot in the leg. Tyler's exhaustion responded to Baxter's words. It was bright and sharp, eating at his muscle and bone. It would be so easy to step out and receive the bullet. He was so tired. Tired of the pain. Tired of the ache. Tired of living.

In the end there was no choice. No choice at all. They had to pay for what they had done. Baxter was trying to goad him into speaking as much as possible, to reveal his position. What they didn't know was his current level of mobility or if he was still in the area. One more utterance of words could end his life as quickly as a razor slash across the throat.

A sense of calm enveloped him, and he leaned out to look at the C-4 one more time. Still no sign of movement. He stepped back and lowered the assault rifle by its strap to the floor. It had grown too heavy for him to use properly. His accuracy would be next to nothing now with the weight. All he had left was the Springfield XDM 9mm. The handgun was more familiar anyway, and it felt good in his hand as Tyler drew the weapon. He checked the chamber and the magazine before lowering it to his side.

Tyler lowered his head and crouched as much as he could without sitting on the floor. He was shielded by layers of crates. His distance from the support beam would help with the limited impact area of the C-4. He could almost hear Baxter's men scurrying like rats.

For one second, Tyler thought he smelled sweet almonds in the air and his mind turned to Emily. Emily, whose gentle nature would never brighten this dark world again. He looked down and saw blood on the floor trailing backwards towards the armory. The proverbial bread-crumbs had gotten few and far between, which was not a good sign. Every second of hesitation allowed Baxter's men to become stronger in their fortification. If he spent any more time, the questions and that hated idea called logic would bring him down before Baxter's bullets did.

Tyler held his breath for three seconds, letting it out slowly. The sounds of multiple footsteps grew closer and then there was a flash of movement. It was time. He held up the detonator and pressed the button.

CHAPTER 44
Decision

THE EXPLOSION WAS not as loud as Tyler would have expected, but he felt the energy of the C-4 pound against his meager wall of protection. The boxes shuddered under the attack but held. The rafters above seemed to crack as dust fell down on him from the ceiling. Tyler felt the ground thrum beneath his feet. He held his hands above his head to stop the ceiling from crushing his skull. Every movie he had ever watched showed explosives with enough power to level city blocks, and the sound was deafening onscreen, but this was somehow muted. Somewhat lessened by real life. The explosion had not yet subsided, but he had no time left. Tyler hoped it had done the job and moved as quickly as he could, the gun held out in front of him, while he stood up.

Warehouse debris swirled through the air, an angry cloud of grime clogging his nostrils. He moved towards the man he had shot in the leg who still lay on the floor. There was no movement from his would-be attacker except for breathing. Tyler could tell by the occasional ragged cough that the prone man was probably in shock. He stepped over the body towards the girder finding himself coughing out dust and blood.

His mind felt clear and focused. The rage inside him roared with new levels of kinetic energy. This time it was cold and soothed the pain. His hearing seemed muffled like he was wearing plugs, but his eyesight sharpened as he crept forward.

The dust parted like a proverbial curtain. Three large dark shapes in front of him swam into focus, and it sharpened into men. Two of his attackers had been thrown against a crate and lay collapsed while the other sat on his knees exhibiting all the symptoms of shock. The man's gaze fell on him, but he didn't seem to see Tyler at all. The man's gun lay several feet away on the floor as usable as the dust in the air.

Tyler walked closer but his attacker's gaze continued to stare through him, even as he raised his gun and struck the man's temple.

The unconscious body collapsed without protest, almost like it was a relief. Tyler checked to ensure the fallen man was out of the fight before moving closer to the site of his destructive trap. His ears rang from the explosion, so he could only imagine what his attackers were feeling right now. If any of them were outside the blast radius, they could have an advantage. He needed to move quickly while he still had the element of surprise left. Dust coalesced around his gun as he speared it forward.

The girder was a smoking ruin of twisted metal. The center was a cut Gordian knot, causing the ends to arch at abnormal angles. The sheer chaos of it all reminded Tyler of Signorelli's The Damned. There was no one else around the site of the explosion. The ground felt uneven beneath his feet and his footsteps left slithering trails in the layer of grime accumulating on the floor. He stifled a cough that itched in his throat and kept walking.

As Tyler walked forward, a muffled wail echoed through the open space. He wasn't sure if the sound was in his ears or his head. The sound congealed into the idea that Chicago's finest had arrived more quickly than he had anticipated. His time was up. The sound grew more intense, strengthening his concern. He could no longer hear his footsteps above the siren's song keeping time with the last of his heartbeats.

A shape stepped out in front of him as he felt a powerful push graze his side. Tyler sighted his gun and fired before he fully recognized the shadow as Will. The gun jerked to the side and Tyler cursed the poor shot. Will was screaming something as he fired his gun in answer. Tyler held his breath and fired again. Will continued shooting, cracking the gun over and over. He thought he felt another push, but he was numb. Numb and half dead. He fired again and Will flew backwards in an ungraceful arc. There was no sound other than the sirens that had grown impossibly loud.

Tyler knew even Emily would not recognize the smile he felt on his face as he struggled to remain standing. His feet were not working correctly but allowed a broken stumble forward. There was no pain at all, but he wished he wasn't so damn slow. His vision had taken on shades of sepia as though the colors of the world had drained out with his blood. He hoped he was still holding the gun, but he didn't look down to confirm.

Will had gotten up on his hands and knees in a position of prayer. The killer's gun was nowhere in sight and from the way he was breathing, it was unlikely that he could have used it anyway. Tyler's steps brought him close enough to hear the groans of pain and desperation. Finally, he stood over Will and was pleased to see the gun was still in his hand. He raised his arm as though giving a greeting.

"Look at me, Will," Tyler said. His voice was broken and the words came out as a scarred mass of gristle. The smaller man shook his head no and did not move any further into a standing position. Tyler pointed his gun at Will's head.

"Look at me, Will. I want to see the look on your face, just like you saw the look on my family's. Right before they died." There was another shake of the head in denial. Tyler pushed the barrel into the top of Will's head as hard as he could.

"Look at me!"

Will raised his head and Tyler removed the barrel of the Springfield as the man who had burned his family to ash looked up into his eyes. It was not the look of a cold-blooded killer, but rather a scared man who was slightly younger than himself. Tyler saw intelligence in the gaze, but more than anything else there was fear. Fear of death. Tyler pointed the gun into the face of the man he hated more than anything. It felt right.

"Don't kill me. I'm sorry! I am sorry!" The voice was an insect whine of self-pity. It was disgusting. "I was just doing what I was told! Baxter is the one you want. He is a motherfucking monster. I'm just a lackey. Please don't kill me, Morgan. I will testify. I will do whatever you want!"

Tyler wished that Will was cursing his name or even just staring at him with a look devoid of emotion. It was hard to pull the trigger because he knew his wife wouldn't have wanted it this way. His little girl wouldn't have wanted it this way. But they were better than he was in every way. A stronger man would be able to walk away and find what happiness lay in the world, but he had never found the time to become that stronger man.

"Tyler, don't!"

The words came from behind him in a voice that told him his time was up. Without taking his eyes completely off Will, Tyler turned to the left enough to see the gun of Annabelle Herrera pointing at him. She was equal parts terrified and beautiful in her breathless way with a crescendo of sirens heralding her arrival. An azure hue surrounded her which made little sense but also complete sense in his current condition. He was losing his vision, but Annabelle stood out in detail that he didn't want to see.

"Don't do it, Tyler." Annabelle said, "That man deserves justice and jail, not cold blooded murder. Is this what your family would want?"

Tyler replied, "We've already had this discussion, Annabelle. My family doesn't have a say anymore. They lost that chance when they burned to ashes. I already told you that. There isn't anything else to say." Annabelle flinched at his response but did not lower the shaking weapon. Tyler's gun also shook, but it was because of the weight that was bearing down on his body. His fingers felt numb to the point of nothingness, but his arm was on fire, screaming for death. A burden weighed on him greater than any exhaustion or blood loss could. Once he let the gun drop to his side, it would be impossible to raise again.

"I don't believe you." Annabelle said, "I don't believe you are that kind of man. You're right; there is nothing more to say. I can't stop you before you pull that trigger, and we both know it." Annabelle's eyes were a plea and a question as she spoke. "The last question you really have to ask is how many casualties died in that fire? Was it your daughter and wife, or did you also die that day? If you pull the trigger, you are giving up on everything that made your family love you."

The sounds of footsteps and voices had grown louder. There was no chance of finding Baxter, and even if he did, there was nothing Tyler could do about him. This was his final moment. This was the only decision he could still make. His vision had receded to a blur. A smear of shadows that was only focused on his gun and Annabelle's face.

"Tyler please......"

Tyler pulled the trigger and felt the ground rush up to greet him. It was time to rest.

CHAPTER 45
The Void

THE SOUR HINT of ammonia reached his nostrils. Tiny pinpricks of light created a migraine out of the stale recycled air. Tyler forced his eyes open and endured the pain of not being damned quite yet. The steady beep of the machines lying next to his veins kept time with breath as he struggled to take in the surroundings. The hospital room had only shades of gray with the blinds drawn. The neutral tones of the room added layers to the shadows that had seemed brighter than the sun itself a few seconds ago.

Tyler felt the pain in his vision ease slightly, but the headache had already grown to compensate. His whole body ached, and there was no doubt he could not stand, let alone walk out of here. There was a reason it was called mortal trappings when describing life. He was able to lift his head slightly without wincing and look to the side where Annabelle Herrera sat in a leather chair next to his bed. It was like a cheap mirage how she had blinked into existence. In reality, he was either hallucinating, or his vision was seriously impaired by trauma.

"Hello Tyler. I see you're finally awake." Her voice held an edge that he had never heard before. It sounded like a lack of trust. He leaned his head back on the pillow, and she disappeared from view, but her breathing became louder than the machines that surrounded him. Tyler tried to speak, but his vocal cords fought him to a croak. He coughed several times, and Annabelle's hand was holding a plastic cup of water to his lips before he could even begin to protest.

"How long....."

"About three days. Blunt trauma. Blood loss. Dehydration. Lacerations. Contusions. The doctor also had a lot of other more technical terms that I didn't understand. You would have, but you weren't in any condition to listen. You woke up briefly a few hours ago. Do you remember?"

Tyler shook his head no and she continued. "You are a fucking miracle. They didn't seem to think you would pull through; at least that's how it seemed to me. No one would say it, but everyone thought you were a dead man. Lieutenant Rooks has been asking for updates every few hours. When we found out you were awake, I wanted to be the first one to see you. I didn't think he was going to let me, but he did without any complaints. He probably thought you wouldn't talk to him yet."

"I'm not sure." Tyler said. His voice was returning, but the words sounded weak. Drained. He tried reaching for more water. Annabelle made him drink from the cup in her hand. Tyler coughed a couple times, but it seemed the liquid was staying down for now. She was patient even in her mistrust. Questions loomed in front of him, and he didn't want to ask the most important ones. Annabelle said, "You were talking to the nurses and saying Wessler's name. We haven't been able to find him at his apartment, and he hasn't shown up for work. Any ideas?"

Tyler nodded and could only manage a few words before coughing. "Corrupt. He's gone." Annabelle nodded her head and said, "Yeah, I thought it might be something like that. Lieutenant Rooks will want to talk to you more about it, but we can at least put out an external bulletin to start looking for him."

"The heroin?"

"In evidence right now. I think we confiscated all of it, at least from the warehouse. Looks to be millions of dollars in street value. Most of it was already packed up in trucks, but we found some residual and enough manufacturing hardware to indicate that this was their main production point. I think we actually shut the stuff down, Tyler. At least for now. The first serious dent in the heroin production since it started. Pretty fucking amazing. That is the silver lining of the situation."

"Silver….lining….." Tyler said and shook his head as Annabelle tried to offer more water. He had drunk enough, but his throat still didn't work right. It was worse each time he talked. It felt like he was drowning in cement.

"Yeah. I think we caught everyone involved that isn't dead anyway. I don't know the legal ramifications behind this whole mess, but there are going to be so many questions for you. How did you get there? What happened to you after the phone call? Were you present during the explosion? The people who were killed. The list goes on, and I don't have any answers, Tyler."

"Anyone named Baxter?"

"I don't think so, but I'm not sure. They have ID'd everyone that was arrested, and that name doesn't ring any bells. Was he one of the guys who did this to you?"

Tyler frowned, but nodded his head, saying nothing. Robert Baxter had disappeared like all the monsters of the world. The bastard was either lucky or had conjured some sort of unholy intervention. Maybe both.

The space between them grew with each second until Tyler could barely feel her presence in the room. He stared at the clock on the wall, but couldn't read the time. Annabelle was waiting for him. Waiting for him to ask the question that they both didn't want to discuss. Not all the plastic cups of water in the world were going to make the words flow smoothly, however he owed her this much.

"The man……?"

"Will Thompson. Yes. The man you tried to kill. The man going to jail, not the morgue."

Tyler's mind swam back into focus. He struggled to speak. The words would not come despite his will. He turned his head to look Annabelle in the eyes, and the truth was written there. He had failed. Will was going to prison instead of what Tyler had planned for him.

"Your gun was out of bullets. You...you pulled the trigger, but nothing happened." Annabelle looked away as a tear ran down her cheek. "You collapsed on the floor with a smile on your face! A smile! That's when I knew......You have no idea how close you were to death. You weren't even aware that the gun was empty. But I knew. That's why I wanted to be the first one to talk to you, if you lived through all of this."

"I..."

"I am not going to say a word, Tyler. What could I really say anyway? Purely observational and speculative in a case that is going to go on forever," Annabelle said, her face wet and her eyes reddened. He wanted to turn away more than anything in the world, but it wasn't right. He deserved this shame.

"Ultimately, I don't know what is going to happen with all of this. What I do know is that I believed you were a good man. Deep down inside, I thought, despite all the pain and torment you were going through, you would not let yourself sink to that level. You were still the best detective Chicago had ever seen. When I saw you standing over that criminal...that man, with a gun in your hand, I knew you would do the right thing. I knew you wouldn't just kill someone in cold blood. Even if it was tied to the death of your family. This wasn't self-defense. This was murder. I knew you wouldn't do it right up until the second when you pulled the trigger. When you smiled, thinking you had killed him. I felt like I died in place of that man."

"Annabelle." Tyler said, but she shook her head for silence. She stood up, rising slowly in her graceful way. The look she gave him was one of a stranger. A police detective looking down on a wounded man in a hospital bed. There was also pity in her eyes. Pity and tears.

"I doubt that God really exists, but seeing what you did makes me wonder if He does exist and just likes to laugh at our torment. You would have murdered someone, Tyler, if it hadn't been for your gun betraying you. That type of damnation doesn't wash off, no matter how much I wish it would." Annabelle's voice broke. "Your family died in a horrible way, but I was convinced you would rise above it. Instead you sank into depths where I can't follow. In reality, all three of you died that day, and now you are the walking dead. A cold-blooded murderer. God help anyone who crosses you. I don't think He is watching over either of us anymore."

Annabelle left without saying another word, though he thought he saw tears fall as the door clicked shut behind her. Tyler stared up at the ceiling looking for patterns in the cheap tile and fluorescent bulbs, but there was nothing to see. He continued staring, wishing for a real answer to appear as the sun set outside in winter's last death rattle for Chicago. The shades of gray disappeared in the darkness above him as Tyler realized he could see nothing there. Nothing at all.

Epilogue

RICH DEMOL HAD never been what you might call a traveler. He had lived in Detroit his whole life and he had no plans to leave either his city or his unscrupulous lifestyle anytime soon. It was this unscrupulous lifestyle that paid for both home and women. It was the thought of those women that made him get up when he didn't really feel the need to be awake so early.

His cell phone had rang this morning, giving him a post-hangover headache, but the voice on the other line had good news. He was meeting with what he thought of as a top dog. Someone who was going to help bring him up in the ranks of product and power. Someone with the means to help him make money. Real money this time. That is what the phone promised anyway. The rest of the details weren't really there, and he didn't care. Rich had thrown on a shirt and was out the door in five minutes to a location that was less than five miles from the apartment. Rich was careful not to make eye contact with anyone around him. It was a practice of his that had served him well over the years. It seemed to work for a lot of people judging by the downcast glances around him.

He had arrived at a bar called Scotty's that wasn't open yet. His meet and greet was supposed to take place behind the building in an alley that had probably seen a mugging or three. The weather had started to warm up with winter melting away to a puddle of mud. He wasn't cold, and he wanted to make sure he was there before the meeting time. Rich made a point of arriving early since it made him punctual and gave him some time to clear his head of any residual alcoholic fumes. The only problem being outside a bar was that it made him think of drinks and vomit, yes in that order. One drink would have helped him immensely right now. If Rich had any alcohol left in his apartment he would have drank a shot before coming here. He would just have to get through this meeting and find a place that sold cheap vodka afterwards. A celebration to his new business proposition in whatever.

The alley was cramped and dark. Rich had met in worse locations before, but this was still something a little outside the norm. Usually a contact would suggest a place familiar to both of them, and it would be crowded. This contact was new so maybe he was inexperienced in selecting ideal meeting places. This second guessing wasn't like him. Rich kept looking for the contact. It didn't pay to think too much about what you were doing when you were in this line of work.

"Hello, Rich."

The voice came from behind him and Rich jumped in spite of himself. He turned to look up at a tall, thin man wearing a long coat. "What the hell do you.....?" Rich said but stopped as he looked into the face of his new business partner. Eyes were supposed to be the window to the soul but there was no soul. There was just nothing. Nothing but a hard stare and a fake smile. Rich had stared down mean bastards before, but he also knew when to keep his mouth shut. If someone was looking at him right now, they would say he was completely focused on the tall man with the cold eyes. They would say there was nothing more important in this world as he listened and began to nod his head.

The End

My Sincere Gratitude

THANK YOU FOR taking time to read my book! We walked Tyler's dark path together in a story written over several years but the journey is not over yet. I hope you enjoyed the novel as much as I enjoyed writing it. If you get a chance to write a review or share my story with others, it is the greatest honor that you could give to me. The power of your voice helps us all share stories and ideas that we enjoy. Now I must go prepare for the next novel as the steps on our journey may grow darker still.......

www.johncoxbooks.com

About the Author

JOHN COX GREW up in the Midwest and currently lives in Indiana. He has a Bachelor's degree in Education from Indiana University where he received an Upcoming Author award for his short story *In the Rough*. He also received a second Bachelor's degree in Accounting from Indiana Wesleyan.

John lives with his wife, son, and an insane Labrador bent on eating the world. He loves noir and thriller fiction, loud music, and writing at 3 a.m.

For more information, please visit his website at: *www.johncoxbooks.com*

Made in the USA
Columbia, SC
19 March 2021